KU-284-642

NIGHTWOODS

CHARLES FRAZIER

SCEPTRE

First published in the United States of America in 2011 by Random House
An imprint of The Random House Publishing Group
A division of Random House, Inc., New York

First published in Great Britain in 2011 by Sceptre
An imprint of Hodder & Stoughton
An Hachette UK company

1

Copyright © 2011 by 3 Crows Corporation

The right of Charles Frazier to be identified as the Author of the Work has been asserted by him
in accordance with the Copyright, Designs and Patents Act 1988.

All rights reserved. No part of this publication may be reproduced, stored in a retrieval system, or
transmitted, in any form or by any means without the prior written permission of the publisher,
nor be otherwise circulated in any form of binding or cover other than that in which it is
published and without a similar condition being imposed on the subsequent purchaser.

All characters in this publication are fictitious and any resemblance to real persons, living or dead
is purely coincidental.

A CIP catalogue record for this title is available from the British Library

Hardback ISBN 978 1 444 73124 8
Trade paperback ISBN 978 1 444 73125 5

Printed and bound by Clays Ltd, St Ives plc

Hodder & Stoughton policy is to use papers that are natural, renewable and recyclable products
and made from wood grown in sustainable forests. The logging and manufacturing processes are
expected to conform to the environmental regulations of the country of origin.

Hodder & Stoughton Ltd
338 Euston Road
London NW1 3BH

www.hodder.co.uk

Limerick City Library

3 0002 50028154 8

NIGHTWOODS

WITHDRAWN FROM STOCK

Also by CHARLES FRAZIER

COLD MOUNTAIN

THIRTEEN MOONS

For Annie

You can't even cross a river
Without having to pay a toll.

—ARCHILOCHOS (SEVENTH CENTURY B.C.)

I

LUCE'S NEW STRANGER CHILDREN were small and beautiful and violent. She learned early that it wasn't smart to leave them unattended in the yard with the chickens. Later she'd find feathers, a scaled yellow foot with its toes clenched. Neither child displayed language at all, but the girl glared murderous expressions at her if she dared ask where the rest of the rooster went.

The children loved fire above all elements of creation. A heap of dry combustibles delighted them beyond reason. Luce began hiding the kitchen matches, except the few she kept in the hip pocket of her jeans for lighting the stove. Within two days, the children learned how to make their own fire from tinder and a green stick bowed with a shoelace. Tiny cavemen on Benzedrine couldn't have made fire faster. Then they set the back corner of the Lodge alight, and Luce had to run back and forth from the spring with sloshing tin buckets to put it out.

She switched them both equally with a thin willow twig until their legs were striped pink, and it became clear that they would draw whatever pain came to them down deep inside and refuse to cry. At which point Luce swore to herself she would never strike them again. She went to the kitchen and began making a guilty peach pie.

LUCE WAS NOT MUCH MATERNAL. The State put the children on her. If she had not agreed to take them, they would have been separated and adopted out like puppies. By the time they were grown, they wouldn't even remember each other.

Though now that it was probably too late to go back, maybe that would have been a good thing. Separate them and dilute whatever weirdness they shared and ignited between them. Yet more proof, as if you needed it, that the world would be a better place if every-damn-body didn't feel some deep need to reproduce. But God in his infinite wisdom had apparently thought it was an entertaining idea for us to always be wanting to get up in one another.

Also, the children were here, and what was Luce to do? You try your best to love the world despite obvious flaws in design and execution. And you take care of whatever needy things present themselves to you during your passage through it. Otherwise you're worthless.

Same way with the Lodge. Luce didn't own it. She was the caretaker, sort of. Some would call her a squatter now that the old man was dead. But nobody else seemed interested in keeping it from growing over with kudzu until it became nothing but a green mound.

Back at the edge of the previous century, the Lodge had been a cool summer retreat for rich people escaping the lowland steam of August. Some railroad millionaire passing through the highland valley in his own railcar had a vision, or possibly a whim, to build an earthen dam, back the river up, fill the upper end of the valley with water right to the edge of the village. Then, on the far side, build a log lodge of his own design, something along the lines of the Old Faithful Inn, though smaller and more exclusive. He must have been a better railroad executive than architect, because what he built was a raw outsized rectangle, a huge log cabin with a covered porch looking down a sweep of lawn to the lake and across the water to the town. Evidently, rich people were satisfied by simpler things in the yesteryears.

Now the millionaires and the railroad were gone. But the lake remained, a weird color-shifting horizontal plane set in an otherwise convoluted vertical landscape of blue and green mountains. The Lodge persisted as well, a strange, decaying place to live in alone, though. The main floor was taken up by the common rooms, a voluminous lobby with its massive stone fireplace and handsome, backbreaking Craftsman armchairs and settles, quarter-sawn oak tables and cabinets. A long dining room with triple-hung, lake-view windows and, behind swinging doors, a big kitchen with a small table where the help once crowded together to eat leftovers. Second floor, just narrow hallways and sleeping chambers behind numbered six-panel doors with transom windows. Third floor, way up under the eaves, a dark smothering rabbit warren of windowless servants' quarters.

WHEN SHE LIVED ALONE, Luce didn't go to the upper floors often, but not out of fear. Not really. It was little but bedsteads and cobwebs up there, and she didn't want to believe in ghosts or anything similar. Not even the portents of bad dreams. Yet the fading spirit world touched her imagination pretty strong when she was awake at three in the morning, alone in the big place. The dark sleeping floors, with their musty transient pens and cribs for the guests and their help, spooked her. The place spoke of time. How you're here and then you're gone, and all you leave for a little while afterward are a few artifacts that outlive you.

Case in point, old Stubblefield, who had owned the Lodge for the past few decades. Luce visited him several times during his dying days, and she was there at the end to watch the light go out of his eyes. In the final hours, Stubblefield mostly cataloged his possessions and listed who should get what. His concerns were largely real estate, all his holdings to go to his sole useless grandson. Also a few valuable objects, such as his dead wife's silver service and lace tablecloth, perfect but for a slight rust stain at one corner. Barely noticeable. The silver candleholders were a heavy weight on Stubblefield's mind because his wife had loved them so much. Oddly, he left them to Luce, who didn't love them at all and probably never would.

Easy to be disdainful and ironic toward others' false values. Still, Luce hoped that when she was at the same thin margin of life she would be concerned with looking out the window to note the weather or the shape of the moon or some lone bird flying by. Certainly not a bunch of worn-out teaspoons. But Luce was half a century younger than old Stubblefield, and didn't know how she'd think and what she would value if she made it that far down the road. All her life, the main lesson Luce had learned was that you couldn't count on anybody. So she guessed you could work hard to make yourself who you wanted to be and yet find that the passing years had transformed you beyond your own recognition. End up disappointed in yourself, despite your best efforts. And that's the downward way Luce's thoughts fell whenever she went upstairs into the dreary past.

BEFORE THE CHILDREN, Luce had learned that after dark she'd best keep to the communal lobby, with its fireplace and mildew-spotted furniture and tall full bookshelves and huge floor-standing radio with a tuning ring like the steering wheel to a Packard. She dragged a daybed from a screened sleeping porch to form a triangle of cozy space with the hearth and the radio to make herself a bedroom. The bookshelves held a great many well-read old novels and a set of Britannicas, complete but for a couple of volumes in the middle of the alphabet. Also, nearby, a Stickley library stand with an unabridged 1913 Webster's. The places where you naturally put your hands on the soft binding were stained dark, so that all you could figure was that decades of guests finished a greasy breakfast of sausage biscuits and then right away needed to look up a word.

At bedtime, lamps out, the rest of the big room faded into darkness, only the fire and the radio's tubes sending a friendly glow up the nearby log walls. Luce finally fell asleep every night listening to WLAC out of Nashville. Little Willie John, Howlin' Wolf, Maurice Williams, James Brown. Magic singers proclaiming hope and despair into the dark. Prayers pitched into the air from Nashville and caught by the radio way up here at the mountain lake to keep her company.

Also good company on clear nights, the lights of town. Yellow pinpoints and streaks reflecting on the shimmer of black lake water. One advantage of the village being over there on the other side was the proximity of people as the crow flies, but no other way. By car, it took the better part of an hour to go around the back side of the lake and across the dam and around the shore to town.

The distance seemed shorter when Luce first got to the Lodge, due to a rowboat she found in one of the outbuildings. Town became only twenty minutes away. But the boat was rotting and loose-jointed, and on her first few trips across, she spent as much time bailing with a saucepan as rowing. And she was not much of a swimmer, at least not good enough to make it to either shore from the middle. She dragged the boat up onto the shoreline and let it dry for a few days, and then one evening at dusk, she poured a cup of kerosene on it and burned it. Flames rose chest-high, their reflections reaching across the still water toward town.

After that, when she had been alone for too many days, she walked the half mile to Stubblefield's house, and the half mile farther to Maddie's, and the mile farther to the little country store, where you could buy anything you wanted as long as it was bologna and light bread and milk, yellow cheese and potted meat, and every brand of soft drink and candy bar and packaged snack cake known to man. A four-mile round-trip just to sit in a chair outside the store for a half hour and drink a Cheerwine and eat a MoonPie and observe other human beings. She always carried a book, though, in case she needed to read a few pages to avoid unwanted conversation.

The past Fourth of July, Luce sat on the porch of the Lodge drinking precious brown liquor from the basement and watching tiny fireworks across the water. Bursts that must have filled the sky in town became bubbles of sparks about as big as a fuzzy dandelion at arm's length. As they began fading to black, the distant boom and sizzle finally reached the Lodge. Friday nights in the fall, light from the football field glowed silver against the eastern sky. A faint sound like an outbreath when the home team scored a touchdown. Every Sunday morning, distant church bells from the Baptists and Methodists tinkled like ice cubes in a glass, and a saying of her mother's always crossed Luce's mind: thirst after righteousness. Which Lola used as a Sabbath toast, raising a tall Bloody Mary and a freshly lit Kool in the same hand only minutes after the bells woke her.

THE DAY THE CHILDREN came was high summer, the sky thick with humidity and the surface of the lake flat and iron blue. On the far side, mountains layered above the town, hazing upward in shades of olive until they became lost in the pale gray sky. Luce watched the girl and boy climb out of the backseat of a chalky-white Ford sedan and stand together, square to the world. Not really glaring, but with a manner of looking at you and yet not at you. Predatory, with their eyes very much in the fronts of their faces and scoping their surroundings for whatever next prospect might present itself, but not wanting to spook anybody. Not yet. Foxes entering henhouses, was the way Luce saw it.

They sported new clothes the State had given them. A blue cotton print dress and white socks and white PF Flyers for the girl. A white cotton shirt and stiff new blue jeans and black socks and black PF Flyers for the boy. Both children had hair the color of a peanut shell, standing ragged on their heads as if the same person had done the cuts in a hurry, with only the littlest regard to gender.

Luce said, Hey there, you two twins.

The children didn't say anything, nor even look at her or at each other.

—Hey, Luce said, a little louder. I'm talking to you.

Nothing.

Luce looked at their faces and saw slight concern for themselves or anybody else. They sent out expressions like they sure didn't want you to mess with them, but maybe they wanted to mess with you. She went to the back of the car, where the man from the State was unloading a couple of cardboard boxes from the trunk. He set them on the ground and touched the smaller box with the toe of his loafer.

—Their clothes, he said. And that other one is your sister's. Personal items.

Luce hardly glanced down from looking at the kids. She said, What's the matter with them?

—Nothing much, the man said. He thumbed the wheel to a Zippo and lit a smoke and seemed tired from the long drive. Ten hours.

—Something's the matter with them, Luce said.

—They've been through a bad patch.

—A what?

Luce stood and waited while the man took a drag or two, and then she broke in on his smoking and said, You're the one that collects a salary from the State to do this job, but you can't even talk straight. Bad patch.

The man said, One doctor thought they might be feebleminded. Another one said it's just that they saw what they saw, and they've been yanked out of their lives and put in the Methodist Home for the time it took to sort things out. The father's legal matters.

—He's not their father. They're orphans.

—It took time to figure that kind of thing out. We got used to certain wording.

—And Johnson? Luce said.

—The trial's coming up, and they'll convict him. Sit him in the big wood chair with the straps and drop the tablet in the bucket. It fizzes up, and pretty soon he chokes out. Immediate family gets an invitation.

—To watch?

—There's a thick glass porthole, tinged like a fishbowl full of dirty water. If there's a crowd, you have to take turns. It's the size of a dinner plate. Pretty much one at a time.

—Count me in, Luce said.

She watched the children rove wordless about the yard in front of the Lodge. Going slow, but in some purposeful pattern, assessing the space like a pair of water witches looking for the right spot to dig a well.

—And that bad patch, Luce said. That's all that's the matter with them?

—All we know.

The man looked around at the relict lodge and the lake and the town across the water, hazy through the humidity, identifiable mainly as a distant low geometric break in the uniformity of green woods. A couple of steeples, arrowheads aimed at heaven, rose above the tiny red brick store buildings and the white houses sloping up from Main Street. Whichever other direction you looked, mountains and forests and lake.

The man waved his cigarette in two circles to encompass all the lonesome beauty and decay. He said, To look at it, you wouldn't think it would take so long to get from town to here.

—It's a long lake.

—Yeah. And all these twisting dirt roads.

—Well, Luce said.

The man said, Beyond here, what? Nothing?

—The road goes on a few miles, but this is the last place anybody lives.

The man looked at the blanched wood sign hanging from two rusty chains above the steps to the porch. WAYAH LODGE.

He said, Indian?

—Cherokee. Means wolf.

—I don't know anything about your finances, the man said.

Luce looked him in the eye and tried to express nothing at all.

—This place doesn't take tourists anymore?

Luce said, It stopped sometime around the Great Depression or the Second World War. I'm caretaker.

—Pay well?

—I get to live here and grow a garden and pick the orchard. And I get a stipend.

—A stipend? he said.

—That's what they call it when your pay's so small they're embar-rassed to call it anything else. Except the old man died. The owner. So right now the stipend is sort of on hold.

—Children can get expensive, the man said. Food and clothes and all.

—I don't guess any money goes with them? Luce said.

—Maybe the grandparents could help out?

—No, they couldn't.

—Then, I don't know. If you could find help with the children, you could move into town and get a better job.

—Yeah, big if.

—Well, the man said.

—So, probably I'll make do. Don't you and the government go worrying too much about us after you get in the car and drive back down to the capital city.

—Do you have electricity and plumbing?

—Is that a requirement? Luce said.

The man shrugged his shoulders.

Luce tipped her thumb toward the off-plumb crucifix power pole at the road and the black swagged wires leading to a white ceramic fixture under the porch eave.

—It's not been the nineteenth century around here for several years, she said.

The man drew his last drag and flipped the butt away, like it wasn't trash at all, it having had such intimate relations with his breath for a few moments. The smoking butt glanced off a pine tree and landed in brown needles.

Luce went over and picked it up by its flesh-tone filter and dropped it into the red dirt of the drive and crushed it out with her shoe. She wiped her thumb and forefinger on the thigh of her jeans three times, which was probably once or twice too many.

The man said, You probably wouldn't believe how little I get paid to do this goddamn job.

—I probably might, Luce said.

THAT NIGHT, JUST UNTIL she figured out how to live alongside children in the Lodge, Luce pulled another daybed from the sleeping porch and put it on the other side of the fireplace from hers. Radio playing low, the children slept pretty well, tired from the long day, but Luce lay hovering at the edge of sleep through three DJs.

The shape of long peaceful days prior to the children kept rolling in, and she guessed it would be naïve to believe that wouldn't change. Days when she had her own life to herself to go walking down the road, free and easy. Though, truthfully, despite all its many joys, life without wheels had a few drawbacks. Hitchhiking, you placed more hope in other people than they would generally bear. You walked and walked and nothing much changed. You had to be attentive to avoid boredom. But for your efforts, there were reimbursments. Elder people and all their hard-earned peculiarities to visit along the way.

In particular, Maddie, living in her own world like it had remained 1898 on and on forever. Or, to be generous, maybe 1917. Her age was indeterminate, as long as you started with old and worked up from there. Her house sat back from the road, and by late summer, flowers grew thick in the yard. Coneflowers and gladiolus and black-eyed Susans and goosenecks all tangled together. In the fall, hot red peppers and brown leather britches drying on lines of cotton twine drooping from the porch posts. Maddie mostly stayed in her country kitchen, with its wood cook stove and dinner table and fireplace, the stones sooted from fifty thousand hearth fires mostly lit by women long dead. The main touches of the current century were a few light bulbs swinging on braided cords from the ceiling.

Maddie wore flower-print cotton dresses all year round and topped them off with pilled cardigan sweaters in the cool months, and she might have been tall and willowy when she was young, before time compressed her into herself, thickening and shortening and bending year by year until all you could see of the young woman she had been were her quick blue eyes, faded almost to the color of steel. Some days she'd be in a mood. All she wanted to use were the sorts of words she'd grown up hearing. *Yonward* and *thither. Hither. Sward.* On a really bad day, half of what she said, you had to figure by context. Early on, Luce viewed Maddie's homeplace as mostly imaginary, life still circling around hog killings, oil lamps, fetching water, outhouses, and all that other old business. Until Luce realized that these days, her life was a lot like that too.

When Luce stopped for a visit, Maddie would give her a drink of cold spring water from a dented ladle and sing her a song. Maddie knew many ancient ballads about girls getting in trouble and being murdered by the men who had lately so much wanted to get up on them. She warbled and keened at an extreme pitch of emotion unattainable by the young, and the verses of the songs went on and on toward a receding conclusion. They were dark-night songs. Knocked-up girls got stabbed or shot or hit in the head, and then buried in the cold ground or thrown into the black deep river. Pretty Polly. Little Omie Wise. Go down, go down, you Knoxville Girl. Sometimes reproduction did not even factor into the narrative. The man snuffed the girl out because he could not own her, a killing offense if the girl's opinions ran counter to his urges. In the ballads, love and murder and possession fit tight against one another as an outgrown wedding band on a swollen finger.

Back then, Luce had thought Maddie's songs were only interesting antiques, but her sister had proved their abiding truth when she came up against Johnny Johnson. Their feelings ran so hot at the start that it must have been sad to watch, though awfully compelling to read about in Lily's occasional letters, where new love's bells jangled like a fire engine's. Lily's spirit neediness expressed itself raw as a kerosene blaze in the material world. *Love, love, love.* That's how she described those few months of desire. Each letter signed in a looping hand: *Love, Lily.*

Now Luce lay awake in the dark, knowing Maddie's murder ballads addressed exactly that situation, and taught that the flame of urgent coupling burned hottest against the woman, no matter how romantic and high and heartsick the anguish of the man might be pitched in retrospect. Luce pictured the killer of Omie Wise through a porthole of dirty green water. A noose around his neck and a trapdoor about to open into a black hole beneath his feet. Oh, what longing and regret he then felt. But too late. And also forever too late for Lily to learn that raging passion predicts nothing but a mess of bad news for everybody.

Luce kept trying to sleep, but hundreds of thousands of katydids or locusts or other screeching insects broadcast a high-voltage buzz into the summer night. She got up and turned on one dim mica lamp and went to an oak cabinet taller than she was and took out a cigar box. The children slept on, and Luce sat inside the circle of gold light, the box in her lap, riffling through Lily's letters from the past few years. Lavender or green or hot pink ink in big happy cursive on coordinating pastel stationery.

Luce opened envelopes at random, reading until she reached a sentence where it became impossible not to criticize Lily's fatal hope and trust in other people. Everybody Lily met was so wonderful, and the shiny future stretched forever. Every page held evidence against her. Luce never made it all the way through any of the letters before she returned them to Lily's precise folds.

Luce decided not to read them again until she could appreciate them more. Some far day when she had become a better person and could feel something besides stinging anger that her beautiful, gentle sister had not protected herself more carefully against a world of threat.

Bud was a handsome man, at least in the retrograde style of the expired southern fifties he still loved so much. High cheekbones, sideburns, upturned collars, and a forelock shaped into a perfect comma down his forehead with a two-fingered swipe of Royal Crown pomade. Bud was nobody's real name. Sometime in youth, a deluded soul had considered him a friend and dubbed him Buddy Buster.

He had a criminal record by the time he was barely a teenager, caught shoplifting a coat pocket of yellow Sun 45s from a dime store. From his first day in high school, Bud kept a small-caliber pistol in his locker, mostly to impress girls and to insinuate himself into the company of bullies and roughnecks. He was successful on both fronts. At fourteen, in an era when it was daring to show up at a party with a beer or two, Bud once arrived with three cases of Schlitz in a stolen car. He announced his presence by cutting a doughnut in the front yard and then jumping out and popping the back end to reveal seventy-two can lids studded into a trunkful of crushed ice, reflecting the porch lights like the crown jewels of a minor country. Which made Bud the hero of everyone except the kid whose parents were gone for the weekend.

And so on, through his youth. Bud endured several bouts of probation and then served nearly two years on a breaking-and-entering charge, made worse because he was carrying his pistol when arrested. The low-security teenager prison was fenced barely stronger than a poultry yard, but Bud chose to serve his entire term. It didn't do him much good, though. He might as well have skipped out. Nearly all the anxious psychological counselor had to recommend was that Bud learn to defer immediate gratification and find a hobby. Such as listening to jabber from overseas on a shortwave radio. Bud said, How about shooting rats at the dump with a shotgun pistol? But that didn't seem to qualify, and not only because shotgun pistols were illegal for some obscure reason. It was more like a mind problem, to be marked down on the counselor's notepad and held against you if you summed up the wrong answer. Like when the counselor delved into your habits of using a public toilet, such as do you flush with your foot and use your elbow to open the door? If yes, woe unto you. You're crazy. From now on, all the doors of opportunity will be rigged to slam shut in your face.

After his release, Bud scrabbled for some years. Short-time jobs and larceny. Selling various forms of dope, kind of as a sideline to pumping gas. And then he got a job with the railroad in the capital city. For a time, he actually drew a paycheck every Friday. He told people he was a railroad bull, but his friend Billy was the bull. Bud had been demoted after only a week. He couldn't be relied upon to kick the asses of hoboes, and not because he was unwilling. It was a matter of prudence. First day on the job, he came up against a big fullback-looking bum who was not the least intimidated by Bud's nightstick and company badge. Bud immediately panicked and ran away, knowing he was overmatched and about to take a beating. And then, soon after, the thing that lost him his position was going too far with a frail old man who'd been riding the rails since the stock market crash in '29. Knocking the man down with his stick and then kicking him with railroad boots past the point of consciousness. After that, Bud's job became more custodial. Pushing a broom, hosing concrete aprons, dumping small containers of garbage into larger containers. His greatest responsibility was using a big Tin Man oil can to lube metal parts that rubbed against each other around the boxcar couplings.

During that strange time of normal employment, he met a pretty young widow with bad judgment and two little children. Nobody who knew Bud considered violence to be his main calling as a criminal. Various forms of theft and violations of substance codes were his specialties. So it was a surprise when Bud married Lily and then soon killed her.

AS A CHILD, Bud was made to attend a church where the preacher spent most of his time at the pulpit talking about Christ's wounds and Christ's blood. The message was clear. Blood mattered above all else, the sacred shedding of it. The rest of Christ's life—his actions, his pithy sayings, his love—became incidental compared to the dark artery offering that covered the globe. Some Sundays the preaching was pitched so fervent and descriptive that little Bud couldn't shake slaughterhouse images out of his mind until the next morning. Which meant dark hours of nightmares interrupted by long sweaty periods of terrified hovering wakefulness until dawn broke on Monday.

At grown-up Bud's new happy church that Lily made him go to, they talked about Jesus all the time, but never about Jesus's blood. That would be embarrassing for this tame bunch of worshippers. Their church featured an arched stained-glass window picturing Jesus standing on green grass in a glowing yellow light beam against a blue sky. Jesus was sad-eyed and pretty, with his arms spread and his palms upraised, long yellow hair flowing to his shoulders and long white robes flowing to his white feet. Little children and lambs and other youngster livestock flocked around him.

For Bud, that vision was unsatisfactory. Disgusting, really, in its cartoonishness. For Lily's benefit, Bud condensed whatever leftover inner religion he had into a bleeding heart tattoo covering the outer face of his left biceps. Fairly painful to receive and impossible to remove. Also a big artistic disappointment, since he had imagined it highly anatomical, but it came out more like a valentine.

Even at that, the tattoo accorded in some pleasing way with his necklace, a big black fossilized shark tooth. On their honeymoon, Lily had found it at low tide down at Surfside and had it wound in silver wire to hang on a leather thong against his sternum. The tooth was millions of years old, but you could still cut your finger on the serrated edges, which Bud did while the tattoo still wept, sealing his thinking about their harmony. Jesus's blood and some big black-eyed shark reddening strange waters. Both expressing the exact same reality. The meaning of the necklace could be summed into one useful idea—adapted from the possibly true fact that sharks die if they stop swimming forward—useful for every single misstep in life. Move on. And the meaning of the tattoo was equally brief, and no argument about it. Everybody dies.

Now, Bud too had drawn considerable blood. He wasn't always proud of it, and though he hadn't actually confessed, things seemed pretty cut and dried in regard to his guilt. In jail awaiting trial, he noticed that everybody treated him like he was a terminal case. So before the court date, he wasted time trying and failing to get his mind right for sitting down in the big chair with a smirk on his face and sucking down a deep breath of gas.

BUD AND LILY HAD become a bad match immediately after the hot courtship ended. In short order, Bud realized marriage was not always going to be a fun time. Lily was not his dream lover anymore, not by a long stretch. Her children could pass for normal back then, but they were still a constant irritant. How could romance prevail with them always needing something contradictory to romance, such as ass wiping and nose blowing?

It could not, was the short answer.

Also, Lily owned her house outright due to the horny grocery-store-manager first husband who knocked her up with twins, then up and died before they were even born. It chapped Bud's ass to live in another man's house, even a dead one's. Troublesome too that Lily had her own money. Some from the dead husband and some from work. She was a beautician. The State had issued her a license to cut and color hair, and she had an arrangement with an older woman down the street to watch the kids during Lily's work hours at the beauty shop.

Bud's strongest argument rested on the fact that he was the man, and therefore Lily should put the house in his name and quit her job. But it got nowhere, especially since Bud's weekly check from the railroad wouldn't at all cover the bills. Pulling a third of his weight was the best Bud could do, which seemed about right to him, give or take. Still, it irked him when Lily headed out mornings into the wide world looking pretty in her tight white beautician outfit and white crepe-sole shoes like she was in the medical profession. Most days, she would put her lipstick on and blot it with a rectangle of Kleenex and throw it in the toilet and walk out. There it would float, unflushed, a perfect red print of her mouth for Bud to take a piss into.

And even more irksome, her hints in conversation with others that what she brought home was so much more than he did. But the two sums drew a little closer if you subtracted tips, which, Bud reasoned, was like taking charity. He told Lily to quit letting rich blue-haired grannies palm her a bill on their way out the door. It was demeaning for her, and even worse for him. Like he was married to a whore.

Lily said, No, I won't quit taking tips. I earn them. It's how the job works. You don't have to eat the groceries I buy with them.

That kind of heartless remark, and the general misery of their marriage, was what lit a fire under Bud's ass, so that before long he got ambitious and came into some money. One afternoon, Bud and his railroad friend, Billy, were smoking reefer and listening to the radio and bitching about their jobs when they should have been working. And out of nowhere Billy proposed a simple break-and-enter deal. Some rich guy he had done a little work for a while back. Surely his house would have enough pawnable stuff—watches and jewelry and silverware—to pay a couple months' expenses and leave ample pocket money while they pondered their futures.

Bud had sort of halfway sworn off felonies. Teenager prison was bad enough, and he sure didn't want to do time with big boys. But it would only be this once, and they'd be careful.

Except Billy's guy was into some shady commercial real estate dealings or other lofty half-legal commerce demanding cash transactions. Stashed in his dresser drawer, alongside his wife's jewelry and a fancy wristwatch, was a size 12 shoe box filled with stacks of money. And a few days after their job, Billy's guy turned up floating in a big lake ten miles north of town, which was a puzzler and sort of sad, though not a major cause of concern.

The shoe box held bundles of bills, all tapped into strict rectangles and banded. Altogether, they stacked nearly to the box lid. The top layers were mostly worn ones and fives and tens. So at the moment they found it, they thought it was nothing more than a little lagniappe to the job. But later, when they dug to the bottom, they found that the final layers were perfect stacks of new hundreds wrapped in red bands.

Billy drove, so Bud counted a stack. That one little half-inch fucker was ten thousand dollars. Who would have guessed?

The first thing they did was go raise hell for a couple of days, and when Bud finally got home, he was still thoroughly drunk and exhausted. Lily, of course, took advantage of the situation and set right in on him. Where had he been? Drinking, obviously. Then she started cataloging all the ways he was worthless.

On fool impulse, as his most potent available argument against Lily, Bud stuck his hands into his coat pockets and pulled out the many bundles of hundreds and threw them on the bedspread. If you were honest and stupid, you worked a couple of lifetimes for that kind of money, doled out by the hour in pocket-change amounts by asswipe bosses.

Lily riffled through a few stacks and then began questioning where they all came from, because she knew for sure he'd never earn that kind of money, no matter if he lived as long as Methuselah.

Bud stretched out grandly on the bed among his winnings, his hands behind his head and a satisfied look on his face, saying nothing. Very shortly, unfortunately, he dozed off or passed out, one. When he woke late the next day, the money was gone and the room started spinning whenever he moved his head. Try to stand and the whole world tipped at a severe angle to gravity. He found himself banging against walls and knee-walking on the way to the toilet.

After a couple more rough days while his head cleared and his appetite came back, he started asking questions regarding the whereabouts of his money. Being cool, since he couldn't exactly snatch it back and hang on to it now. He was the very bird that threw it out there on the chenille, trying to be the big man. And then gave Lily the gift of his unconsciousness, plus two additional vomit-dominated days, for her to plot and hide.

Lily wouldn't say where the money was. Just that it was safe. She had decided not to get too concerned about where it came from. She wasn't the one who stole it. For her, it was found money. Her plan was to hoard it. She said it was their security. Use a little to help pay bills every month. Clothes and shoes for the kids. Insurance. Maybe a fairly new used car every few years. Those dreary sorts of things, on and on. It was like a snapshot of how their marriage had sloped down to its present moment. Lily had lost all her fun. Come into enough money to change your life big-time right now, and all she had the imagination to do was hide it and dole it out in dribs and drabs forever.

Over the next days, Bud became resentful. Where had his goddamn money gone? When she was out of the house, he frantically looked in every stupid place she might think was clever, with no success. Then they fought. Which was what they started calling it when Bud gave her a beating.

The first time, Lily was out of work for three days before makeup would cover the bruises. And the fights continued, sometimes just mild and out of habit, and sometimes for blood. One bad night, Lily conceded partway. The next morning, they went to a lawyer and added Bud's name to hers on the deed to the house, and the lawyer did a fine job of pretending not to notice how her mouth looked, and her left ear, and the way she carried her right arm. The deed wasn't so important to Bud. His money would buy a couple of blocks of bungalows like Lily's. It was the principle of the thing.

Afterward the fights diminished somewhat but did not stop entirely, for Lily would not say where the money went. It was like a partial truce. Except strange days began unfolding when Lily was stupid enough to leave Bud alone with the children, and it became an issue for him to explain bruises and red marks.

Even with all her provocation, Bud would never have stabbed Lily if she hadn't come home unexpected one day. An especially bad moment for her to walk in without knocking. All of a sudden she was shouting, I'll fucking kill you if it's the last fucking thing I do.

And those would be her final words on that subject or any other, since she died in the fight that followed. Blood almost black against the white kitchen linoleum, and Bud gripping a black-handled butcher knife whetted keen to the point of invisibility along the curved edge of the blade. A siren wailing faint in the distance due to a neighbor's phone call out of weariness from the frequent racket. The two children standing in the doorway to the dining room, looking dead-eyed at the scene.

MOTHER. WHAT A VAGUE CONCEPT. Luce had never wanted to be one and hadn't seen hers since sometime around third grade. She remembered Lola rarely, but almost always in a pretty summer dress. Pink polka dots or shimmery lime green. A full skirt, and sunburned freckled breasts swelling above a tight bodice. Sometimes Lola smelled like lipstick and sometimes she smelled like Scotch and sometimes she smelled like the damp moss that grew along creek banks. Her hair changed colors several times a year, like leaves on deciduous trees, which, when Luce first learned the word in fifth grade, she thought meant man-eating trees.

On a bad day, Lola would slap fire out of you at the least provocation. Such as you and your little sister having a row in the backseat of the car. Lola didn't worry over fine layers of justice. She would reach her arm behind her and smack blind at whichever child and whatever part she could reach. Leave red finger marks on your bare legs and arms and faces. All the time driving and smoking with her free hand and shouting about what sorry little bitches she had made. Then five miles later, as soon as you quit bawling, she would pull over and hug until all the breath huffed out your mouth. Lola would ignore you for days, and then she would be right in your face needing your attention. It was still confusing to Luce which one was worse.

When Luce felt charitable, she thought maybe Lola's tragedy was that she lived in the wrong place or had married far too young to the wrong man. Or maybe it was simple, like her beauty, a condition of existence for the people around her to deal with while Lola sailed off carefree toward a blue horizon. But did that need to include having a loud sobbing childhood fight with Lily, wholly your own fault, yet both of you get smacked equally? Lola, barely more than a teenager herself, saying, I'll give you something to cry about.

Lola's only nugget of wisdom to her little daughters was *Never cry, never ever.* So, in the future, if somebody came to Luce wanting to know what to carve on Lola's tombstone, those four words would be it.

LUCE'S THREE-YEAR anniversary at the Lodge was coming up in the fall, and all that time, she had hardly missed any of the modern world. It pressed so hard against you, like somebody standing in front of you screaming and jumping up and down to misdirect your thoughts. Let it all go and it fades away, similar to when you ignore run-of-the-mill ghosts. All they become is an updraft feeling. Nothing urgent. Just smoke as it begins to draw up a cold flue.

What good does the world do you? That was the question Luce had asked herself for three years, and the answer she had arrived at was simple. A distressingly large portion of the world doesn't do you any good whatsoever. In fact, it does you bad. Casts static between your ears, drowns out who you truly are. So she tried to cull daily reality pretty harsh, retaining just landscape and weather and animals and the late-night radio.

Luce was fairly sure about all that, but she wasn't a preacher. Pushing her ideas onto the children held no appeal. Early days, she did try to talk with them, though. Just doing her job as caretaker, asking pertinent questions about their favorite things. She got no answers and realized that they couldn't or wouldn't talk, but unlike the deaf woman in town, who made every possible effort of gesture and facial expression to bridge the gap, the children wouldn't hardly look your way. When Luce tried getting them to speak by pointing and saying the names of things that fell to hand—water, door, hen, beech tree, moon—they looked at her finger. Or if not that, then they looked impatiently into the distance like she was the crazy one. Sometimes she got the feeling they knew more than they let on, and other times she doubted she would ever be able to reason with them.

Luce's first impulse was to be grateful and keep her own mouth shut. Continue running the Lodge like a monastery under a vow of silence. She was used to quiet. But that resolution lasted only a couple of days, and then there was a second dead rooster, and Luce figured that even if she wasn't a preacher, she'd better try to be a teacher.

Maybe these city kids had never seen live chickens before. Didn't realize the direct relationship between the living birds and a fried drumstick or two ecstatic bites of deviled egg, rich with mayonnaise and pickle relish and paprika, which they hoovered up like they'd never had it before, which maybe they hadn't. Luce had learned by observation that the children liked to eat, and they didn't seem to discriminate too much. They liked fragrant cabbage, boiled grey as wet newspapers. Thick slabs of fried bologna cut from a long red stalk down at the little country store. Kohlrabi doused with vinegar so pungent it would bring tears to your eyes. Stewed tomatoes and okra, stringing slime behind when you spooned it out of the pot. Or if Luce didn't feel the least bit like fooling with cookery, sliced tomatoes on light bread with a thick smear of Duke's. Whatever you set in front of the children, they'd put their heads down and eat with the air of hungry bird dogs.

So, on a hazy late-July morning, Luce took them out to search the henhouse for eggs, the first lesson of the week, devoted to how we get our food. The wonder of a perfect fresh shit-smeared egg was not lost on Luce, and she aimed to share it. Even before they stepped through the door, she filled the air with words like a docent. She explained the economics of chickens, talking to the children as if they had sense and hoping that a few words might get through.

First point, they really liked fried chicken and stewed chicken, didn't they? Second point, Luce couldn't afford to go to town and buy chicken from the grocery, and right now, only a few eating-sized chickens roamed the yard. Luce counted them out. Seven. Thus, if you go around killing chickens for entertainment, it's not only a mean thing to do and liable to come back around on you in the future as bad luck and trouble, but it will leave all three of them without fried or stewed or roasted chicken for quite some time.

Maybe Luce was a little fragmented in the delivery, but the lesson was simple. Manage chickens carefully, you'll have eggs most of the time and chicken meat some of the time. Manage poorly, and there will be no more chickens or eggs at all.

The children walked around in the dim brown light of the hen-house and looked on the dusty ledges and in the nesting boxes. The girl found the first egg. She held it cupped in her palm and studied it. Then she smashed her other fist against it and smeared the mess on her brother's face. Immediately, he hit her hard in the stomach and they both started howling at the tops of their lungs without ever pausing in their fighting, which was vicious. They rolled on the packed dirt floor amid the black-and-white chicken droppings and the little white pinfeathers. Luce watched them, and it reminded her of snakes fighting. Real cold, like they were not even very angry at each other, just acting under some shared compulsion as incomprehensible as sex or madness. Luce finally stepped in and snatched them each by the backs of their shirts like they had handles and held them apart.

Many people would council putting the rod to them until the importance of obedience made an impression. That, or lock them up in a dark closet for a few hours until they fell out blinking into the sunlight and did as they were told. Maybe the children had it coming, but if those correctives were applied to her, Luce would just get meaner and more hardheaded. The one angry switching was bad enough, and she'd sworn she wouldn't do it again, for their sake and for hers. So that none of them would have to go around feeling bad all day, or maybe forever.

For the next lesson, Luce took the children out back to the kitchen garden, with its deer fence of leaned and weathered palings. The morning fog had not fully burned away, and dew still beaded on the tomato leaves. The sun was a faint pale disk, the light flat and grey. The children stood shivering with their arms crossed on their chests.

Their faces pale and puffy-eyed, and their hair in points, like they had just rolled out of bed. Luce gave them each a cherry tomato folded in a basil leaf, which they seemed to like. They started making their own, and Luce began filling the air with vegetable lore, learned mostly from Maddie. Luce explained that she planted like Cherokee people did. One corn kernel and two beans to a hill. The cornstalk makes the trellis for the bean vines to grow up, and some magic love between corn and beans keeps them from stripping the good out of the soil, so you can keep on using the same plot of ground a long time. And, of course, squash and melons grow well between corn and beans.

She told the children how you can think about history one way, that it took thousands of years for people to figure all this out by tedious trial and error, generation by generation. Or you can think that some old woman just got lucky one summer and shared the wealth. Either way, though, you have to be vigilant about hoeing and suckering and those kinds of tedious jobs. Otherwise, by August you end up with green life running wild, vegetables to your shoulders and weeds to your knees in the aisles. Copperheads twisting through stalks and vines so that you have to take a shotgun with you to gather dinner.

So much more produce than we could ever eat by ourselves, Luce said. Yet the garden keeps on making stuff, whether it's wanted or not. Squash and cantaloupes collapsing where they lay. The sad internal structure of a rotting tomato haunting your dreams. If you didn't learn the art of canning, you'd better get comfortable living with the guilt of wastage. Which reminded Luce of a day long ago when she and Lily were home alone and somehow broke the kitchen faucet. A fat stream of water splashed into the sink. They could not turn it off, no matter how hard they twisted the handle. Childhood panic. Lily reached a glass to Luce and said, Don't just stand there, start drinking.

Which led Luce to ask the kids, So, what do you remember about Lily? I've got so many stories like that one. I remember a lot.

The children wandered deeper into the garden and didn't seem to hear a word of Luce's ramble. But at least they weren't trying to light the cornstalks on fire. The girl scrunched her cheeks and brows to hold two cherry tomatoes like red eyes for a few seconds, and the boy looked like he was trying to decide whether it was scary or funny. He picked up a fallen beefsteak tomato and splattered it against her shoulder and she retaliated. More playful than violent, so Luce even lobbed a couple herself.

The day they visited the orchards up the hillside, Luce explained that trees behaved more rationally than vegetables. Slow and careful. These had been let go for decades, and the limbs had grown crisscrossed and shaggy with dun-colored moss and lichen, yet they still made about as many fuzzy peaches in summer and bright speckled apples in fall as she could eat, whether fresh or dried in brown leathery rings or canned. Even without pruning and fertilizing, the elderly trees would probably go on for at least one person's little lifetime, offering themselves forward against the uncertain future with grim persistence.

The children walked straight down the old rows, the girl first and the boy right behind. At the end of the orchard, they continued the line into the random woods until Luce ran ahead and waved her arms, herding them back to the Lodge.

On a drizzly day toward the end of the week, Luce walked them in the woods, making water the topic of her ramble. It's what makes life so rampant around here, she said. The children kept leaving the crooked trail and diving straight into wet brush and tall weeds until they were soaked, and Luce kept shooing them back to the path, all the time explaining how most years, you got eighty or ninety inches. A hundred is not at all remarkable in a temperate rain forest. All the moons from spring to early fall, everything plumps with water. Think jungle, and then go a degree onward in the direction of a deep green world so wet you could wring it out like a dishrag if you could get a good grip on either end of it. Giant hemlocks and sycamores and tulip trees. Rhododendrons. Moss and ferns. Understory too thick to see more than twenty feet into the woods, until killing frosts reveal the bones of the place. A steamy greenhouse of plants and creatures. Flip any rock or dead log, and myriad beings go crawling down individual vectors toward the darkness they crave. Sit in a yellow sunbeam, and the damp air around you thickens with myriad beings dancing up into the daylight they love. Life likes the wet and rewards it. Archaic forms incompatible with the modern world persist here. Hellbenders, deep in the creek beds. Panthers, high on the ridges. Even dead blighted chestnuts resurrect themselves out of the black forest floor, refusing to accept the terms of their extinction. Hope incarnate. All, Luce explained, due to moisture. Some summer days, the air carried so much of it you couldn't strike a paper match. Briefly, Luce entertained the idea that maybe a fascination with fire was fine here. A harmless oddity, like a family streak.

But, really, it wouldn't do. So the next day's lesson began with her admitting to the children that the attraction of fire was not lost on her in the least, the beauty and mystery and power of a strong blaze. Same type of thing with fire as with chickens, though. So easy to get things out of balance and suffer the consequences. Burn down the Lodge, and they're all liable to find themselves sleeping on the ground in the woods.

Luce took a hearthside galvanized bucket filled with thin splits of fat pine kindling out to the porch and emptied it on the floor. She and the children sat cross-legged around the jumble. On the fly, Luce made up a game like pick-up sticks in reverse. The goal was to lay the most complicated pattern of kindling—cones, squares, triangles, goofy pentangles, or whatever form sprang into your mind—just like building a fire, but no matches or flint and steel or bows. Rule one: if you burned your sticks, you lost. And if your complicated shape collapsed first in the delicate laying of pieces, you lost. If it held together into a perfect geometry, and you finished first, you won. In case of a tie, the structure with the most pieces won. Simple.

She declared the prize to be either a fried bologna sandwich or a cereal bowl of vanilla wafers. Winner's choice. Sharing optional. And, as an afterthought to the rules, if you decided to build something that looked like a little Abe Lincoln log cabin or a hay wagon or a hog pen or a '57 Studebaker instead of a fire, you got extra credit.

The children looked at the wood splits but didn't touch them. They went to the porch rockers and rocked for the next two hours, looking glazed into the distance.

THERE USED TO BE so much time and space in a day. Whenever Luce wanted, she'd walk down the road and check on Stubblefield. He was so lonesome for company after his wife died that every time Luce stopped by, he set a bottle of good Scotch on the kitchen table and killed a hen. She'd be there for hours listening to his tales of wild youth, and eating the crisp salty legs and breasts he dredged in corn-meal and fried in lard. Spending an entire afternoon that way suited Luce fine, because she was lonely too, but in a somewhat different way.

Now, though, Stubblefield was dead and the children had come, and suddenly she couldn't let up for an instant. The children rose with the sun, so Luce did too. Pay a moment's attention to your own life, and they would burn the place down or run off to get lost in the woods or drowned in the lake. Watchfulness was something Luce had mostly applied to nothing but the natural world. Birds and leaves and weather. An occasional deer or bear or screaming panther. Distant lights in the sky at night moving contrary to the expected. And the sweetness of it was simple: the natural world would go on and on just fine whether you watched or not. Your existence was incidental. Nature didn't re-quire anything at all other than the bare minimum deal in return for life. Be born, die.

Neither did the children care whether you watched their doings. But the catch was, they might be dead within the hour if you let up your attentions. Little pale damp lifeless bodies lying at the lakeshore or beside deep-woods streams. Peanut-colored wet hair swarped across blue foreheads.

What a mess if the children found a way to die. What would you need to do? Probably, walk to the store and call the sheriff's office. Afterward, start dealing with the horrors of law and mortuary. Stubby little caskets fitted into abbreviated holes backhoed into the ground. Order a stone.

And that wasn't exactly idle daydreaming, either. The children were worse than horses in their ability to harm themselves against the most benign elements of their physical world. The girl tore off the bail to a little zinc bucket and pierced the wing of her nostril with it, apparently experimenting to see how far she could run it up into the cavities of her head. The wound bled like the fountain of life itself until Luce stanched it with a press of pigeon moss. Then, as if bleeding were a contest, the boy cut a triangular gash at his hairline on the edge of the smokehouse tin roof. He stood hollering, with blood running down his face and dripping off his chin onto his white shirt. Blood on the point of the roof, which was ten feet above the ground and the boy was not much better than three feet high. The only ladder on the place was six feet tall. None of the arithmetic worked out. You could drive yourself crazy trying to figure the angles. What a damn needy world Luce suddenly occupied. A pair of suicidal old men would be easier to caretake than these two youngsters.

Still, Luce held firm to the belief that quiet and solitude were good for you, offering peace, or at least hope for peace. Mainly because people were what they were and you couldn't change them. Most of the time, they couldn't change themselves, even if they were desperate to be somebody different from who they were. So, best keep your distance. Nevertheless, here were these little children who didn't remind her in any helpful nostalgic way of sweet Lily.

Most nights Luce couldn't even be sure they would sleep until daylight. They wandered, part nocturnal in their comings and goings, sharing the habits of raccoons and house cats. By morning she'd have to hunt for them like hen eggs. Find one balled up in a nest of quilts on the sleeping porch and the other laid out like a corpse at a viewing beneath a hunt board in the dining room. Had to start locking the doors at night instead of only latching the screens.

It was hard not to think about giving the children back to the State. Luce wondered sometimes if they would even notice. As long as they had things to tear up or set afire and nobody to disagree with them, they seemed content. They particularly liked being outdoors. It was one of their major opinions. On stormy afternoons, when lightning forked from black clouds, they would sit together and look out a window, their gloom about Luce keeping them inside expressed by the droop of their posture.

They had come with names. Dolores and Frank. Luce had probably once known that but had forgotten, since in letters Lily always referred to them simply as her babies. And, yes, Luce owned, they were pretty messed up. But to put matters in perspective, she thought back to people she'd had to share her daily world with. In comparison, how messed up were the children really? Lots of human beings got through the day a bunch more messed up than Dolores and Frank. They weren't criminals or drunks. Being uncommunicative and taking an interest in fire were neither crimes nor sins, just inconvenient. And Luce didn't have to love them. She just had to take care of them.

These days, around noon, Luce began counting the hours until bedtime. Lights out, children asleep. Think your own thoughts and listen to WLAC. John R. and Gene Nobles with their wondrous music and offers of a hundred baby chicks delivered C.O.D. to the P.O. in no more than a few days at a price too low to be believed. Luce had been tempted to order a boxful of chickens, but pictured a hundred yellow fluffs of life packed like ping-pong balls, dying one by one, hour by hour, waiting for her to come pick them up. Open the lid, and the survivors would be looking up into the light, necks stretched and yearning, and sort of treading water above the dead ones, whose nearly whole view of life on earth was the black inside of a cardboard box. So she had taken a pass on the fabulous and depressing chicken deal.

The music, though, was brilliant and beautiful, bright and wild, opening deep into her heart. It strove upward toward some indefinable, or perhaps unmentionable, light. Even exhausted from a long day with the kids, Luce would stay up late as she could, listening until she finally fell asleep.

CITY OF LIMERICK PUBLIC LIBRARY 99382

WHEN SHE AND LILY were little girls, not quite a year apart, Luce was the wanderer. At six, her last year of perfect freedom, she explored the lake town without restraint. If some shade-tree mechanic's feet stuck out from underneath a jacked-up Nash getting a new clutch, Luce would soon have her head under the car, studying the dark miraculous complication of greasy parts. She once sort of borrowed without permission a frontier clothes iron from an elderly woman living in a log cabin. The kind of iron with a space inside that was meant to be filled with hot fire coals. It fascinated her. Some simple forgotten relic of the past that could be made to work again. Luce carried the iron around until she found a house with a fire going. It was muggy June at the time, and it took a fair amount of walking and knocking on screen doors. And then she managed to burn a red second-degree triangle into her thigh that would leave a faint permanent mark, now visible only when she had a tan.

Probably that same day, Lily had been content to stay home and count her toes. She liked being safe inside. She could sit all morning dressing and undressing a frizzy-haired baby doll with only two outfits and just one blue eye that would open all the way. Lily liked naps and vanilla wafers.

So, anyone back then paying attention to the two girls—which was nobody—would have predicted that Lily would never leave the lake town. Someday way in the blue-haired future, she would rest in the hillside cemetery with a view across the water toward the Lodge and the mountains beyond. Luce would be the one to take off into the wide world at the first opportunity, probably with some man, the first of several husbands. Be buried in Anchorage or La Paz or whatever distant city you cared to name.

But Lily was the one who disappeared. A couple of weeks after her high school graduation, she bought a bus ticket with savings from her carhop job. No word of her whereabouts for months. Not like there was a mother at home to worry about her, and their father was busy or else figured, you get out of school, you're on your own.

Luce stayed home. No money for more school, and no precedent for it. Nobody in her family had ever darkened the doors of any college. Also, she held some underlying suspicion that people were about the same wherever you went, but lots of places were way less beautiful than right here.

She took various jobs. Counter work at the drugstore and the post office. A brief stint as secretary for the town's insurance agent. She quit at the drop of a hat if she felt the least slighted. The amazing power of saying kiss my ass and walking out the door. She dated the kinds of local guys her age who had family businesses to inherit some-day. Son of the dry cleaner. Son of the dime store owner. Two of four redneck brothers who stood to inherit the paving business that got all the road contracts in this whole backwater of the State. She had a pretty serious thing for a while with a doctor's son who had been off to UVA and wanted to become something or other that he couldn't quite put into words, a teacher or philosopher or entrepreneur nudg-ing the world in a better direction. His claim to fame, other than not wearing socks with his Weejuns, was that for an entire semester he had lived in the dorm room right next to the one Poe had occupied. It seemed like real love for a whole summer, and then he went back to graduate school. By Thanksgiving the letters, in both directions, had dwindled to nothing.

Everything else lasted about two months and then either blew up or fizzled away. Luce decided she lacked passion, which was a word she hated. Ask her what she craved, and she'd get a little frantic about things like books, the woods, music. Plants and the seasons. Also free-dom. Not being bought and sold by some idiot employer, not having the moments of her days valued in fractions of a dollar by somebody other than herself.

———

LUCE, WITH DOLORES and Frank drifting and wavering along ahead of her—kites in the wind, hen and chicks—stopped by one day to let them meet Maddie. They found her busy at the stove, frying thin strips of something dredged in cornmeal. The black iron skillet crackled and spit, and the room smelled of good food sputtering in yellow pork fat. Hickory fire so hot little wispy circles of blue flame escaped around the cast-iron stove lids. Dolores and Frank crowded close, and Maddie had to sweep her forearm against their bony chests to move them a safe distance back. When a batch of strips browned, Maddie lifted them out of the lard with a slotted spoon and cast them onto layers of newspaper covering the kitchen table.

Luce couldn't help but read anything put before her, and an ad on one page caught her eye. A simple graphic pair of round spectacles from an optometrist named Finklestein. Above the ad, little boxes of tiny print with estimates of weather in the near future and the past month's rainfall amount in inches, and all the fascinating business about moon phases and where Venus and Mars and Saturn and Jupiter would be in the night sky on whatever day this yellow sheet commemorated. Luce looked to the top of the page for the date, and she would have been twelve.

When Maddie had finished four heaping batches of the strips, she salted them and dashed hot drops of green-pepper sauce on them, and then poured four tall glasses of cold buttermilk. Beads of condensation ran down and printed dark rings on the newspapers. Maddie and Luce and the children sat and started eating with their fingers.

Luce tried to guess the name of the meat. It was good. Crisp and greasy. Inside the brown crust, pure white as a shaving from a bar of Ivory soap. But it had little flavor of its own. Mainly a chewy texture.

—What? Luce asked.

—Spinal cord, Maddie said.

—Of what?

—Hog.

—Hum.

—Not many people bother to eat it anymore.

—It's way better than I would have guessed, Luce said.

—Probably, if you breaded cardboard in cornmeal and fried it in lard, it would taste pretty good too.

Dolores and Frank downed their buttermilk and ate their share of fried spine clean down to the paper and then sat sniffing their fingertips, remembering a grand moment just passed.

—I like it when people like my cooking, Maddie said.

She got up and went rummaging among various boxes and bags in cupboards and dressers, looking for her fairy crosses. She collected them. Knew a secret spot, a runneled dirt bank deep in the woods. After a hard spring rain washed the crystals out of the ground, she could find as high as three perfect crosses out of the many X's. She threw the X's back to the ground because they were bad luck. She kept the crosses in a shoe box. But someday, she would let them go back to the wild, scatter them in the woods so they could become miracles again for future pilgrims.

When Maddie found the box, she dug around making a selection, and then gave Dolores and Frank two of the smaller ones, perfect and identical in the intersections of their angles. Also two shiny brown buckeyes from a tree struck by lightning and thus sacred.

Said, Carry them in your pockets for protection.

Then she brought out the main welcome gift she had bought on a recent rare trip to town. A child-sized straw cowboy hat, bright red. She set it on Frank's head and said, Welcome to the lake. Luce could tell Maddie was awfully proud of the gift, but she also saw trouble written all over Dolores's face. Luce said her thank-yous and hustled the children out the door and up the road toward home, thinking that a few weeks ago she would have made the same mistake. Not having children of her own, it had likely never occurred to Maddie that she'd better buy two hats.

Before they got much past the first bend, Dolores slapped the hat off Frank's head, and then they rolled in the dirt. Luce, pretty hot, grabbed them by their collars and separated them and stood them on their feet. Then she took a slow breath and decided that for the rest of the afternoon, they each had to wear the hat exactly fifteen minutes. She mashed the hat on Dolores's head and clicked her fingernail five times against her watch crystal. Said, Dolores, you have to wear the hat until three thirty-two, then Frank has to wear it. Don't cross me on this.

Dolores took the hat off and tried to give it to Frank, who wouldn't take it. Luce made her put it back on, and Dolores walked tragic and sad-hearted, dragging the toes of her sneakers in the dirt, her face down and shadowed by the brim. At five to go, Luce started counting off the minutes. Dolores's mood suddenly brightened, and dread over-whelmed Frank. At the moment of transferring the hat, Dolores danced three happy steps.

Back at the Lodge, they sat in the porch rockers, sulled up and sad, rocking slow. Partway through the walk home, it had quit mattering anymore who wore the hat. All the joy had drained out of it.

Luce sat with her feet dangling over the porch edge, looking at the blue lake and the green mountains, keeping time and enforcing the exchanges. Trying to hide how delighted she was to find that the children understood and actually complied with her totally arbitrary rules, an important skill for living in the world with other people. Unless you retreated to your own private wilderness. Except there was no wilderness.

Arbitrarily, Luce decided that one more exchange would finish making the point, and afterward, she gave the children the choice of what to do with the hat. They carried it to the cook stove and used a piece of kindling to stuff it down an eye onto the bed of coals. The straw flamed up yellow through the open hole for a few seconds and then was gone for good.

CHAPTER 4

BUD'S LAWYER WAS A SMART and ruthless old white-haired bastard. Drove a new black Coupe de Ville, and had gotten drunk with every governor back into the late twenties, regardless of political party. He'd taken Bud's case only because he figured one way or the other, he'd end up with Lily's house to sell. Said to Bud, right at the outset, Not a great deal of money in a little two-bedroom bungalow, but sadly the modern world has become largely a matter of volume.

The State's man was so fresh out of law school that he still went back to campus for parties thrown by friends who had not yet graduated. He seemed stunned to find himself in court. During the course of a morning, Bud's lawyer convinced the jury of men that Lily had been little better than a whore. All in all, they inferred, she probably deserved killing, at least within the shadow of a doubt the old lawyer had laid out as a confusing yet binding covenant between God and man regarding the administration of justice on earth. Case in point, Lily had conceived not one but two children by another man. Also, hypothetical boyfriends were alluded to vividly and with only a hesitant objection from the boy lawyer, who seemed crushed when the judge ruled against him. When it came to the murder weapon, the old lawyer asked a simple, compelling question: If you live in a house, aren't your fingerprints on everything, including the knives? Crazy dope-addict killers wearing gloves could never be ruled out. And, further, the only possible eyewitnesses, when questioned by police detectives, had not testified to his client's guilt in any way.

The old lawyer failed to mention that the witnesses were children who either could not or would not utter a single word or even acknowledge they had been asked a question. When the State's man went into those inconvenient facts, the old lawyer pulled out a doctor's report labeling the children as feebleminded. After that, the State's man sat quiet, like he knew he was taking a beating and just wanted it to be over.

Three days later, Bud walked out the courthouse doors. Hardly two o'clock, humid and hot and the sky dull white, still wearing his grey trial suit the lawyer had bought for him, and carrying a paper poke with his clothes and effects from when he was arrested. Outside, an elder woman sat on a bench feeding peanuts to pigeons, and when a group of them took to the air their wing beats were like muffled applause.

Many high feelings rushed through Bud. Mainly he felt giddy disbelief over his impossible good fortune at the hands of the justice system. What a grand idea democracy is, where every fool who can't get out of jury duty gets to have his opinion counted. Especially the two fools who held out and voted not guilty. And the judge didn't even ask for a bond while the prosecution decided when and if to retry. He just said, Don't leave the state, son. Also the splendid matter of the little retard bastards keeping their jaws shut. Though, of course, the lawyer had to piss on Bud's parade by reminding him that even if they don't retry soon, there's no limitation on murder charges. Ninety years old, they can drag you out of your sickbed and have another go at you.

And then, a more forward-looking early thought. Where was his goddamn money? Where else but with the mute witness kids?

Bud walked down the street to the bank and checked Lily's account balance. It was exactly what he'd guessed it would be. He zeroed it out, which only bought him a beat-up Remington revolver and one box of shells at a pawnshop. Only enough left over for a club sandwich and a Coke at the Woolworth's counter.

Homeless and penniless, but armed and pondering deeply, he wandered the streets of the capital city. The lawyer already had papers for the house, so about all Bud could claim were the furnishings. Flea-market shit. Selling scratched chifforobes and stained mattresses was not how he cared to spend time. He knew Lily had family up in a hillbilly mountain town. Minus a mother who'd had the sense to fly away many years earlier to places unknown. So, nothing left here worth fooling with. But he had a damn hoard somewhere. Dusky dark, Bud hot-wired a new Chevy coupe and took off west.

THAT FIRST NIGHT, in a thunderstorm, Bud hit two filling stations, one right after the other, for the day's receipts. Pretty simple transactions, when it's just you and one guy at the register, and you're the one waving the gun. Afterward, Bud kept driving west on slick black roads for a couple of hours, and checked into a linoleum-floor motel in time to flop on the plaid bedspread and watch *The Twilight Zone*. Next morning, he did two more filling stations and a country store. Fifty miles onward, he drove the Chevy down a red dirt road and pushed it over a steep clay bank into a brown river. He knew enough about sinking cars from teenage joyriding to roll the windows down and open the trunk and hood. The car bobbed briefly, and then went all the way under, nothing but fat bubbles breaking the surface of the water. A rainbow sheen of gas trailing with the current. Reluctantly, Bud pitched the Remington and the unused ammo to midstream. Then, figuring you can't be too careful, he pulled out the red bandanna he had worn over his face for the stickups, cowboy-movie-bandit style. He knotted it around a rock and threw it into the river and walked on to the nearest town.

At the first used-car lot, he bought a happy-faced green Ford pickup from deep in the previous decade for two hundred and sixty dollars cash. He put the title in the glove box for future reference by any interested party, such as the highway patrol. They were welcome to have a look. Title and tag were clean, and he had been turned loose and was unarmed. The law was his friend, and he was off to start a new life in his farmer pickup with the wood sideboards grey as old fence palings. Such was the attitude he would strike if he got pulled. But he didn't plan to get pulled. He drove carefully and no more than five over at all times.

NIGHT AND RAINING AGAIN. Bud had driven across two mountain passes and through a dark twisting gorge. All the way, the narrow road hung either at the brink of a long drop or else ran right alongside a rush of white water. Few signs of life out in these black mountains. If there were houses, the folks shut out the lights and went to bed early. Probably no TV this deep in the vertical country. The radio in the piece-of-shit truck barely worked due to a possible short in its wiring, so mostly it picked up a lot of static and one strong blast of race music, and then, in between patches of silence, strange gibber that sounded like Cuba or Mexico or Texas, one.

The gas gauge alternated between half a tank and empty. Pecking at it with a forefinger clarified nothing. There hadn't been an open station for two hours, and not even any closed ones lately. The only business for miles, a dark roadside shack with a hand-lettered plywood sign offering boiled peanuts.

His map said the town had to be not far ahead, but for all the evidence the road offered, it might well go nowhere from here. Drive and drive through winding steep cliffs, and then without warning the pavement would end. And immediately beyond it, in the yellow converging headlight cones, would be a patch of tall weeds ending in a solid wall of trees. Damn nature all around. Not even a sign saying DEAD END. Probably because you would surely know already that's where you were.

So it was a welcome moment when Bud crossed a low gap and dropped toward a lakeside town, streetlights and neon glowing ahead. At the edge of town, a giant towering sign cast a distorted image of itself onto the wet pavement. Twisted tubes in pink and lavender and yellow outlined an Indian wearing a feather headdress, and under-neath, flowing blue letters spelled out the title of the place. CHIEF MOTEL.

Bud checked in, and the room had a surprise television, though when he turned it on, he found only one snowy station featuring a man in a gas station uniform guessing the weather. Then an old melan-choly Wolfman movie, to which Bud fell asleep and dreamed one of his favorite innocent clarifying dreams involving Jesus's blood bathing the world and making it fresh and clean. It was like the picture on the paint can, except it was blood pouring over the North Pole and drip-ping off the equator.

Bud woke late morning with a feeling of certainty about his future. He swung his feet to the floor and sat up and said aloud, I don't know when, but I do know how. Then he started reflecting. In a minute, with less conviction, he said, Maybe I don't know how, but I do know where.

L<small>UCE DIDN'T CLAIM ANY UNDERSTANDING</small> of young children, or even one useful bit of knowledge about them, and though Maddie had plenty of opinions to share, they were largely theoretical. Luce couldn't even look back to her own childhood and remember anything practical in regard to child care. She wondered if Lily's children had even pushed out their baby teeth. When did they stop doing that? She was like her father in degree of ignorance. He used to say that when Luce was born, the first time he saw her, she was asleep. He asked the nurse how old they had to be for their eyes to open.

Luce did know that if Dolores and Frank were able to go to school, they would immediately take the common childhood diseases one right after the other. Measles, mumps, chicken pox. What a mess that would be. They were pretty, and that's about all they had going for them. Speckled and lumpy and scabby wasn't much to look forward to.

As an experiment, Luce tried to teach the kids to count, get them to number their fingers, say their age. No dice. Bedtime, she tried to play Little Piggies with them, adding numerals to the old rhyme for educational purposes. This biggest one went to market. This number two little piggy stayed home.

But the children attended poorly and found no delight in having their toes handled. In fact, just the opposite. They drew their feet from her fingers and pushed them under the covers and scooted close together, shoulder to shoulder, ready to flee inside themselves if Luce insisted on continuing with the game.

The first time Luce tried to take their clothes off to help them bathe was a bad day. They cried bleak, silent tears. They could bawl like calves or wail like beagles when they were frustrated or mad, but this was something else. She stopped undressing them immediately, but they went off into their own heads, dazed, and stayed there for hours.

She found, though, that if allowed to undress themselves, they didn't mind being buck naked outdoors. Pour a pail of chill spring water over them in the backyard while they soaped themselves, and all was okay. But it was still muggy August. Come a November morn, frost white on the ground, then what? A pair of children could get to smelling pretty high over the course of the cold months, was Luce's guess. But mainly she began thinking about how bad their bad patch must have been for them to go down so deep where fear and pain couldn't reach.

AFTER THE BATH INCIDENT, Luce never saw the children cry again. It was not a channel they used to communicate. They expressed their feelings in ways besides whimpering and chin quivering and their eyes watering up. They might fly at you with balled fists and try to fight. They might go running away toward the woods. They had a sound like a growl, and also various hollers and hoots and screeches. Or they might give you a slow look that suggested if they weighed a hundred pounds more, they would kill you where you stood. Most of the reasons regular children cry—pain, fear, embarrassment, frustration, anguish, regret, sorrow, guilt—didn't seem to apply with these two. They showed little fear and no embarrassment. And especially no sorrow or regret or guilt under any circumstance.

On the happy side of things, they forgot bad emotions of their own almost immediately. Not that they came running to hug you around the knees shortly after some violent moment. Asking forgiveness, even by way of facial expression, was not a possibility. More like, they invested no feeling at all in what had happened and expected you to do the same. Let it go. No apologies. *Repent* was a lost word in their lexicon. They did what they did, and moved forward despite whatever trail of ashes they left behind. And Luce wondered if maybe that was what they had to teach her. No looking back. Life goes one way only, and whatever opinions you hold about the past have nothing to do with anything but your own damn weakness. Nothing changes what already happened. It will always have happened. You either let it break you down or you don't.

A simple enough lesson, yet hard for Luce to learn. She couldn't make her thoughts stop running back into the past, craving to be happy about something long gone, feeling sad or shameful for things she should have done differently. If the children came to harm under her care, she would not be able to let it go and move on. Not ever. Guilt would haunt her to her deathbed. It's what she would be thinking about instead of teaspoons or moon phases or birds. Living life unfettered by the past would be splendid, but she couldn't do it. She didn't even really like the children, much less love them. But she loved Lily and would raise her children and not be trash. And her own parents came directly to mind at that point in her thinking.

Apart from Lola's bitter slaps, benign neglect had been about the worst of it during Luce's childhood. And that had its reimbursements. Mainly, limitless freedom, even at age five. Who wouldn't wish for that at any age? Out roaming without anyone calling your name way on into moonlit evening, if that's what you wanted. Maybe a hug or a tone of concern in a parental voice now and again would have been helpful, but on the other hand, Luce had never been laid into by an angry grown man when she was five or six.

Her parents were too busy with each other to pay much attention to her one way or the other. That was a few years before Lola disappeared, when her father had just returned from the war, back when most days involved empty Blue Ribbon cans and Wild Turkey bottles rolling on the living room floor and the radio too loud and her parents hollering at each other and sometimes snatching at each other's persons under the influence of great conflicting emotions.

In short, Luce suffered few adult requirements against her until the State dictated that she must go to school. By then, she had been free-range for nearly seven years. The first day of first grade was not bad at all, a certain joy to be had in milling about confused with the other children as the buses emptied. Overseen by a stern tall lady teacher in flashing metal glasses and dressed all in brown with a sprig of violets on her lapel. In the morning, they sat at desks and drew pictures with fragrant new crayons and sang songs, a few of which Luce already knew from when her father came home late at night in a good mood. "Camptown Races" and "Buffalo Gals." Dinner was some kind of soft grey breaded meat and mashed potatoes drenched in white gravy, with green beans that squeaked when you bit them. And all the yeast rolls and butter you could eat. Good food.

But for all that, even though Luce had sat in careful concentration all day to determine exactly what school was all about, when the three o'clock bell rang, she'd seen all she needed to see. The confinement was intolerable. One little room all day long. Everybody breathing the same tired air together. As the teacher began lining children up for the buses, Luce felt compelled to announce her judgment of school to all in attendance.

—Just so you know, I'll not be back.

For a while afterward—as if that one day fell into the same category of frequency as a total eclipse of the sun, possibly a once-in-a-lifetime occurrence—Luce went back to doing what she did before school burst into unwelcome existence. Play with homebody Lily in the mornings. Then, in the afternoon, solo walks in the woods to watch the change of plants and their colors as the season drove forward toward fall. Study odd bugs and flowers. Throw rocks in the creek. Look at whatever birds and animals and reptiles presented themselves to her, and also the way weather goes always different from moment to moment and day-to-day, and the bigger circle-shaped repeated patterns of season and year. See whether or not she could smell squirrels in the trees on damp days.

Put to it, her parents would have said they did indeed care whether

Luce attended school. Sure they did. It was just that fights and hang-overs and sweet makeups intervened. In the specific misery of day-to-day life, they couldn't wake up at six in the dawn and give a great shit whether she went that one particular day or not. But one day leads to another, and so on. No way around it. It's that merciless thing that time does. And then suddenly the leaves are falling off the trees and it's October. A tall man in a Harris Tweed overcoat and a tie comes knocking at the door to set matters right.

The man didn't talk to her parents beyond about three exchanges of questions and answers before he saw how things stood, how young they were, particularly Lola. He'd seen it all before. He pulled little first-grade Luce aside and leaned down and looked her in the face. He asked her in a low voice if she wanted to grow up to be like her parents. Even then she knew to blow air out her nose and say, Not hardly.

—Then you need to go to school every day, the man said. He squeezed her shoulders and looked her in the eye and said, You go, whatever it takes. I'll push them, and I've got the law on my side. But there will still be days where it will be up to you. And next year, you'll have to help your sister.

So thereafter Luce attended, whether her parents had yet roused themselves of a morning or not. Some nights, to save time and signify her resolve, Luce would go ahead and dress for the next day before she went to bed. And waking wasn't a problem. Anybody can turn out the lights and think a time in their head when they want to get up and do it. They only have to try. Luce could already reach the stovetop, and it is no mystery to make a pot of especially good oatmeal if nobody stands over you worrying about whether you're wasting too much brown sugar and butter.

The lady schoolteacher with the flashing glasses turned out to know a valuable thing or two, such as how to teach you to read. Though she had her faults, like everybody else. For example, how she chose to deal with a pale quiet country girl in a faded flower-print cotton dress who had never seen ice cream before. Thinking to take it home to share with her little brother, the girl carried her dessert

ice-cream sandwich from the lunchroom back to class and put it beneath her desk, where it melted all over her books and papers and
made a thick muddy puddle on the wood floor. What that mistake got
her was grabbed by her upper arm and marched out to the hallway.
Everybody became quiet. And then bam, bam, bam. The long paddle
was an inch thick and had twelve holes bored in it.

In addition to the regular paddlings, there were horrific arithmetic
flash-card battles where half the class stood on one side of the room
and the other half on the other. The teacher went down the lines calling for answers, pitting side against side, holding up big white cards
with heavy black number problems on them, either plus or minus, depending on what area of ignorance she decided to probe. You got one
wrong, you sat down in shame. The last one standing was the winner,
though Luce was not alone in wondering what you won other than a
feeling of glowing superiority. And further, you were culled into reading circles called Red Birds, Blue Birds, Yellow Birds, and Black Birds.
In no particular order. Except it was obvious, even to a bunch of first
graders, what the order really was. And discovering that little decep-
tion was, in itself, a valuable lesson about authority to tuck away for
future use. Even though Luce was never anything but a Red Bird.

In recompense for such moments of terror, there were lots of
framed pictures hung around the room to admire at your leisure. Pale
stunned Washington, with his strange white side hair, and sad wise
Abe, with his weary, baggy eyes and patchy beard like a bum. Also,
Blue Boy, who would have been stomped into a mudhole at recess if
he'd shown up with even a trace of the attitude he expressed on his
smug face, not to mention that outfit. The State provided many free
storybooks, especially the ones concerning Jack climbing the beanstalk
and the Pied Piper leading the children away to a happy land inside a
mountain. There was also a record player and stack of records, including a set of 78s with an accompanying picture booklet telling the compelling story of Peter and the Wolf. Though you could play them only
on rainy days when recess was impossible and the class was half crazy
by midmorning from the physical pressures of confinement.

Also in the category of reimbursements was this: sometimes the teacher had about all she could take of education and would request that the students read quietly while she went up the hall to have a smoke in the lounge. In her absence, everybody went wild. The deep country boys, the ones from kerosene-lit cabins way up some dark holler, would dance on the teacher's desk just to show it could be done. Little rebel boys three feet tall in blue jeans with cuffs turned up nearly to their knees so they'd be able to wear them for a few years. And too, if you're counting happy moments, once a month they all marched quietly in a line down the hill through a stand of dark pines to the town library, where each one got to check out two books all their own for two entire weeks.

Yet, as much as she began to enjoy school, Luce figured that she must never forget the main lesson she was learning, which was very simple. The way they get you is, you trade your freedoms for entertainment.

—LOOK AT THIS, Luce said, holding up a curved meerschaum pipe with wizened bearded elf faces carved on the yellowed bowl. It was like a small saxophone. The children didn't particularly look, but they didn't not look either. They were liking the dusty clutter of the Lodge's upper floors, and the pilfering.

Docent Luce had taken them exploring, digging into leather trunks left in attic spaces under the eaves and in storage closets. Foretime lost-and-found stuff like tarnished silver-and-ebony brooches the women thought so little of that they left them strewn in the bureau drawers. Tan floppy-thighed jodhpurs and black boots with rusting eyelets threaded with rotting laces. Which suggested that rich people must have come costumed to the mountains back then.

They found a gramophone with a brass horn shaped like a morning glory blossom and a stack of records in brown paper sleeves. There was still a record on the platter, and Luce blew the dust away and turned the crank and lowered the needle. From the brass cone a man's voice sang "Pucker Up Your Lips, Miss Lindy," the sound scratchy and thin. The children focused on watching the record spin and the needle ride the groove. They sprawled on their sides on the floorboards with their heads propped on their hands and seemed relaxed and soothed by the crackling music, ghostly from the past. When three or four notes of the chorus came back around, they'd hum along faintly, blank-faced.

Luce went through the entire stack of records, being the DJ. She played Peg Leg Howell, King Oliver, Bix Beiderbecke. A tiny orchestra wheezing away at "The Ride of the Valkyries." Then some rube duet singing about corn husking, which Luce knew for a fact was no fun at all and tore your hands up, but the rubes seemed to be having a good time making up a happy fantasy about it. Yodelers and blues screamers from soon after World War I, and crooners going back beyond raccoon-coat days, an age lit entirely by the light of the silvery moon. And finally, Jimmie Rodgers's "T.B. Blues." It was the only song out of the whole bunch that Luce knew anything particular about, so she explained that Rodgers had lived nearby once upon a time, and then died of tuberculosis, but nevertheless sounded awfully jaunty and belligerent singing about it.

When all the records had been played, both sides, she carried the player and records and a maroon leather album of photographs downstairs.

The photographs were from a summer long ago, and that night after the children had gone to sleep, Luce looked at them carefully, one by one. The corners of the pictures were affixed to the black pages with little scalloped black paper triangles, the glue licked by dead tongues. In the pictures, the Lodge looked nearly new. World War I wasn't even close to happening yet. A whole different world, but occupying this same space right here. A picture of five girls in high-necked white dresses sitting on the front steps drying their long, shampooed hair in the sun. Two girls dozing together in a hammock with books spread open across their narrow waists and their tapered fingers trailing unconscious from the bindings. Girls batting shuttlecocks across a net on the lawn, skirts to their ankles and ribboned hats on their heads. Girls paddling canoes on the lake. Whiskered men in striped summer suits smoking cigars on the porch after dinner. A lovely grown woman walking across the lawn in a pale summer dress, the hem skimming the grass, her dark hair bunned off her neck and her face blurred by the motion of turning to look at the camera as the shutter clicked.

CLEAR AND MOONLESS, an hour before sunrise. The children woke and rattled around the lobby. Sliding a mica-shade lamp two inches to the left, a rust-colored piece of pottery four inches to the right. Reordering the Britannicas by some system less obvious than the alphabet. The kinds of things they did when they were hungry or bored. Luce eventually quit pretending to sleep, but she'd be damned if she was going to set the precedent of cooking before the sun came up.

She took the children out into the dark dewy yard and pointed at groups of stars. Particularly Orion, visible briefly before dawn for a few weeks during late summer like a portent of winter. When Dolores and Frank both looked at Luce's finger instead of the sky, she moved behind them and aimed their eyes with her hands against the sides of their heads.

Just talking, figuring maybe a word now and then might register, she said, There, rising just above the ridge. Broad shoulders, narrow waist. The Hunter. He's chasing that little patch of stars up ahead of him. The Seven Sisters. People with good eyesight can count them. Twenty-ten. Everybody else sees a few lights shining through haze. There's a story goes with them.

Luce had gotten well into the narrative when she realized that the sisters' suicides were coming up soon. Editing on the fly, she told it so they turned into stars without having to die first. But they were still pursued across the sky from early autumn into spring by Orion and his dangling sword. The important point was that for an awfully long time, even before people thought up the story, Orion and the sisters have gone around and around, night after night, and he still hasn't caught them, and he never will.

NEXT AFTERNOON, the children disappeared. They had been sitting on the front porch playing the records and Luce was in the back-yard feeding chickens and admiring the late-summer lushness of the woods all around. Poplar leaves already one degree off their highest pitch of green. And then she went into the garden and picked a few yellow squash for supper. More squash erupting than Luce and the kids could eat, and they all liked yellow squash an awful lot, especially tossed in cornmeal and fried crisp. They could eat it five days a week that way. And the other two days, stewed with green peppers and onions. Luce had six fat squash cradled in her arms and was setting them on the back porch when she realized she couldn't hear the old songs anymore.

She found the porch empty and the Lodge too, best she could tell in a quick pass shouting their names. She ran down the lawn to the lake. Along the shore. Up the creek and over the ridge and back to the Lodge. Shouting all the time as she went. Red-faced and blowing air. Frantic and terrified.

Luce ran back to the house, but they hadn't returned. She drank water from the spring dipper and walked the other way along the lake-shore and up the next creek and over the next ridge and back to the Lodge. Nothing. She was less frantic and more exhausted and shamed within herself, for she had let them go.

She had let her attention turn away for a moment, and suddenly they were nowhere. Bears and panthers out there in the mountains. Not to mention snakes. The children were capable of hiding behind a stout tree trunk and not making a move or drawing a breath while you walked ten feet away yelling your lungs out, calling their names to the world with evident desire to reunite with them.

Luce went back down by the lake, where they surely had no better sense than to drown themselves, and found them standing at the bank throwing rocks at each other. She ran and tried to hug and kiss them and they would not look her or each other in the eye. They stood stiff against her hugs with their necks twisted around, as if something mildly interesting was happening down the road.

Luce followed their eyes and saw rising above the treetops a shape of black smoke against the ash-colored sky. It might have looked more like a funnel or a mushroom, but in her mind it was an exact projection of old Stubblefield's empty house, which stood on the other side of the ridge.

Light rain misted west across the island. Cool for the season. The Atlantic olive drab, and either way you looked, a thin band of black seaweed wavered along the tideline into the distance like one long cursive sentence in a lost alphabet. Stubblefield put on a raincoat, glanced in the mirror, and wished somebody else looked back. Outside, he passed the rusty showerhead where end-of-summer beach tourists should have been washing off sand and salt. Except it had been rainy for so long that they all checked out and climbed into their station wagons and drove home.

Over the dune to the empty beach, and then he slogged north in wet sand just above the runout of waves. The past winter, locals had referred to Stubblefield as that man who walks at night. This summer, he had been that man who swims at night. But he wouldn't be doing either in this weather. A few hundred yards farther, and he turned inland at the beach shop. Air mattresses and Frisbees and hula hoops. In the window, a Coppertone display with the little tan girl's white ass uncovered by the dog tugging at her bikini bottom. A page taped to the inside of the door said, *Be back when the weather clears.*

Well, you could only hope. And Stubblefield really appreciated the casual attitude toward business. But at some point you quit counting on anything too far in the future.

He walked toward town. Past a lighthouse and the entrance to a historic fort. Lots of contention here, back in the past. Some progression of displacement involving Indians, Spaniards, English, and, lately, us. For better or worse. On down the sidewalk past a salt marsh, the high school, a hamburger joint, a church.

At the beginning of Centre Street, Stubblefield reached the milestone of the movie theater. An ordinary-looking small-town façade. But behind it, all was provisional, the building like a big Quonset hut, a corrugated metal barrel-vault. It leaked in the rain, and he believed he had seen bats, or at least big moths, flying through the projector beam and casting shadows on the screen. A half-sheet for a coming attraction: *The Defiant Ones*, with Tony Curtis and Sidney Poitier.

On down the street, the drugstore. A modern low brick-and-glass building, out of place among the Victorian mansions and nineteenth-century storefronts. Up near the front window, paperbacks in two spinning wire racks, comic books and magazines fanned on shallow shelves to display a teasing strip of their bright covers. A quick flip through *Hot Rod*, and then *Stag*. Each world no more or less fictive than the other. At the counter, Stubblefield bought an envelope of Stanback powders and a Jacksonville *Times-Union*. Walked out with the powders in his raincoat pocket, the newspaper folded under his arm as if it were the *Times* of Los Angeles or London or New York.

He strolled on in the rain to the monumental post office with the WPA mural on the lobby wall depicting conquistadores in crested helmets and Seminoles and palm trees. At the wall of little brass-doored cubbyholes, he twisted the knobs in the correct combination and pulled out his mail. Then down to the dock, the boats in for the day. Widely spaced raindrops pocked the stretch of intercoastal that separated the island from the mainland. Stubblefield bought a pound of shrimp, paying right across the gunwale of the boat. He held three sheets of classifieds out to the crewman, who scooped heaping double handfuls onto the paper and said, That look about like a pound to you?

—At the very least, Stubblefield said.

Some of the shrimp were still tail-kicking, antennae twitching, the little black eyes fading. Cockroaches of the sea, but nevertheless tasty. Later he would boil them with Old Bay and peel them and dip them in ketchup with enough lemon and horseradish to bring tears to the eyes and an expanding ache to the sinus. He folded the paper around the dying things, tucking the ends into a neat bundle, the paper already turning wet and grey when he stuffed the package down in his raincoat pocket and felt the shrimp move against his hip.

He checked the front page banner to be sure of the day—Tuesday— and stopped in for one quiet vodka tonic in the brown light of the bar near the docks. His deal was simple. Sunday and Monday, nothing. Friday and Saturday, three or four or so. But Tuesday and Wednesday and Thursday, only one while he read the paper and opened his mail. Afterward, no dawdling. Pay up and leave.

Stubblefield sipped his drink and tore the envelopes open. Bills, mostly. Including one for a telephone pole he'd knocked down somewhere on the Mississippi coast last year, totaling a lovely green Austin-Healey in the process. Four dollars a month to the phone company nearly forever. Then, a letter from a lawyer up in the mountains expressing condolences for the death of his grandfather and informing him of his inheritance. Various parcels of land, plus the farmhouse and outbuildings, the Wayah Lodge, and the historic tavern, remnant from stagecoach days.

All in sad neglect and disrepair. Those were the lawyer's exact words.

Stubblefield imagined the corncrib he had played in as a boy melting into the dirt, the springhouse caving in, kudzu overwhelming the garden.

Farther down the page, and more positive, a mention of monthly rental income plus a percentage of net from the historic tavern. Now called the Roadhouse, according to the lawyer, and mainly a late-night sort of place featuring live music. But a potential liability despite its being the only profitable piece of the inheritance.

What Stubblefield read into the euphemisms was that the tavern, bought by his grandfather as a folly, like collecting eighteenth-century china or old black-powder firearms, had become an illegal bar in a dry county. Which made a fitting inheritance, since his grandfather never was the kind of hard-shelled man to deny himself or another the simple joy of a drink at the end of day.

From toddlerhood until he was eighteen, Stubblefield had spent every summer at the farm. He quit visiting after his grandmother died and it began to seem that his grandfather wanted to ride out the tail end of life with the fewest possible outside distractions or inconveniences. So, a summer being three months long, tot up the numbers. He figured he had spent approximately several years of his life up there in the wet green mountains. How lovely and unexpected to inherit all that familiar picturesque ruin. Still, Stubblefield felt guilty about not attending the funeral, even though nobody had thought to inform him until it was too late to make the long drive.

The lawyer's letter concluded with an unwelcome paragraph. A matter of various unpaid taxes and outstanding bills. And, yet, so little cash money left in the bank accounts. What to do? Please inform.

Stubblefield thought about it, all the shit of ownership. And then remembered his Stanback. He ordered another drink and washed down the healing envelope of bitter powder with the first sip.

FEATURING HIMSELF A BACKROADS, scenic-route guy, and the sun shining again, Stubblefield went indirect. A couple of days driving up the coast, stopping to eat or drink at beach joints and walk in the towns. Jekyll Island, Savannah, Beaufort, Charleston. All the beautiful old places very much like the beautiful place he had just left. Victorian houses, Spanish moss in live oaks, fishing boats at the docks in the afternoon, and waterside fishhouses frying up the day's catch. The Atlantic changing shades by the hour, verdigris or slate or taupe. Those kinds of special colors.

At Sullivan's Island, he walked through the dank fort where Poe served time in the Army. And then on to Isle of Palms, where everybody drove a station wagon full of kids in bathing suits, the back-end windows pressed tight with inflated beach balls and floats in shiny primary colors. He parked and swam parallel to the beach, on and on until he couldn't do it anymore, and then he rested in the wet sand at the water's edge and swam back.

He drove inland, past sunset through the sandy pine flats and rolling hills, thinking about the mountain lake and the big white frame house. Green trim around the windows and along the fascia boards, a rusting 5v galvanized roof. A deep porch all the way across the front, in whose shade he had turned a geared crank to produce ice cream on summer afternoons. The homeplace was a leftover from some dusty ancestor who bought great swaths of land at auction when the State sold off the Cherokee holdings back in the early eighteen-whatevers. Later, in the deeps of the Civil War past—or probably the Reconstruction, if somebody needed to get precise—his people had owned a whole quarter of a huge mountain. A pie shape of ragged landscape stretching point-first from the summit eastward. Thousands of acres, maybe tens of thousands. But, back then, steep land was worth about a nickel an acre, if you could find a buyer. Over the decades, though, it got a little more valuable, and eventually it did get sold, all but a few fragments, by old Stubblefield's elder brother.

One year shortly before the Depression, the brother had taken an affection for mournful cowboy music. He was in his middle thirties, a dangerous time of life. Most afternoons from early spring to late fall, he sat on the porch of the farmhouse, lounging in a striped canvas campaign chair and drinking multiple shots of good Scotch. Reaching out periodically to crank the handle of a Victrola, spinning stacks of 78s. "Bury Me Not on the Lone Prairie," "Red River Valley," "Streets of Laredo." If, someday, people could see by his outfit that he was a cowboy, his life would be a success. Then, without warning, he was gone, having quietly sold most of the mountain land for much less than it was worth. Decades later, old Stubblefield discovered his brother's whereabouts and went to visit. He found a tall bowlegged white-haired man living in a little bungalow in downtown Rawlins, Wyoming. The brother's life had been a great success. He wore Levi's except to church and a John B. Stetson hat every day of the year, pale straw in summer and brown felt otherwise. Each of the many times Stubblefield had heard his grandfather tell the story, it concluded with the observation that his little grandson bore great resemblance to the cowboy. Which, until now, Stubblefield had taken as a compliment.

NEXT MORNING, STUBBLEFIELD rounded the bend past the barn and the corncrib, both time-blanched and sagging toward earth.

Sad disrepair, yes indeed.

So he expected more sadness when the house came into view. But it never did. Where it should have been, a big empty space of air shaped itself in Stubblefield's mind exactly like his grandparents' house, except invisible. And below that, a black circle of ash and charcoal on the ground, surrounded by unmowed grass. A few burnt stubs of roof joists pitched at low angles to the sky. Century-old oak trees in the yard, their leaves scorched on the sides facing the empty space. Boxwoods all burned down to nubs beside eight sooty stone steps climbing to nowhere.

Stubblefield parked in the j-hole by the gate and walked to the edge of the burn. He squatted and studied the circle where better than a century of life had happened, some of it his own. The ashes at the edge lay soft and light and pale. Every hint of breeze puffed up a mist of ash that seemed to Stubblefield like the contents of a cremation urn tossed to the wind. He reached deep to throw another fistful into the air, but drew his hand back fast and empty. Burnt. Still damn hot down in there. He quickstepped to the singed springhouse and soaked his hand in the cold clear water rising from deep underground flows.

L ATE DAYS OF SUMMER. A social occasion in a raw new clearing at the edge of town, the margin where everything turned to jungle and sloped steep to the high peaks. A couple dozen vehicles parked between the bulldozed ground and the road. Chevys and Fords mostly. A few outlier cars, like a low-slung Hudson coupe and a tiny pink-and-white Nash Metropolitan, and even a weird pale yellow Vauxhall. Also the worn-out green pickup with sideboards.

A full moon peeped over the ridges to the east, and the sky was dark enough to show one bright planet. But plenty of light left for shooting. Everybody stood around with pistols in their hands, hats on their heads, and cigarettes drooping from their mouths. Men in jeans and flannel and khaki in front of a red clay bank still showing teeth marks from the D6 blade. Lots of beer, and a few nostalgic mason jars of corn liquor. Burnt matchsticks pinned paper targets to the bank. White background with thin black concentric circles around a dense black center hole. Their rows against the red wall looked modern and artlike. Or to another turn of mind, not at all artlike. More like problems in geometry class requiring a solution, and the correct answer was a perfect empty hole through the black dead center.

Bud, new to town and drawn to congregation, had driven by and then turned around and parked. He mingled about, hoping to overhear gossip about Lily's family and where the kids might be, having already struck out earlier at the barbershop and the pool hall. In short order, he became more than half drunk on handouts of beer and a very generous paper cup of Wild Turkey.

He lacked a gun, but that didn't stop the bully in him from needing an airing. He walked over to a short slim man with a sweaty Pabst in his left hand and a big .45 like a brick in his right. The little man leaned against its weight. Bud said the first thing that popped into his head.

—Hey Lit, some of these old boys say your feet's so small you buy shoes in children's sizes at the store that sells Florsheims.

Lit smiled, raised his eyebrows, and sipped his beer. He moved up real close into Bud's air. Inches apart. The top of his head level with Bud's collarbones.

—Which ones say that?

Bud took one involuntary step back. He said, Nobody.

—Nobody said it? You just took a flying fuck of a guess at my name and where I buy my shoes?

—Somebody might of said something. I don't recollect all the specifics. It was supposed to be funny.

—Funny? It's the same shoes for less money. You ought to feel funny paying full price.

Bud looked down at little Lit, his angle against the weight of his big pistol. Drawing himself together, remembering his higher degree of suavity among the hillbillies, Bud said, Slim, you need a twenty-two. It would fit your hand better. One of those purse guns.

Lit closed the back step Bud had taken. He reached his .45 out, and Bud took it from him and turned it from one face to the other and studied it, like a message might be written in the diamonds of its grips.

Lit switched his beer to his shooting hand and pitched the half-full can toward the clay bank. It rolled, spewing, just a score of feet.

Lit said, Can you hit that?

—In my damn sleep.

—Well then, if it's that easy, can you empty the clip into it?

—Step back and watch me.

Bud squared up and started shooting, pulling the trigger as fast as he could jerk it out.

The first round hit the can fine and knocked it spinning up against the bank. Then with every shot, the .45 began rising on him, like it wanted to haul back and strike him in the forehead. He fought to hold it down, and he lost. By the time the clip emptied, the barrel pointed about where the moon would be come midnight.

Lit said, Yeah, that's how I figured.

—Shit. Let me see you do it.

Lit took back his empty pistol and packed it in its holster and snapped the flap over it.

—I tell you what, Lit said. When you can do it, I'll do it.

Lit walked away. Immediately, several shooters came over to Bud with fresh beers. One of them said, Natural mistake. He was off duty and out of uniform.

—Off duty from what? Bud said. Pumping gas?

Laughing and delighted, they talked over one another, telling the new man the famous story about Deputy Lit and the burglars. How when Lit was first hired, many people around town thought him a figure of amusement due to his size. But that ended one night when three men set out to rob the dime store in the dark hours after midnight. The burglars carried guns for some fool reason. Lit surprised them in the alley as they came out the back door with their loot. Nineteen dollars, mostly in ones, from the cash drawer. And a brown paper sack of stuff they had scooped in leaving. A fat roll of a thousand Daisy BBs, a hawkbill knife with a fake bone handle, a red-and-white paper cylinder of Royal Crown pomade, and a pink rabbit's-foot key chain. So, altogether, make it twenty-three dollars and change. It shouldn't have amounted to much trouble at all. A fine would have taken care of it if the magistrate was in a good mood. Except when Lit turned his light on them and told them that they were under arrest, one of the burglars misjudged and pulled his pistol. Lit was afoot and off duty, making one last check of town on his way home. He had his flashlight and nothing else. Nevertheless, the flashlight was longer than Lit's lower arm from elbow to fingertips, heavy with D batteries stacked down its black metal sleeve. When Lit was done, all three men ended up in the hospital, and the one that pulled the pistol nearly died. He never thought right from that mistaken moment forward. Even now, you could see him most days sitting on the bench outside the pool hall, a slow simple fellow with a deep pink dent in his forehead, smiling at everybody, a friend to mankind. Afterward, a rumor passed around that Lit had been a Ranger in the big war, which meant he could kill you barehanded ten different ways without breaking a sweat.

—Shit, Bud said at the end of the story. Shit, shit, shit.

One of the tale tellers, struggling to keep his mouth straight, said to Bud, You know what I think?

—What?

—Lit must have taken a shine to you.

So, Bud reckoned, a bad move for starters, calling attention to himself with the law. But don't look back. You make your mistakes, and then fuck it. You don't dwell, you move forward.

And sure enough, as night settled in and the marksmen quit shooting their guns and drank more beer and ran their mouths, they taught Bud something welcome. They bitched about how difficult and expensive it was to get beer and bonded liquor, this being a dry county with nothing but vast national forests and several layers of other dry counties at every quarter of the compass. You either had to drive hours to reach the outer world or else pay the one bootlegger a horrendous markup. It took Bud about three seconds to recognize a ripe situation. And then a day to find the Roadhouse and learn that it served drinks, the local law looking the other way. And only one more day to learn the bootlegger's name and pay him a friendly visit.

OLD JONES WAS A BALDY ELDER who had cut his teeth on moonshining back at the edge of the previous century. He wore pressed bib overalls and a starched white shirt and a black suit coat. Farmer below, businessman above. He sat rocking on his porch, looking at the view across the valley. Said he was thinking about cutting open a watermelon if Bud cared to have a slice.

They ate the melon spraddle-legged, letting the juice drop between their feet and disappear into the porous porch boards. Jones got pretty talky about his early days of moonshining, the copper kettle and copper coil. Eluding revenuers for decades and never serving a day of time. Even now, cooking off about fifty gallons every fall when the evenings grew crisp and he and his white-headed buddies wanted to get away from the wives and camp out in the high mountains for a couple of weeks, running their coon dogs and recollecting lies from their youth. Oh, the happy late nights holding fresh bottles of corn liquor up to firelight and complimenting one another on the fineness of the bead. Now the money was in bootlegging. Hauling bonded stuff. No art, just commerce.

When Bud grew weary of listening to folklore and turned to business, he bore down pretty hard. Times have changed, was his main theme. Less bullshit, more profit. The new world had gotten dangerous, and Bud embodied the new. In the end, he nudged the bootlegger into retirement with a combination of fairly specific threats and promises involving a slightly vague percentage of an expanded liquor empire run by Bud on sharper modern lines. Long story short, the former bootlegger could sit in his porch rocker and do nothing but collect a monthly check.

—Good God, Jones said. Don't you know this is a cash business?

Bud left with a little brown leather shirt-pocket address book. Inside, a long list of standing orders reaching forward into infinity from everybody in town interested in getting their liquor without committing themselves to a day's drive. Two fifths of Smirnoff every two weeks. One of Johnnie Walker Red and two of Bacardi monthly. Half gallon of Popov weekly. Page after page. Each order with a name and a number, if you considered 7 and 14-G to be phone numbers, which Bud didn't. So, what a happy surprise when actual liquor customers answered his calls.

By the end of his second week in town, Bud had made four long runs in the pickup and found himself amazed at how fast you make friends when you're the bootlegger. Amazing, as well, to be gainfully self-employed so soon after arriving in town wondering how far he could stretch a pocket of greasy bills from his gas station stickups if he lived frugal, which was never likely to happen. Yet, in a matter of days, he had income.

Jones's little brown book made the new vocation possible, so Bud stopped by one afternoon and peeled off a few twenties as a first fraudulent percentage for the old boy, who was an entertaining little shit when you compared him to the run of regular people. Sat on the porch with him, drinking a tumbler of his shine mixed fifty-fifty with lemonade, and Jones told every bit of local gossip he knew. Always an appealing trait, but especially now, when anything about a couple of new kids would be so interesting.

When Bud finally got ready to leave, already down the porch steps on the way to the truck, the old man said, You ever wonder why there hasn't been but one bootlegger in this end of the county?

Bud said, Nope.

Old Jones said, Twenty years ago, if you'd come to my house saying the things you did last time, you'd have found yourself at the bottom of the lake by midnight.

STEADY MONEY GOT BUD to wanting a Mercury, equipped with every hot nonstock item a car can have in regard to carbs and cams and transmissions and hubcaps. A Hurst shifter with an eight ball. Kind of car that could twist the speedometer off the end without breathing hard.

But then he took a woman he'd met at the Roadhouse to the drive-in one night, *Thunder Road*, which proved so instructive that Bud fended off her groping at his trousers to attend to the lesson. Robert Mitchum had a shit-hot car, and the movie showed exactly where that got him. Dead was where. Glorious, but nevertheless dead. Fact of nature, hot cars draw trouble. So, better than getting away from the law in white-knuckle races over twisted mountain roads was never having to run because you looked plain as dirt and they paid you no heed.

Next day, Bud settled for getting the truck's radio and gas gauge fixed. He bought a brown canvas tarp to cover his load and a dozen bales of hay to strew for camouflage in the bed. As for cash investment in his new business, that was it.

He wanted to feel the glow of his accomplishment, but he made the mistake of projecting his thoughts into the future. He ran the numbers in his head, and found that hauling liquor paid considerably better than lubing boxcar couplings, but even if he worked until he was as old as the former bootlegger, he'd never make back what Lily took from him. And he'd always live like he had the muzzle of a gun to his head, those two idiot kids with their grubby fingers on the trigger.

CHAPTER 8

IMAGINE, LUCE SAID. What if a locomotive pulling flatcars loaded down with fresh-cut logs came chugging through right now. You'd smell dirty coal smoke and cinders. And then, when the cars passed, new-cut oak and poplar and maple, all crisp and clean. The ground shaking and the rails clacking against the big wheels and the sleepers shifting under the weight.

The children paid no attention to Luce but stood with their heads bent, studying a fanned branch of hemlock needles. They began backing slowly away, as if the branch were dangerous, a bear or snake.

—Luce said, What is it?

Dolores and Frank turned and continued walking down the sunken bed of an abandoned narrow-gauge logging railway from early in the century, which even now made a good trail for the daily jaunts through woods and fields they needed as bad as a high-strung pair of spotted bird dogs. It drained their energy into the ground like electricity and settled them.

Luce kept hoping that if she talked enough about the relict places she had discovered in her days of freedom, language would rub off on the children. And they seemed to like the walking, and would follow creeks and streams for great distances, slogging through them as if they were trails. Wet to the knees, mossy underwater stones shifting beneath their feet, they bobbled along and for balance waved their arms like lunatics. And if they weren't doing that, they had to be herded down the curves of trail to keep them from making one of their straight-line marches, regardless of terrain impediments, like they were being pulled by a string down some passage nobody could detect except maybe dousers with their wise twitching sticks crossing and parting to find underground watercourses and other transmissions of unknown powers.

This day, Luce's next history stop was a magic place in the river where a Cherokee fish weir still showed its downstream V during times of low water, and where Luce believed she would always catch a fish. Which she demonstrated by cutting a springy pole from a beech and using a string and hook from her pocket and rock bait she'd taken from a secret place in a creek a ways back that old Stubblefield had shown her one day on a walk together, acting like he was giving her the combination to a safe full of money, saying only three people knew the spot and two of them were dead. The result, a rainbow trout she pulled out of the water and showed the children, to no particular impression, despite its brilliant agonizing in the sunlight. She worked the hook from its lip and let it go back into the history it arose from.

Later, after struggling up to a gap hardly anybody crossed anymore, she showed them a rock cairn where she said people used to mark the end of their climb by adding a stone. It stood knee-high and spilled in a circle six feet across. Luce told the children that if they dug into the pile to the earliest stone, it might well reach back as deep into time as the hairy cavemen who dressed in furs and had enormous feet.

Farther on, along a stretch of trail Luce had walked at least a dozen times, she noticed something new to her. A stout old oak partly screened by younger trees, the first four feet of its trunk hollow and the crown nearly dead. What Luce first thought was a low limb, much thicker than her torso, ran parallel to the ground and then made an unnatural upward right angle. At the L, a knob of scar.

Luce went to the tree and raised her arm and cupped her hand on the knob. She realized the odd limb was really the deformed trunk and knew this was a trail tree. One day two or three hundred years back, in a different world, somebody bent down a sapling and torqued it in the middle and sliced it partway through at the angle and tied it to a stake in the ground with withes or ligaments to make it grow that way forever. When the cut healed, the scar kept growing, like an old man's nose, and it was where the nose pointed that mattered. *Go this way*, was the message nobody had received for a long time.

—Where does it aim? Luce asked the children. Maybe to a sweet spring, or a rock overhang sheltering a good camp where we might find an ancient fire ring, scribbles of lost languages, or drawings of animals on the rock. Maybe a cave of treasure hidden from Spaniards in the days of conquistadores marauding for gold.

The children stood within themselves, without apparent interest. Luce said she was ready to follow the tree's suggestion, if neither of them had a better one of their own. She threw her right arm forward, her forefinger matching the way the tree pointed.

The children took the lead and walked straight through general hardwoods and clumps of laurels, galax and its dank body smells. Luce came behind, keeping her eyes open, though nothing presented itself worth deforming a tree to indicate. Following the line, they crossed a creek and climbed to a shelf of land, a dry place with hickory and lo-cust and a few pine trees. Open woods.

Then down into a wet cove. Dense old-growth hemlocks. The limbs of the big trees lapped over one another, shutting out the light. All Luce could smell were the astringent needles and wet rot. Dolores and Frank kept marching forward under the trees. The light was fil-tered and green, and their footsteps fell silent in the dead needles that lay a million years deep. Dodging giant fallen trunks, nurse logs sprouting moss and ferns and new hemlock saplings from their own brown decay. The children kept to the line. They went downslope until the contour of the land leveled into a clearing. But not really a clearing, a blank space in the world. They stopped short at the edge of a drop.

As long as she could remember, back to the freedom of childhood, Luce had believed that if you walk in the deep woods long enough, you'll inevitably come to places of mystery or spirit or ritual. But she hadn't ever found a place like this, and she hadn't expected to feel so scared when she did. It was a perfect round hole down through the earth. A deep cylinder of still air encompassed by dark rock. Not a lot farther across than you could throw a softball. Far down inside, black liquid lay still as the face of a mirror. The hole was set about with hemlocks, their trunks dark and massive. The children went right to the lip and looked down, and Luce felt scared and reached for them, expecting them to flinch, but they didn't. They let her hold their clammy little hands with crud in the creases.

She walked them all the way around the pit's lip, looking for a slightly sunken track through a corridor of younger trees. If the place had once been a quarry, wouldn't there be signs of an old road or rail bed for hauling out the shattered rock? Spalls and shards scattered on the ground. But Luce found no sign of disturbed ground and no obvious break in the circle of tree trunks, so stout that many of them must have begun life back before the flood of white people into the landscape. The rock inside the hole was free of half-round drill marks or raw grey jags sharp as knapped flint from blasting. Nothing but serene smooth stone with lichen and a few ferns growing in nooks and crannies.

Luce let go of Dolores's hand and picked up a rock the size of a grapefruit and lobbed it out into space, and then grabbed back the hand. The rock arced and fell and fell and fell and then broke the surface of the black liquid with no splash, like there was forty-weight down there. She guessed her rock would keep falling slowly through the thick liquid in total darkness nearly forever. People shoveling wells or outhouse holes or graves, when they got past knee-deep, joked about digging to China. But however deep the black hole went, Luce figured China wasn't near weird enough to be where it came out.

Luce realized she hadn't said a word for some time, so she tried to devise commentary. Something about young warriors coming here alone to spend the night and test their courage. Or maybe ceremonies with big bonfires and drums and dancing. That's what the tree aimed people toward. What she didn't say was that the message of the tree was surely *Don't go this way.* And the sign that meant *don't* had been lost to time.

———

THAT NIGHT IN BED, WLAC playing low and not helping much, Luce couldn't sleep for thinking about the black hole. She didn't spend a second wondering what creatures lived down there. One look and she knew nothing lived there. Life would only be in the way. The black hole was before life and beyond life. If you dipped a ladle of that water and drank it, visions would come so dark you wouldn't want to live in the world that contained them. You'd be ready to flee toward the other darkness summed up in death, which is only distant kin to the black hole and the liquid it cups. A darkness left over from before Creation. A remainder of a time before light. Before these woods and these mountains and the earth and even the sun, there was a black hole filled with black water. The black held no reference to the green world around it. And what did the green world mean if the black was and forever had been?

It was a question Luce could not immediately answer. But she knew the black hole pulled at you. You stand up to it, or you go down. If the children found their way back there alone, they would drop themselves into it like stones, and fall and fall into the dark. It was altogether their kind of place, and the job that had been put on Luce's shoulders was to keep them from the lip of rock and the face of black water below. Upon which God does not move, not even a quiver.

In the hovering between sleep and wakefulness, lucid but dreaming, Luce's mind got away from her, and all kinds of empty shit she had meant to put entirely behind her forever swam up and lived in her head again.

IN TOWN, PICK UP the phone to make a call, and a woman's voice would say, Number, please? The owner of the phone company could conjure warts using stump water and a mumbled formula of words. Also, he owned the only tennis court within fifty miles, a rectangle of red clay covered in weeds and fenced with rusting sagging chicken wire, which he had built in the glowing decade of the twenties, when he was also in his twenties. The whole phone company involved fewer than a dozen employees. When you went to pay the monthly phone bill, you walked through the dark upstairs hallways of what had been a hotel back in World War I times but was now nearly abandoned. The oiled strip floors creaked against the nails. At night, three-fourths of the milk-glass light fixtures remained dark, and just one door had light behind it. Inside the room, across one entire wall, a rat's nest of colorful wires and silver sockets and silver plugs with cylinders of black Bakelite to grip them by. Every telephone subscriber around the lake and down the valley and up the coves had a hole, which meant somewhat fewer than seven hundred holes. If 7 wanted to talk to 30W, it was a matter of making the connection, the correct plug into the proper socket.

Day shift and evening, there were two operators. Graveyard shift, one. They mostly looked like the tough young women in black-and-white detective movies. In the corner of the room, a sort of illicit sagging cot covered with a patchwork quilt for the night girl's naps. Graveyard was an easy job, if you didn't mind the hours. Almost nobody used the phone after ten, but you never knew. Had to sleep light. Shady business during the deeps of night. Emergencies or trysts or threats to be conveyed. Sad lonely girl sleeping with one eye open at three in the morning anticipating some sad call.

For a time, a few years after high school, that graveyard girl was Luce. She lived in a room over the drugstore, beside the movie theater, so on her way to work the daring late-night moviegoers from the second showing would be coming out onto the sidewalk under the bare glaring marquee bulbs. Main Street's three stoplights flashing yellow. On Sundays and Wednesdays and Fridays and Saturdays, when the features changed, a guy Luce barely remembered from school would be lofting a long pole with a pliers jaw on its far end to take down the red letters saying the name of tonight's movie and to put up the ones announcing tomorrow's. Happy when two or three letters in a row from the previous title worked for the next, like women washing

dishes getting to an unused knife or teaspoon and calling it a hallelu-
jah. When Luce came out the street-level door to walk two blocks to
work, the night owls stood yawning and checking their watches and
thinking of bed, and the letter guy got to watch her walk away. Probably the high point of his evening.

Luce didn't mind the late shift. It gave her a great deal of freedom.
She usually got two or three hours of sleep after midnight, and at
eight she went back to her room and slept a few more and then had the
afternoon and the evening to fill however she wanted. For example,
the grand little Carnegie library with steep steps to the double front
door. Inside, high ceilings and tall windows and full bookshelves and
a stern tiny librarian who always wore black and peered through her
spectacles in judgment at your choice of book to see if it was worth
anybody's time or if you were a foolish and suspect person to be wanting to take it home with you. Those years, nearly all Luce read came
from the travel section, and for a while she couldn't decide whether
Kon-Tiki or *Around the World on a Bicycle* was the best thing ever written.

Despite the librarian's disapproval, Luce read a great number of
westerns, such as *Wanderer of the Wasteland*, and planned one of these
days to get on a bus and head out there. Amazingly, the one road running right through town went all the way to anywhere you wanted to
go. From her study of library atlases, Hinton, Oklahoma, seemed like
it ought to be a fine town for her, though that opinion was based on
absolutely nothing but how well the empty spaces fell around it when
you looked at its dot in relation to other dots and the web of roads
spreading across the whole continent.

Then one day Luce went up the street to pay the power bill for her
room and saw a government topographic map of her immediate landscape framed on the wall. It came as something of a revelation. She
had to study awhile to place herself in the quadrangle. When she
found the town, it was a red speck at the edge of a thin blue slice cut
into great overwhelming swaths of mountain green in various shades.
Thin black contour lines crowded dense in waveforms to represent

how steep and complex the mountains stood all around. Below the dam, the valley lines spread wide apart and the flat farmland was a wedge of palest green. A blue river wiggled down the center of the valley and off the page, spilling over the edge of the world into blank space.

A tiny island in the vast sea is what Luce thought the town looked like. The map that described her entire range rested on the wall more like art than information. And Luce took it as a clue to why she had never left, that being one of the big questions in her mind during her time as an operator.

LUCE'S RAPIST WAS A YOUNGISH MAN, and married. Mr. Stewart. Luce knew him well. He had been one of her high school teachers. Fresh out of college back then. Luce, like most of the girls, thought he was cute and sort of funny. Mr. Stewart taught chemistry, not at all Luce's best subject, so she settled for an easy B in his class.

There wasn't any question in Luce's mind what had happened. He came in awfully late for paying his bill. And it was clear he had confusing expectations. He smoked, nervous and abrupt. Flirted a little, talking about how much prettier he thought she was now in comparison to high school, and yet how pretty she was when she was seventeen. If Mr. Stewart had not been married, Luce might have gone out with him. He was no more than six years older. No big deal. Go to a movie. A football game on Friday night. But Mr. Stewart was not single, and that was that.

He took a final long drag on his cigarette and dropped it to the floor. Suddenly he was reaching and grabbing and pulling at her. Then pushing her across the room to the narrow cot, where it was all yanking at her clothes and groping. Then grabbing her wrists, and his weight on her. She distinctly remembered shouting, *Quit*. Shouting, *No*. Over and over. Maybe she even screamed it, but who would have heard? And she tried to shove him off her, but he was so urgent. She turned her face aside to keep him from kissing her. She refused to cry for the moment it took him to be done.

It started so quickly and ended so quickly. He had not removed any of his clothing, so all he did was stand up and zip and apologize and leave. His check for the month's telephone service lay faceup on the table. Three dollars and sixteen cents. Also a gold Saint Christopher's medallion on a gold chain.

Funny thing. Soon after Mr. Stewart left, the clapper on the bell started striking, announcing a call coming in. Luce stood up from the cot and pulled her skirt down. She couldn't think. Her mind felt distant from her body, and her body felt distant from everything in the world. The cigarette butt still smoked on the wood floor, and she crushed it out with the toe of her shoe on the way to the switchboard. She put the headset on and jacked in the plug and said, Number, please?

It wasn't until after midnight that it came to her. She was sitting there in the chair on a damp place doing her job just because a bell rang. Luce stood up and took off her headset and walked out, leaving the door standing open. Didn't call her backup girl. Luce wasn't really premeditating much at the moment. Mainly, she figured, phones dead for one night, so what?

And normally, she would have been right. Except this night the high school burned down, and there was suddenly all kinds of need for people to make phone calls. Switchboard all lit up. And true, most of it was still useless chatter at three in the morning because sirens screamed and the sky was yellow with flames. But one call in particular was an actual urgent emergency message to the closest larger town, requesting a ladder truck and a crew of firemen to help out. The school became a heap of scorched brick fallen in on itself, and the oiled oak floorboards and wall laths and beams and joists converted to ash and charcoal. The pile smoked for weeks.

Naturally, Luce's name became mud, regardless of whether the truck and crew would have arrived in time to make a difference or not.

Small towns will go a long mile to take care of their own, but there's a bright line you dare not cross, and Luce found herself on the far side of it. She might as well have left all the black plugs and silver sockets as they were and gone straight to the school with a gas can and a book of matches instead of walking down the empty street to her room and showering in the dingy bathroom used also by a waitress at the diner and a counter girl at the drugstore fountain. Then trying to sleep, and wondering what to do about Mr. Stewart. Finally falling hard asleep with the radio on, not even hearing the sirens.

Luce never went back to work. For two days, she kept trying to tell herself that if Mr. Stewart had been a stranger instead of her teacher, she might have reacted differently. Maybe in that moment of shock, she hadn't fought hard enough. But no matter how she tried to revise the moment so as to heap the blame on herself so she wouldn't have to try to make Mr. Stewart pay, she kept circling back around to the truth.

Also, she couldn't help replaying things she'd never forget. Him licking up her neck and biting her ear. And after he was done and gone, touching her lobe and looking at the drop of blood on her finger, black in the dim light. Also how, back in school, when he waved his hands to make a point, the skin of Mr. Stewart's fingers, and the nails too, were scurfed chalky white from the chemicals he handled all day for experiments. Thinking how, from now on, it would be a fact that those fingers had been in her.

She walked up to the Sheriff's Department. Sat in the chair opposite Lit's metal desk and told her story, looking him in the eye the whole time.

Lit started trying to act a little fatherly, but Luce would have none of it. She said, We pass each other on Main Street and barely speak. I saw you last week outside the post office, and we sort of nodded to each other, like to an acquaintance. We never were close, not before or after Lola took off. Let's do business and let it go at that.

Lit said, Well, if that's the way you want it, then I'll tell you that this sort of charge is hard to make stick. You say one thing, he'll say something else.

—Of course he will.

—You might not know it, but the last graveyard-shift girl, the one that only stayed here a few months, was sort of an amateur whore. Mainly, when her rent was coming due.

—So what?

—It doesn't help, is what.

Lit described how it worked. Some man hears something in the pool hall or barbershop or gas station, puts off paying his phone bill until late. Knocks on the door and steps inside. Says something smooth, like, I been a-thinking about you. Gives the girl the monthly payment, plus a gift. An item of jewelry or something else easy to hock. She didn't take cash, just gifts. Fifteen minutes later he walks out the door to the sidewalk with an attitude like Adam cast out of paradise.

—So what? Luce said.

—I'm talking about expectations. Maybe there was a misunderstanding of some kind, Lit said.

—I guess he misunderstood that I was the same kind of whore as the last night girl. But I don't see how that changes anything.

—Hard to convict. One says one thing and the other something else. Might help some if this was the first time.

—First time I got raped? Luce said.

—That wasn't my point.

—I got your point.

—I was thinking about a jury. It can matter an awful lot to them, especially if a defense lawyer lays things out real vivid.

—Good God.

—I'm just saying, it's a hard case.

—I guess it is, unless criminals generally confess right off. But is there anybody in Central Prison serving time for rape?

—White ones?

—Yes.

—A damn few, Lit said.

—Maybe one or two, though?

—You said you want business, but I can't leave it at that. I'm say-ing, it won't be easy on you if it goes to court. A little shit of a lawyer can do to you in a couple of hours what you won't let go of for the rest of your life. People get all kinds of crazy ideas, and facts don't matter much. Stewart's got a place in this town. He wears a coat and tie to work, and you're a nightbird living in a single room with a bath down the hall.

On her way out the door, Luce said, You go straight to hell.

A week later, her first evening as caretaker of the Lodge, Luce sat on the porch after a supper of light bread and yellow cheese. Paint flaked off the stair rails and pickets in dry petals, the bare wood weath-ered and bleached, and the grain raised. Rocking chairs equally weath-ered and skeletal, with sunken bottoms of twisted kraft paper woven in an intricate angular pattern by somebody now likely dead. What she had wanted was grilled cheese, but the whole tedious matter of lighting a fire in the cook stove for just a sandwich set harsh priorities.

The day was slowly going dark and chilly. Luce wrapped a quilt around her shoulders and poured amber liquor from an important-looking bottle into a little stemmed crystal glass. Old Stubblefield had told her to use whatever she wanted, and she had found the bottle that afternoon as she'd searched through every room, every closet and cor-ner, under every bedstead. Hours of searching. She hadn't wanted to go to bed imagining hidden places and getting herself all worked up. Down in the basement, back in a corner tangled with busted-out cane-bottomed dining chairs, she had found stacks of wooden crates, each holding dusty bottles of Scotch or red wine from France.

Luce rocked and looked across the water toward town, judging the separation to be about right. A mile by one measure, an hour by an-other. She sipped Scotch considerably older than she was, the taste of time in its passing, in harmony with the outer world, where poplars were already half bare and long grasses drooped burnt from the first frost. The call of an evening bird, and the sun low. Bands of lavender and slate clouds moving against a metallic sky, denoting the passage of autumn. Fallen leaves blown onto the porch. The planet racking around again toward winter.

That first evening, as she continued to do for so many of the next thousand, Luce sat through all the degrees of sunset. Venus and the crescent moon and some other planet all stacked and falling through an indigo sky, the three spaced equally down a bowed path toward a jagged line of black ridges. Distant sreetlights in town came on, tiny and yellow, reflecting in streaks across the still water. Long past dark, Luce believed she had watched the seasons collapse, one into the ashes of another. To the east, winter star patterns rose, coming back around again. Orion chasing the Seven Sisters, old reminders of an abandoned order like a deep indelible pattern in the ground. An Indian trail, a long path. She went inside, reluctant, feeling eluded by so much.

In dim brown light, an old man scrabbled in a wooden bin, searching for the shiny two-cent nut that would thread onto his rusty bolt. Two boys in Keds and Wranglers studied red-and-white boxes of bicycle tubes for the correct size to fix their flats and give them their freedom back. Along with nails and brads and staples, the space behind the narrow storefront was crammed with lawn mowers, shotguns and rifles, a glass-fronted case of pocketknives, latigo dog collars, ripsaws and keyhole saws and bow saws, two-man crosscut saws so long they hung from pegs near the ceiling almost to the floor. Wooden spirit levels six feet long with silver bubbles floating in mystery green liquid. Many sizes of awls and planes and adzes and chisels. Wonderful adjustable wrenches in several sizes with knurled spirals to twiddle back and forth endlessly, imagining all the variety of nuts they were capable of turning. Brute murderous monkey wrenches two feet long with jagged teeth in their jaws. Sledgehammers and double-bit axes. A general odor of metal and oil, and also some funky underlying man smell that sparked an unwelcome prison memory for Bud.

His shopping trip was not for a little poke of finishing nails or a ball-peen hammer. He'd come to lay down an alibi. So he picked up a cheap rod and reel and the biggest, gaudiest bass lure, for purely artistic reasons. As an afterthought, a filet knife because of the thin, elegant blade.

At the register, Bud shouted, Three fucking dollars for this fucking piece-of-shit Zebco?

Heads turned.

He tried to pay with a hundred, which the cashier couldn't possibly break. He grumbled some more and finally pulled out a fist of ones and walked out to the car with no doubt that everybody in the store would remember him outfitting for a fishing trip.

Then, the lengthy scenic drive around the lake. Because, after much patience and discretion, he'd finally picked up a whiff of gossip about a couple of new kids with some woman that had to be Lily's sister, living in an old-time lodge. Some place with a leftover Cherokee name.

IT WAS THAT DAY at the very tail end of August when the sun angled a degree lower and the quality of light made people begin saying, Fall's about here. Bud spent a half hour casting with his plastic Zebco, thrashing his big lure against the water, two shades bluer than the sky, and looking over his shoulder at the bark-shingled shake-roofed hulk. Like a bunch of dead trees decided on their own to shape themselves into a building.

What he kept on seeing was nobody. So the plan from that point was simple. Knock on the door, Zebco drooping at his side. No way Lily's sister could know him. If she answered, ask if she minded him fishing in the lake below the Lodge. Or, better yet, seek advice on bait. For bass, are you better off with worms or bread balls? Some bullshit story. It didn't really matter. Just riff along in the moment and leave. Important thing was, if nobody was home, go treasure hunting.

So, two polite knuckle taps at the screen door. Rod in hand, Bud grinned through the distorting veil. The bottom half bulged outward from kids pushing against it to open the door. Bright outside and dark inside. Bud had his face close, toking on a Lucky. Smoke clouding his face and filtering in through the screen. He tapped again. Nothing.

Bud grasped the handle and rattled the door. Hook in eyelet. No problem. The thin springy blade of his new filet knife fit perfectly into the wide crack between the stile and frame. He lifted the hook and opened the door enough to stick his head in, drawing more of his smoke with him.

Around his cigarette he said, Hey?

Still nothing, so he stood inside the door and waited, listening for the slightest movement. Hearing nothing, though, other than the silence of an unoccupied building.

He started creeping the lobby, and immediately it became clear that the Lodge enclosed a lot of space. And that was just the first floor. So, needle in a haystack when it came to half-inch bundles of hundreds. And what a bizarre place to live. Like a museum nobody wants to visit. Evidently, they all slept in the lobby. Single beds reminiscent of jail cots with faded quilts, arrayed near a monumental stone fireplace.

Ears cocked, constantly checking out the windows, Bud looked in the obvious places. Beneath a thin layer of powder in the Ivory box and the oats in the Quaker drum, behind the coal furnace and inside the antique refrigerator with the wheel of coils on top. Hoping to smell fresh cash, he sniffed the heat registers and got only cinders and mildew down in the ducts. He felt all over the fireplace for loose stones and stuck his hand up the flue to check the smoke shelf for bundles of money.

Bud looked for the personal and found a bureau, its drawers full of stuff that must have been the sister's. Boring everyday clothes. Also a disappointing underwear drawer. Not even one item deserving the term *lingerie.* In the bottom drawer, carefully folded and mothballed, a red-and-black cheerleader outfit from back when the pleated skirts fell almost to the ankles. Yet when the girls twirled, what splendid glimpses.

He considered the dizzying possibility that his money had been split up, hidden in a dozen places. Such as what? A fat book with the center pages cut into a perfect bill shape with a razor? Bud riffled through the Webster's. Not there. Roll bills into a tight fat cylinder and stuff it up the ass of a baby doll? He checked the children's few things, but apparently these two hadn't become baby-doll children. So, where was his goddamn money? No way could he imagine Lily being clever and devious.

Bud ghosted around, learning the terrain. Staying careful all the time to leave things undisturbed, invisibility being a great advantage, at least for now. But, in time, he got itchy. Eventually, he couldn't help himself. He went to the back porch and found a red can of kerosene. He took the precious cheerleader uniform from the drawer and carried it to the fireplace. Careful not to overdo, he drizzled it no more than taking a piss, then returned the can to its place. One match, and the uniform blazed. At some point, Bud stepped onto the hearth and stomped the fire out, careful to leave a few red-and-black scraps, a perfect spooky calling card. People start doing all kinds of interesting things when they're scared.

CHAPTER 10

H—OW MANY ACRES? Stubblefield said.

After hearing the gloomy accounting of his new debt, which made the power pole in Mississippi look like nothing, it was the only question he could think to ask that might result in a happy answer

—In toto? the lawyer said.

—Yeah. One big pile of toto.

The lawyer, a bald buddy of his grandfather's, gazed at Stubblefield as if some glum preconception had been confirmed. The lawyer adjusted his many papers, making new shapes of them on the green blotter covering most of his desktop. He wore a puckered seersucker suit, blue and white stripes. A square-bottom knit navy tie two fingers wide fixed tight to his wash-and-wear shirt with a gold clasp displaying the geared wheel of the Rotary club. His face was nothing but sags and wrinkles and brown patches, but up top, the skin stretched tight and shiny, and caught the reflection of the slowly turning ceiling fan. Stubblefield couldn't take his eyes off the shapes of the fan blades circling the tanned pate like an outward expression of thinking. Or a little boy's beanie with the propeller spinning.

The lawyer licked his thumb and paged through the stacks. He uncapped a tortoiseshell pen and made notes on a yellow tablet as he went, columns of numbers in a style of handwriting long obsolete. Big loops and whorls in blue ink flowing from the split gold nib. He was precise to the point of annoyance. All manner of fractions down to thirty-seconds.

Whereas Stubblefield always kept to whole numbers and rounded up and hoped for the best. Fifteen, Stubblefield thought. Or sixteen. Somewhere in there. It was just a flying fuck of a guess, but the riverside fields were good-sized.

The diddling with numbers went on so long Stubblefield asked for a magazine, and got another glum look.

But eventually, the lawyer said, Fifteen hundred fifty-six and seven-eighths, on the nose. He held his hands out flat, palms down, and then slowly spread them apart. A vestigial gesture. Some gambler move meant to indicate that the deal was unquestionably clean. Riverboat cardsharps in Mark Twain days spread their hands in such a manner, was Stubblefield's take.

—A lot of rich bottomland, the lawyer said. And there's the lakefront property and the farm. Pretty remote, though, and just thirty-nine and a quarter. Sad about the house and its contents.

—Uninsured, I'd bet, Stubblefield said.

—Yep. Too bad. Hate to see the historic structures go down. Our collective past, shallow though it is. Old wiring or lightning, one, got it. But what you do is divide that parcel for vacation building lots. It's called progress.

—I thought progress meant things getting better, Stubblefield said.

The lawyer made a fluttery motion in front of his face with his right hand like shooing gnats. He said, There's also the Lodge and the Roadhouse. But the thing to get in mind is that the taxes are your most pressing matter.

—Sixteen hundred acres is not nothing.

—No. Nobody said it was. And because it's not nothing, the county has been running a tab for longer than usual.

Stubblefield might have raised an eyebrow a sixteenth, or a mouth corner. Some slightest twitch interpretable as smugness concerning his new holdings.

The lawyer paused and lifted one knobby-jointed forefinger to indicate that he was thinking. Then he said, That last statement of mine calls for revision. It could lead to a misinterpretation of how things stand around here. The tab that's been left running is entirely because your grandfather was liked by a great number of people. Liked a great deal. If he owned one acre, we'd all be acting about the same. But now he's dead, and you're the one with his name attached to this pile of deeds. You're nearly unknown. Nobody feels any responsibility toward you. The people in the courthouse are working themselves up to take as much as they can. And they might succeed in getting everything. So, my point is, we need to sell something to pay the taxes. Soon. Three or four months, outside. The Roadhouse might entirely cover it, and we'd be better off shut of it. It's a mess waiting to fall on us.

—It's the only thing bringing in any money.

—Selling the Lodge won't nearly cover the taxes. But it might buy us some time. Go look. Your grandfather has a hermit spinster he liked an awful lot living there as caretaker. But the place is getting in bad shape. About all she can do is call me when something is nearly coming apart, and I send a man up. Out of my own pocket, lately, which we can talk about later. And go look at the Roadhouse too. Then we'll sell something and get the taxes off our backs. After that, we line up five-year ag leases on the big bottomland tracts along the river.

—Ag?

—Corn, soybeans, tomatoes. Doesn't matter to us what they try to grow as long as the checks clear. This goes like I think it will, there'll be a drop of our tomatoes in the ketchup we pour on our hot dogs two or three years from now.

—You put ketchup on hot dogs? Stubblefield asked.

—I more assumed you might. The point is, I tried to get your grandfather to do this for the past five years, but he was tired of thinking about his land. He let it lie fallow. There's jack pine growing on some of it. Goddamn Chinese trees of heaven twenty feet tall. It hurts my sense of management every time I drive down the valley. For better or worse, it's all yours now. Decide on something. There's not but about two ways to go right now.

—What's this going to cost me?

—Maybe I should have been more clear, the lawyer said. You'll be making money.

—Your part, I'm talking about.

—It's your land, but you don't know what to do with it. So, probably I'm a fool not to say fifty-fifty. I'll go twenty-five, and don't insult me by coming back with fifteen.

—What do you do for your part? Stubblefield said.

—Nearly everything but own the land. All major decisions to pass through for your agreement, of course.

—Well, Stubblefield said. I'll have to think about it. I might just sell out and be done with it. Move on down the line.

—You'll get low dollar if you want to do it fast.

—Goes without saying.

Stubblefield stood and was at the door on his way out when the lawyer said, You don't even remember me, do you?

Stubblefield turned and looked more closely, but nothing registered.

The lawyer said, Go way back. Fishing in your grandfather's boat. You were a snotty kid. The bass were biting and we were going to have a fisherman's dinner of Vienna sausage and saltines and RC Cola and then keep casting. But you wouldn't eat that food and got fussy. Nothing would do but your grandfather had to go in to the dock and get hot dogs and french fries and shit from the cafe to suit you. And when we got back out on the water, the fish were gone. So, standing here looking at you, all grown up, the question I ask is simple. In the long run, how different is a goddamn hot dog from a Vienna sausage?

Stubblefield pondered his younger self. Sorry? he said.

REACQUAINTING HIMSELF WITH the landscape after years of absence. That's how Stubblefield justified spending a stretch of afternoons driving and thinking and being confused every time he cast his thoughts more than a day into the future. Checking out the two properties would have to wait. Summer lay heavy, every cove and ridgeline claiming its own particular green world for only a few weeks before the first frost burned everything up.

September was low season, but Stubblefield tried not to get sucked into that kind of thinking. Low, high. Though it did mean a good rate on the garage apartment he had rented in town. He had never been here this time of year. Back then, he'd had to leave at the end of August for the start of school, so the week before Labor Day became its own tiny season of gloom, like a hundred Sunday nights crowded together. Now, Stubblefield suspected, September might become his favorite month, if he drove enough and paid attention.

He found that the steep country remained beautiful and sometimes hard to travel even in these latter days, and he also regained the old feeling that life could be enlarged by burning a few gallons of twenty-cent gas as an offering to the mountains. A spiritual transaction, like the Sioux with their tobacco, or like his own ancestors who'd had a hard time letting go of the deep idea that particular landforms and plants and animals and weather were sufficient within themselves, leaving no great need to affiliate with larger outside abstractions.

One favorite route went with the flow of the river down the dim gorge, sunlit only at midday, the twists of the road like swirling toward a drain somewhere ahead. Then later, an exhilarating tire-squealing race up the switchbacks of the Jorre Gap, toward the clear thin light of the upper altitudes where dark balsams grew. One afternoon, he drove the dirt road all the way up to the fire tower on Juala Bald. He had gotten the impression as a boy that legendary Indian things involving giant flying lizards or spear-fingered monsters happened up there. Now illicit lovers drove the winding dirt road for trysts in the midnight hour, at least that was the story he'd heard at the barbershop. But, then, to hear the barbershop loafers tell it, lovers went all kinds of places. Around the lake, down the gorge, along the river. The complex mountain landscape, with all its nooks, offered infinite possibilities for romance. And yet, Stubblefield had nothing of the sort in his life, except listening over and over to his scratchy copy of *Kind of Blue* and getting sad. Love, at least sustaining it, had not been his best talent. His best talent had yet to be determined, unless you counted unrealized potential.

At the tower, he climbed the winding open metal stairs to the tiny high room and knocked on the door. The sleepy-looking ranger seemed less than happy to have a visitor, but he opened up. Stubblefield stood breathless. Windows three-sixty, revealing dizzying vistas, green valleys thousands of feet below, blue mountains circling farther and farther until they faded into sky.

The ranger, hardly older than Stubblefield, behaved not at all lonesome and talky but like he'd been interrupted on a busy afternoon, though the entire horizon appeared free of smoke plumes. His hair lay lopsided on his head, mashed flat on the left and sticking out in greasy points on the right. Sort of a dirty-sheet smell to the place, and a skinned-over bowl of cold tomato soup on the table. Huge black binoculars fixed to a tripod, a long desk below one bank of windows, covered with many pale green topographic rectangles and scattered pages of notebook paper dense with tiny pencil scribble. Barely visible atop a peak in the distance, another tower. The radio crackled and the far ranger started talking about weather, a change coming. The faint voice said, We get a week of rain, maybe we can get off these damn knobs for a few days.

Stubblefield looked down toward the town and the lake. He held his hand at arm's length from his face, and it nearly covered them both. Everything else was mountains and coves and valley, already shifting away from the highest pitch of summer green. Where would the big ag-lease fields and the Lodge and the Roadhouse be down there? The round black circle of the burnt farmhouse?

Thinking that surveying his new holdings from such a distance would be clarifying, Stubblefield said, Mind if I take a look through the binoculars?

—Sorry, no can do. Sensitive instrument.

The ranger looked at his watch. Impatient, like time was pressing.

—Big date? Stubblefield asked.

The ranger said, Maybe you could ease on out about now.

———

FOR A WHILE ON THOSE late-summer drives, Stubblefield began believing he had fallen into an adventure. Near the top of Jorre Gap stood a lone log cabin, a tourist shop selling folkloric products, according to a hand-lettered sign by the road. Local honey, handmade pottery, rabbit-tobacco door wreaths, quilts, arrowheads. But the shop was closed. It had either failed or had taken a recuperative pause after Labor Day and was waiting to reopen early in October, when the leaf lookers drove up from the flatlands. Passing the tourist shop, he noticed a face behind the window, indistinct in the shallow light. Stubblefield's initial reaction was to declare it a girl's face, and possibly a pretty one. As he switchbacked from gap to valley, he wondered why his first thought was to distinguish man from woman, pretty from not pretty? Probably because he was so damn lonely and because the schematic of our fool brains inclines us that way. Always looking for any opportunity to cast our sad little package of hope into a future we won't inhabit.

Stubblefield soon abandoned all other beautiful routes in order to drive over the gap every day. He found that unless the light was too faint or too bright, the girl was always there. Then he began to wave as he passed, and thought he saw a response. He started detecting a kind of agitated air about the woman. Not that she thrashed about or anything, but she seemed frazzled and distraught.

Stubblefield found himself constructing a story. A beautiful but emotionally disturbed young woman locked away in the cabin by day while her family went about the necessary business of life, jobs, and all that kind of crap Stubblefield had so far mostly avoided. But not a very serious disturbance, just a romantic manic-depression that might be lightened by Stubblefield's presence. He imagined her neglect and dishevelment represented, movie-like, by a stray strand of hair, a two-fingered smudge on one otherwise perfect pale cheek. She probably sat all day in a rocker glooming out onto the infrequently traveled mountain road. His passing and waving would be a thing anticipated and remarked upon. He imagined her only company a radio tuned all day to the local station, the only one available until the sun set and the world blossomed outward. Midmorning, the *Mortuary of the Airwaves*, with the names of the deceased and their survivors announced over plodding organ music that made death sound like something with big slow feet. Midafternoon, *Tell It and Sell It*, with the hesitant voices of callers seeking buyers for used mattresses and dinettes and forlorn puppies. In between, nothing but country songs with tales of burning love and faded love and the longevity of yearning long past any possibility of fulfillment.

Stubblefield could save the troubled girl from all this. He would take her to his cottage, which is what he had started calling the garage apartment. She could bathe away her smudge in his tub while he sat in the living room drinking coffee and listening to *Kind of Blue*, which would be exotic to her. She would come to him, flushed from the hot water. He would be all cool and cook a simple dinner, which they would eat at the table out back under the walnut tree at dusk.

So, the upshot was, somebody ought to do something for her. But still, Stubblefield didn't want to meddle too deep in local matters. Back here, that was a good way to become a shotgun victim.

Yet, finally, one afternoon, Stubblefield worked himself up to visit the sheriff's office. He said at the front desk that he had a concern about someone's safety, and he was told to go see Lit, in the second office down the hall. The deputy sat behind a metal desk, and when he stood to shake hands, Stubblefield towered over him by a foot and found himself stooping a little to reach Lit's hand. Lit wore his dark hair combed straight back, shiny with Brylcreem, comb tracks straight as soybean rows. No jewelry, not even a wristwatch. His faded chino uniform was starched and pressed sharp, with a silvery shine along the seams at pockets and fly and cuff and collar where somebody leaned hard on the steam iron. Stubblefield tried to call up the name of some little slim twitchy mammal that could squirm through the cracks of a henhouse and kill every bird in the place. Mink wasn't it, but close.

Lit gestured Stubblefield down into a chair across the empty desktop and listened blank-faced to the detailed story.

—Exactly where is this cabin? Lit said when Stubblefield finished.

Stubblefield gave all the numbers of the roads and the turnings, including his best estimations of distances from major landmarks and intersections.

—We've been knowing about that situation for some time, Lit said, nodding. But there's not much we can do until there's an actual crime.

—Somebody needs to do something to help her.

—I believe it would be helpful, Lit said, if you would go check on that girl. As a private citizen, you're not as restrained as I am. Hands tied behind my back, if you understand me.

—Yes, I do, Stubblefield said.

—Report back, Lit said.

Stubblefield drove directly to the cabin. Pulled two wheels onto the grassy shoulder. The afternoon sun broke rips in the cloud cover and cast a yellow glare on the glass, obscuring the desolate girl. Stubblefield walked onto the porch and knocked at the door. Nothing from inside, not a rustle. He circled through the high grass to her window, set in checked logs. He cupped his hands around his temples to shed the glare. His nose mashed its print against the glass.

What stared back at him was a dummy, the unclothed top half of a mannequin. Its frazzled dark nylon hair blown out on one side, like a hard-used brunette Barbie. One arm was broken off at the shoulder. The other lacked a concluding hand but was cocked back as if in the act of throwing something through the window directly at Stubblefield's head. Yet what beautiful smooth nippleless breasts. And blue eyes painted impossibly wide with thick lashes like a Venus flytrap.

Stubblefield drove back to the sheriff's office. Lit was waiting at his desk. He sat pitched on his chair's hind legs with his hands behind his head against the wall. Expressionless except for a quiver of tension around his pressed lips.

—Appalachian humor? Stubblefield said.

—Welcome back to the Lake, Lit said.

CHAPTER 11

THEY SAT WET-BOTTOMED on a big flat rock at the edge of the creek, swapping a mossy crawfish back and forth. Dolores let it clamp its pincher onto her lobe like an earbob, then pulled it off, her eyes watering from the pain. She passed it to Frank, who let it grip his lower lip with both claws until he yipped like a beagle. Then into the creek again to flee backward, tail-kicking. Frank lay prone, put his whole face in the creek and opened his eyes to a green-tinged world, mica-flecked sand and gravel. He breathed out, and silver bubbles rose toward the surface, tickling up his face and into his hairline.

Sprawled in the grass of the creek bank, faces to the sun, they communicated in their manner with each other, trying to remember Lily. The color of her hair, her eyes. Chilly mornings when they ran in and climbed shivering into bed with her. How warm she was. She smelled like wet grass, fallen leaves. The memory remained vague, just her presence and her absence. A ghost that doesn't wish you harm but can't do you any good either. A beautiful white haze. They held memories in their heads like boxes. Some they were happy to open whenever they wanted, and some stayed closed and dark.

They circled to the smokehouse, where Luce had stored the unopened box of Lily's things. They ripped the cellophane tape with the point of a rusty nail pulled from the wall and sat on the greasy dirt floor in the dim pork-smelling air. They sorted through treasures. A white rabbit-fur muff, a blue leather jewelry box that opened in tiers of little empty blue velvet compartments, a green hat with a black

wide-mesh veil inside a hatbox, a blue velvet handbag with seven identical thin silver bracelets inside. A lumpy fox stole with beady-eyed
heads and dangling tails. Two hard-shelled cases, like small pieces of
luggage. Everything smelling of Lily's perfume, Lily's powder.

Dolores held her thin arm up and dropped the bracelets one by one
past the elbow and then tipped her arm down to spill them jangling
over her hand to the greasy dirt floor. And then again, over and over
and over. Frank upended the muff and wore it like a hat, and then he
wore the hat like a muff. Then he set the green hat, punctuated with a
gold hatpin, on top of the muff, and pulled the black veil down over the
white fur. Lily, though, was nowhere to be found.

Not curators by nature, they reached for contact with her by de-
constructing her things. Breaking the golden hinges of the blue leather
jewelry box and pulling out the blue velvet compartments. The hatbox, with its octagonal walls and thick lid and double floor, became a
flat stack of pasteboard, hunter green striped with cream. They separated the hat into its components, green felt and black satin and veil-
ing. The locked white train case, nearly as big as the hatbox, took
some work, but it finally yielded many fragrant tubes and boxes and
squat cylinders and, finally, two pink circles of pleated satin lining.
The locked pink case held hair, two blond wigs and a ponytail exten-
sion, plus circles of white lining. The lumpy fox stole with beady-eyed
heads and dangling tails was tricky, but eventually, after much picking
at stitching with the rusty nail, it became three separate flat animals
with no insides.

They continued their work until bits of Lily's life covered the
smokehouse floor. Lily, though, stayed far away. Frank took a big powder puff from the train case and held it as high as he could and shook
it. A pale shape formed in the air and then disappeared. They began
heaping the stuff back into the big box, leaving until last the fake ponytail and useful stacks of paper tinder wrapped in red bands. Frank
held the tail up and tipped his head back and brushed his face lightly
with the ends of the long hairs. Dolores held one stack of tinder near

her face and thumbed bottom to top and let the dry flammable leaves flutter her cheek.

Back at the creek, they lay on the bank, turned their faces to the sun, and remembered Lily hugging them tight, both at the same time, until their stomachs tingled and they laughed uncontrollably. Lily saying over and over, Love you, love you, love you, till the day I die.

II

CHAPTER 1

A LATE-SUMMER AFTERNOON. Tall stalks of ironweed and goldenrod bordering the dirt road nearly ready to bloom. Stubblefield drove one-handed, sipping a beer, trying to keep the Hawk from dragging its sensitive underparts against the rocks. Raking its shiny flanks against the various jungle shrubs encroaching on the passway. He had worked most of the way through a green eight-pack of Rolling Rock pony bottles, a gift from the Conway Twitty–looking dude leasing the Roadhouse and very much wanting to keep his jolly position, it being so central to a certain half-legal local social whirl.

Jollier still to be the owner of the Roadhouse. During Stubblefield's tour, the potential for entertainment seemed clear, even hours before opening time, no music from either jukebox or live band, neon off, back-room pinball tables dark and silent. Daylight blared gritty through the opened door and cast a vampire-killing trapezoid onto the nineteenth-century wood floor, the splintery puncheons hip-wide and wrist-thick, cut from trees nearly two hundred years ago and made to last. Still bearing adze marks from bearded pioneer ancestors. The festive stale odors of spilled drinks and tobacco smoke soaked so deep into the thick boards that some archaeologist with sharp instruments could scrape down the layers of wood and identify McCallum's Scotch spilled by some horseback trader in the days of the Cherokee Nation. Might as well put up a sign: SERVING HIGH TIMES FOR TWO CENTURIES. Stubblefield imagined cashing a check every month, and yet no other responsibilities on his part than to be *el patrón*.

The Hawk rounded a turn, raked its oil pan alarmingly on the high center of the two-track, and drew to a stop. Projected on its windshield, a brown log fortress set against a green mountainside. Down a weedy slant of lawn, the lake lay glassy, about halfway between the color of sky and the color of mountains.

Some memory of country etiquette learned in childhood from his grandfather kicked in, and Stubblefield tapped the chrome horn ring, the briefest of friendly toots, before getting out of the car. Even then, he couldn't bring himself to walk right up the footpath and climb the steps and knock on the front door. He waited below the porch and called out, Hello?

Across the lake, mounds of pale grey and silver clouds rose in convincing mountain shapes so high into the sky that Stubblefield became confused about what was heaven and what was landscape. Have to be in Tibet to validate some of those upper peaks.

—Hey? he said.

Off to the far side, past the row of rockers, two small heads popped up over the rim of porch boards. Hair like dried shucks, and dark eyes glaring at him. Then they ducked back down. Stubblefield walked around to the end of the porch, but the children were gone. Whose children, by the way? Grandchildren of the hermit spinster's?

In the backyard, no children. Just a clutch of chickens pecking at the ground and a slim girl. Or, rather, since she appeared to be about Stubblefield's age, a woman. Wearing black pedal pushers and a white blouse and scuffed black penny loafers. Standing at a chopping block splitting kindling with a double-bitted axe, the shape of its flared blades echoing deep into Iron Age history, some Viking or Celt thing. Whack, and two yellow-faced pieces of pine fell away from each other and landed in a pile of their fellows.

—Hey, Stubblefield said.

The woman swept back dark hair with her wrist and glared, about as welcoming as the children. She said nothing for an uncomfortable stretch of time.

—So, again, greetings, Stubblefield said.

Just then, he realized that an empty pony bottle still dangled from his right fist. He shook it, pretending to throw it away but it wouldn't go. A Red Skelton bit surfacing into his life all of a sudden.

The woman raised the axe to whacking level and propped its helve on her shoulder.

—Help you? she said.

—No, Stubblefield said. Or, possibly, yes.

—Which?

—My name's Stubblefield.

—He died.

—Grandson.

—Ah.

—So, I guess Grandpa, what? Mentioned me?

—A time or two.

—And he hired you to, what?

Nothing from the woman but a neutral straight-on look. Put a level to her eyebrows and the bubble would stay inside the lines.

Stubblefield glanced off toward a set of fading ridges or clouds or whatever. Some big bird passed overhead. A shadow of wings brushed him but he didn't even look up to see hawk or raven or buzzard. Instead, he watched the shadow waver away across the grass and become broken up by the ragged garden.

As if making an apology, he said, I guess I own this place now. And I need to . . . He paused and started to say, Make some decisions. But before he could get all confessional about what hard choices they were likely be and what a mess his grandfather had dumped in his lap by dying with everything in such disarray, he factored the lack of upwelling sympathy in the woman's demeanor. The axe, but not just the axe. Something about her eyes. So Stubblefield revised his sentence on the fly, like lighting a fresh cigarette off the butt of an old one, and said, Have a look at my inheritance.

—Look all you want, she said. It's yours. And by the way, there's a fair chance the children burned down the house.

She set another section of pine onto the chopping block and

whacked it, scenting the air with piney odors, sharp and clean. And then before Stubblefield could go, What? in relation to the house, some instant memory flashback washed over him. Something about the sway of her hair, or a glint of light off angles of cheekbones and jawbone. Seventeen memories came rolling in from some useless brain attic that usually opened up only to inform Stubblefield exactly where he was and what he was doing and what the weather was when he heard a particular song for the first time, even back to early childhood. Hearing his mother singing, *When the red red robbin goes bob bob bobbing along along* while she ran meat through a hand-crank sausage grinder, October sunlight beaming aslant onto the green tiled kitchen floor, segmented by the crossed black shadows of the muntins.

But no music kicked off his Luce memories. They rose to him like watching an eight-millimeter movie thrown onto a white wall by a Bell & Howell, the only sounds a soft clatter of sprockets engaging holes in the film and the hiss of the film feeding off one spool and snaking its way onto another.

IT IS SUMMER'S END. But not reckoned by some vague astronomical moment when the autumn equinox passes and nobody even looks up or feels an onset of chill. Reckoned, rather, by Labor Day, after which the pool closes for the year and school resumes. Which feels much more like something irreplaceable just died.

As for locale, it's the town swimming pool beside the mile-long grass airstrip. Two dozen pretty teenage girls walking around the concrete apron, the water dark green. A Labor Day beauty contest back when girls wanted to look like Marilyn Monroe or Ava Gardner. All the bathing suits identical except for color, body sheaths cut low across the chest, modesty panels stretched quivering tight. Deep reds and blues and greens, and then the less interesting pastels. The most popular girls are curvy armloads levered up onto stiletto heels. Scarlet pouty lips. Breasts scooped like double cones of vanilla almost to their chins and glowing with Sea & Ski. Hair domed and flipped and sprayed into crunchy helmets. Pinched waists and asses like upside-down valentines.

Aluminum megaphones on creosote poles at each corner of the pool's chicken-wire fence blare some fake Latin samba cha-cha saxophone shit played by heroin-addict New Yorker jazzmen daydreaming they're living in Rio or Batista Cuba. Anyway, whatever the music, even if it were a Sousa march, only pretty girls drive Stubblefield's picture show. They walk around the rim of the pool, each one a Helen of Troy, launching a carload of high school boys to spray-paint her name on the water tower.

A red-and-white antique biplane lifts off the green grass airstrip into the pale blue sky above the dark blue mountains. Four shirtless teenage boys ready for football season set off running down the length of the landing strip, constantly angling their Timexes, worn on the undersides of their wrists, to see how close a pace to Bannister's four minutes they are achieving. Townfolk gather around the pool fence and hang over the rails atop the sunbathing platform, applauding all the loveliness their lives encompass.

Luce is one of only two beauties wearing sunglasses. Green lenses set in black cat eye frames. And, by a long stretch, she is the only one eating a frozen Mars bar from the concession stand while she parades. Her lips candy-apple red, and all twenty nails painted to match. Black swimsuit. A swoop to her do so that one eyepiece of her glasses is nearly obscured by a dark wave of hair.

So, what high and mixed emotions for young Stubblefield that day after the beauty show. Driving his grandfather's Packard back around the lake to the farmhouse, the hopeless and glowing vision of Luce burrowing deeper into his head by the minute. And then the gloom of his mother's arrival the next day to take him back to Jacksonville for the start of his final year of high school.

KEEPING COOL AND LETTING the memories unreel, Stubblefield wandered off to check out the Lodge. Floor to floor, opening a door now and then, barely attending. All the way up to the sad, airless servants' quarters under the eaves. Back downstairs, he studied the lobby, the daybeds near the fireplace and the elderly radio. Kerosene lamps mixed in with a few mica-shaded electrics. Woodstove in the outsized kitchen, iron frying pans big as car wheels, and a flashlight by the back door. By the time he finished scouting around, he was dizzy from trying to hold the current image of Luce and the one from the past in his head at the same time.

When he returned to her, Stubblefield started trying to say some vague things about the Lodge's potential and its liability, talking like he was all business, using the bald lawyer's vocabulary. Assets and profit and shit. Imaginary money. He broke off and said, I guess when the power goes out, you don't hardly notice.

—I miss the radio.

Then Stubblefield decided to tell Luce about his memories. Except it wasn't exactly a decision. He blurted something stupid before he could catch himself. Like, Great God, do you remember that beauty contest back when we were in high school?

ON THE WAY HOME he kept striking the steering wheel with the heel of his hand and trying to remember exactly what he'd said. His face felt flushed red as a lipstick kiss. Was it possible that he'd concluded his memories with, You were so beautiful back then? Had he really committed that unforgivable past tense?

But he remembered her response pretty clearly, at least in précis. How embarrassing that she ever did something that silly. But, good God, she was seventeen. At that age, we're mostly high-pitched and crazy. All the urgent chemicals raging around the blood course. And that's why we do dangerous and embarrassing things, as if simultaneously we're immortal and going to die tomorrow. And that's why we look back on that time so fondly from the dimmer years to come. Remembering the days when we were like Greek gods. Mighty and idiotic.

Something like that. It was a fairly awkward conversation.

But Stubblefield was quite sure Luce had concluded by saying, I'm not the same person as that girl. Sure, too, that he had collected himself enough to state a firmly held belief. We are who we are. Ten or eighty. What we see in the mirror is all that changes. Same fears and hopes running around inside like hamsters on a wheel.

—Well, that's depressing, Luce had said. But whatever. I didn't win that day.

—They chose wrong.

—The sunglasses?

—Could have been the Mars bar.

After Stubblefield had turned and started to walk away, Luce said, either to his back or to herself, So, a flame still burns?

Even in that dizzy moment, Stubblefield at least retained enough clarity to know sarcasm when he heard it. Or would that be irony? Fine line, sometimes.

He had kept walking, but raised a hand as far as he could reach above his head, made a leveling motion, and said, Yea high.

As he rounded the corner, he saw the children sitting in rockers at either end of the porch, glaring and intemperate like pickets guarding the flanks. Stubblefield thinking, If they had muskets they'd shoot me down.

Later that night, back at the cottage, Stubblefield remembered that he had seen Luce one other time. The summer after the beauty show. His final summer at the lake. A teenage burger joint in town. Luce leaning over the jukebox, studying the songs. Her long hair falling forward, hiding her face until she hooked it behind her ears and he recognized her profile. She had on boy clothes. A white button-down shirt, the tails untucked over faded jeans. Black penny loafers with dimes in the slits. And the memory, when it came, kept spooling all the way to her dropping the nickel in the slot and the fans of shiny 45s rotating until one fell onto the turntable and Johnny Ace began singing "Never Let Me Go," scratchy and hollow, since the record had been in the Wurlitzer for some time. Luce slow-danced solo, doing the

Stroll, back to her booth to rejoin her friends, some dismal triple-date arrangement of cheerleaders and football players. As for weather, it was raining that long-ago night when Stubblefield walked out to his grandfather's car. The neon of the cafe set the water drops on his windshield alight with pink and lavender.

MIDMORNING, LIT ROLLED SLOW down a gravel road, letting farmers harvesting crops see their tax dollars at work. It was one of the perks of the job, plenty of time for driving and thinking. That plus the cruiser, a lawman special with the big-block engine set up so hot that citizens couldn't just walk into a dealer and buy one like it. At idle, the two banks of huge pistons rocked the whole car slightly from side to side, despite the extra-firm suspension.

Lit felt like shit. He'd downed about a pot of coffee already, and it hadn't really raised his mood. He dialed the volume on the two-way down so as not to interfere with his thoughts about law. How, most places, it could be bought for a price, high or low. Which was a fact Lit knew could be tested all the way from little county deputies right up to Supreme Court justices and rarely fail. But it failed with him. He was not at all corrupt. If some lawbreaker tried to slip him a twenty to get off, Lit was not above pulling a blackjack out of his hip pocket and laying him out twitching in the road.

And deputy was fine with him. No higher ambitions, mainly because you had to get elected sheriff, and then the fools who voted in your favor thought you were beholden to them. The sacred public trust and all that tired bullshit. Deputy was just a job like any other. The sheriff got unhappy with you, he could fire you. You got unhappy with him, you say kiss my ass and walk away.

The current sheriff was a plump old boy who made a lot of money off a gravel pit and a bunch of crooked State road contracts. The unpleasant part of being a lawman didn't interest him whatsoever. That was Lit's job. The part where somebody deserved getting beat to the pavement and grabbed up by the scruff of his neck and thrown into the back of a patrol car and taken to jail. It was the part Lit was proud of and expert at, quickness of movement being such a great and unexpected equalizer.

Lit's failings as a lawman mostly involved his being prone to form his own judgments. He'd look away if a mainly all right guy went astray and yet nobody got much damaged by it. Such as the shiny new bootlegger taking over the local liquor business. Lit judged it no big deal. Bootleggers were a fact of life. Can't sell what people don't want, and nearly everybody needs to find a way to shift their mood up or down a few degrees now and then. Or even daily.

As for the really wonderful uppers and downers, they had recently become illegal if you didn't get them through a doctor. But back in the war, the government passed out Benzedrine like jelly beans when they needed you flaming bright seventy-two hours in a row, killing people that badly needed killing. So it was plain wrong that now you had to pay a doctor for a script and then pay a pharmacist to do nothing but count pills and put them in a bottle. In the long fights of France and Italy, nobody kept count. You just dug them out of buckets by the fistful. One bucket for go, another bucket for no-go.

Lit was a man of peace. At least he wanted to be someday. World War II had given him the gift of all the conflict most men would ever need. He'd witnessed all kinds of horrible shit, and he'd committed quite a bit of it himself. Such was life at the time. But back then he was so young. His blood called for other blood. Even now, he couldn't believe how much fun some of it had been. A perfect dream, unmatched ever after, driven by the fervent hormones of youth and amphetamines.

That was some while back. Yet in these latter-day peacetimes, Lit still never quit wanting him a handful from the go bucket. It was a great chapter of his nostalgia for the past. Back in his youth, when he was always jacked up and happy.

Until recently, in lieu of pills, you could go to the drugstore and buy a Benzedrine sinus inhaler over the counter. Crack it open and be in business. Now the government had outlawed them, made you a criminal to get even a taste of what they once glutted you with. Where was the sense in that law? Probably some drug company or doctors' union figured it out. And who gets fucked? Everybody but drug companies and doctors. And the old bootlegger was useless. He dealt in nothing but fifths and pints and fluid ounces.

When the gravel met pavement, the valley road, Lit didn't even think about where to go next. He turned back toward town. This shiny new man needed checking out.

AN EMPTY BLUE SPAM CAN sat atop a locust fence post behind Bud's rental, yet some firearm malfunction stood in the way of amusement.

—You don't think about a revolver being broken beyond repair, Bud said. They're damn simple machines. Not much more than a hammer connected to a tube. But this pistol is done for.

Morose and not aiming in the least, Bud randomly snapped the trigger six or eight times to no effect.

—Point that up in case it does go off, Lit said.

—Shit, it's dead broke.

Bud snapped three slow dejected snaps. And then a hopeless fourth, which fired with a fierce crack.

Lead whooshed weird and supersonic past Lit's left ear.

Bud looked at Lit and then held the pistol two-handed up to his face, studying its profile, his expression a caricature of fear and amazement.

—They damn. It's been healed.

Lit, unamused, put up his forefinger and wagged it at Bud.

—Set it down for a minute, he said. I've got questions. Such as, where are you from?

—Down along the coast. Several little towns in three different states.

—Why come here?

—Nice place, with business opportunities.

—Any relations in these parts?

—Nope.

—Mind if I take a look at your driver's license?

—Not at all, except it went through the wash.

Bud dug his wallet from a back pocket of his jeans, and it came out cupped to the shape of his ass. He opened the wallet and extracted his license. Reached out a limp pale rectangle, which Lit declined to touch.

Not much use anyway. Little piece of pasteboard where somebody typed your name and height and weight and hair color and eye color. So, Lit's watchman duties half-ass fulfilled, he went directly into his spiel about how you can't sell what people don't want to buy and how dim the local laws are. Nothing but the whim of ignorant voters keeping all these steep counties dry when you could drive a couple or three hours in any direction and legally buy alcohol. Or whatever else you need to lift your mood if you don't get too fussy about every little ordinance. Then he shared several opinions about World War II and its sensible drug policies. The recent idiocy of banning inhalers.

As he talked, Lit began feeling like Bud was reading his mind. Like maybe signals passed between them along the order of Freemasons with their deep verbal codes and intricate handshakes. At that point of possible understanding, Lit looked at his watch and said, Time to go and do.

THREE DAYS LATER, the black-and-white sat at the street again. Lit, bleak and furious in Bud's garage, attacked a stubborn inhaler with a chrome nutcracker. It was Lit's cracker, conqueror of a thousand inhalers, but now something about the diameters mismatched. Either Bud's new tubes were slightly slimmer or Lit's cracker was reamed out from hard use. Lit worked with great focus, damning capitalism and government nonstop.

—How you doing? said Bud.

—Hanging in there, like a hair in a biscuit.

—Don't you ever get tired of that stuff?

Lit looked up from his work and made a great exaggerated expression of incredulity and went back to cracking.

Swallowing the woolly strip inside was the goal, the thing that set Lit's day up and gave it a forward motion, an aim.

Lucky for Lit, clever entrepreneurs had recognized in advance the profit to be made when inhalers were driven to illegality by the government. For a year prior, a fellow Bud knew down in the low end of the state had bought case upon case of the little tubes from every drugstore around. Now there was a mighty steep markup to be taken. Getting higher all the time in ratio to the dwindle of supply.

—On the dim day when these all go away, then what? Lit said. Twenty cups of coffee before lunch, is what.

Bud bent from the waist, his head in the bright circle from a caged shop light hooked to the upraised hood of the truck. He studied down the open barrel of the carb like he actually knew how all the springs and needles and jets and butterflies and floats deep in there actually worked in concert to make the truck go.

He said, Some of these bits you're meant to twist one way to mix the air and gas lean, and the other way goes rich. And then some bits, you'd better let alone if you ever care to drive again.

—Damn government, Lit said, working the cracker with elbow and shoulder action. Feeling all wretched because you fight for your country and then you come home wrung out to alleged peace, and they leave you to your own poor devices to find the daily fire. Sad times when heroes pay high money to bootleggers.

—Hell, I'll do it for you, Bud said. I thought maybe you enjoyed the challenge.

He took the inhaler from Lit and dropped it on the concrete floor and stomped it flat. He stooped and picked the ribbon out of the bits of broken shell and flicked dirt off with a middle finger and then blew on it and handed it back to Lit.

Lit meticulously twiddled the paper into a perfect tight spiral, reflecting how he intended his thoughts to go for the rest of the day. Delicately, he placed the spiral on his tongue and swallowed, tasting the delicious eye-watering tang all the way down.

When his eyes quit watering, Lit said, Coffee's not the same thing at all.

Bud said, When they make coffee illegal, you come to me. I'll have it.

—For a price.

—Damn straight. Name something worth having that's not got a price. The first rule of life is, you got to pay. In my opinion, the more that's made illegal, the more capitalism works as it was intended.

—That doesn't really move me one way or the other, Lit said.

—You know, you don't need these inhalers. It's not really my line of work, but I can get you pills if you want. White crosses and that kind of thing. Trucker stuff.

Lit glanced skyward, said his thanks to the divine light suddenly bathing him.

RIGHT AFTER HOOKING UP with Bud's wonderful constant resupply of uppers, Lit stayed awake for three days and nights. Work hours, people driving through town five over got all kinds of angry barking shit right in their faces to go along with their speeding ticket. Later, about three in the morning, the TV test pattern accompanied by radio music seemed pretty fascinating after some beers cooled Lit down without having the power to put him all the way to sleep, which would have taken a fist of army downers to accomplish.

—Need me some no-go. *Mucho, mucho* no-go, Lit repeated to himself, until he found the rhythm in the words, and it seemed like a good start for the chorus to a country song, except you probably needed to figure a few more lines. And a bridge. Songs needed bridges, but Lit wasn't certain what they were. He decided maybe Bud would be a good place to start looking for a cowriter. Bud looked pretty musical, especially his hair. And even if they couldn't make up a hit song together, Bud could for sure get some downers.

IT TOOK LUCE A WHILE to believe that the children were not mean, they were scared. Or, maybe, to hew closer to the harsh truth of a bad day, they were not *just* mean, they were *also* scared. The scared part was what they guarded against showing Luce or anybody else outside the pair of themselves. Luce thought of her new understanding as a hypothesis. They want to travel on, put an end to days where every moment begins in fear. Shift the load somewhere else. So they strike a wood match and hold its power between thumb and forefinger. Which leaves about five seconds to decide how best to be its agent. No wonder flammable things like nostalgic cheerleader outfits and wonderful old farmhouses got lit up and burned to ashes.

Give anger a furious voice, why not? The argument for finding joy in those strong blazing minutes of destruction was not lost on Luce. Afterward, though, nothing but a black circle in the green woods to show for it. And the after is what she couldn't quit worrying about.

Left to the thoughts that arise from fire, maybe in fifteen years the children would be making everybody who brushed up against them scared or hurt or dead. End up in Central Prison, sitting on the wrong side of the green porthole, buckets of acid between their feet, eyes as blank as burnt holes in carpet. So, like prep for a high school debate, Luce started thinking about ideas to argue against fire.

———

A BLUE-SKY SEPTEMBER DAY, color in some of the trees, especially poplar and dogwood. Luce and the children walked past the edge of what was once a cornfield, but now the lovely hopeful processes of plant succession had transformed it into a Brer Rabbit briar patch. The arcing canes etched a tangled geometry where bright migrant finches, yellow and black, darted for the last drupelets of withered blackberries. In a cleared space about the size of a stage, a pony mare harnessed to a long pole paced a circle centered on a simple machine made mostly of wood, a mill designed for crushing cane to make molasses. A nearly forgotten folkways practice from the past, but not an irretrievable past. Short of poisoning all life or blowing it up, people could keep doing it on and on, if they wanted to. Like when you're on the wrong road, you turn around and go back.

Luce believed that the children could learn something here. A calmness. Some seasonal lesson about time flowing forward pretty steady, and this day connected to all the others, and the years connected too. Not every day needing to stand all by itself and be its own apocalypse.

Maddie wore a broad-brimmed man's hat and tended a slow fire of wood coals under a big three-legged iron cauldron of simmering cane squeezings. She sat on an upturned stub of log with her shanks crossed and her boots unlaced, and when Luce and the children arrived, she tipped her face out of the shadow of her hat brim and winked a pale eye at them. She scraped at a raw split cane with a pocketknife and then licked the white marrow off the blade. When the pony came around at less than the necessary pace, Maddie tapped her with a long stick, a gentle reminder of the job they were doing together. The air sweet with the smell of the crushed stalks heaped in bright yellow piles and the boiling molasses syrup and wood smoke. No sound in the immediate world rose louder than the grinding of the cane press, and it so muffled as not to obscure the shuffle of the mare's feet in the dirt and the occasional pop of the hickory fire.

Normally, the children would have offered a lot of emotion back at the fire, but the mare drew their attention so strong that they ignored everything else. And, Luce hoped, not because it was occasionally being struck with a stick.

The pony was a stocky elderly Welsh cob, dusty black and already growing her winter shag, even before the first frost. She was descended from pit ponies, bred to pull mine carts, but was several New World generations beyond that ancestral brutality—being lowered by a belly strap down into a horrible dark shaft to live a brief life beyond the light of day. Her nose was pink as a rose petal over yellow teeth nubbed from cribbing. Pale patches at hip bones and shoulders where her hair was worn down almost to the hide by time and work. She sported a wide barrel and a deep neck, and her back swagged low between her shoulders and her hips. Her expression struck Luce like she held no illusions, having seen it all. Yet her ears aimed forward, alert and hopeful for the next significant thing to appear, even though right then, walking in a circle, she just kept seeing the same old scenery come back around every thirty seconds.

Maddie looked up from tending her bubbling molasses and saw the children's interest. She came over and said to Dolores, You can ride her, if you care to.

Maddie grabbed Dolores at the armpits and swung her onto the mare's down-slung back. Dolores neither fighting Maddie's touch nor falling numb and surrendering to some black personal hole down deep in herself. She sat on the mare's back and grinned.

Frank, watching his sister, raised his arms to be lifted as well.

The two of them fit perfectly into the sway of the mare's back. Dolores, in front, grabbed a handful of mane, and Frank squeezed his arms around Dolores's waist and pressed his face against her back with his eyes closed at first, as if to feel only so much sensation all at once. Maddie gave the mare a pat, and the children went riding together around the circle like normal children would do, enjoying the view from higher up than they were used to, smelling wood smoke and burnt sugar and the pony herself and the manure trod into the dirt.

When the ride ended and Maddie set the children back on the ground, Dolores looked up at her, all open-faced.

Maddie said, Her name's Sally, at least as long as I've had her.

Dolores nodded solemnly, like that name seemed perfect to her. She said, Sally Sally Sally. Then Frank said the name too, but just once.

THAT NIGHT AT BEDTIME, Luce said, Tell me something. What kind of weather suits you two best?

They stared at her as if she were a fool, and then they looked at each other. Neither of them said a word.

Luce said, I know you can talk. I heard it.

Nothing but blank faces from the kids.

—I'm the one that puts food on the table, Luce said. That's not any kind of threat, simply a fact. It's one of the things I do for you. I'm asking a question about weather. Do me a favor and answer, just because it would make me happy.

Wheels turned behind the dark eyes. Dolores finally said, very weary and put upon, as if the answer were obvious: Lightning.

—Good, Luce said. That's a sort of weather. Now, Frank, your turn.

—Lightning.

—Still a good answer. So, Frank, next question. What's your favorite color?

The boy turned his head to the side and did a little spitting thing like a smoker who rolls his own cigarettes getting a fleck of tobacco off his tongue.

Luce waited and waited.

She said, Frank, you're being called on to name a color. There's not a wrong answer, and nobody's going to hold anything against you. So say one of them.

Without looking at Luce, Frank said, Black.

—Yes, that's a color. And one of my favorites too.

—Fire color, Dolores said.

—Well, let's call that red and orange and yellow. So good choices, and thank you both.

She touched them each lightly at the brow, just a graze of fingertips, and turned out the light near their bed and sat awhile in the dark, listening to the radio playing soft, enjoying the rare feeling of finishing a day knowing you've done about as good a job as you know how to do. Though with all that fire and lightning talk, maybe she'd better keep sleeping with one eye open.

WANTING TO KEEP language rolling forward, Luce figured bedtime stories would make a good starting point. She wished she had some family heirlooms to tell, but Luce had missed out on ancestors. No barking-mad great-grandfather to sit by the fireside of a frosty winter's night passing down the folktales of their people, fishing his pink-and-white false teeth out of the bib pocket of his overalls so he could properly wheeze harmonica sound effects to a tale that involved a steam locomotive. As folkloric as it got for Luce were Lola's Wild Turkey ravings and Lit's bloody World War II stories.

Luce went scavenging through the lobby bookshelves and found a collection of violent Old World tales. Fe, fi, fo, fum, I smell the blood of an Englishman. She read them all, front to back, trying to imagine which ones Dolores and Frank might find useful. Share lessons children had learned for centuries regarding power and vulnerability. People got beaten and killed awfully cavalierly in the old stories. The fragility of the human body, all the threat and fear loose out there in the dark, and also sometimes in the daylight.

She started with "The Boy and the North Wind," figuring that at the very least she might get them to say, "Beat, stick, beat" with her when it came around in the tale. It was a glorious moment, and who wouldn't want to own such a stick and strike down stronger enemies? But Dolores and Frank paid no attention to it, or to the one about the princess who vowed not to smile for seven years.

Eventually, though, by trial and error, Luce hit a rich vein. For a full two weeks, all the children wanted to hear at bedtime was "The Three Billy Goats Gruff." Luce used suitably different voices for the small, medium, and large goats. For the troll, she spoke in a quiet menacing growl. She did sound effects of the goats trip-trapping on the bridge, and she was especially convincing when the big goat roared that he would use his horns to poke the troll's eyes out his ears, and his hooves to stomp the troll to bits, body and bones.

The children quivered and drew the quilt up to their noses, and Luce could feel them squirming toward her, their feet reaching under the covers to touch her hip where she sat on the edge of the bed. When the big goat laid the troll low, they drew a deep breath and let it out slow. By the third night, she had them joining her to shout the final lines. *Snip, snap, snout. This tale's told out.*

CHAPTER 4

STUBBLEFIELD COULDN'T HELP HIMSELF. After he met Luce, every few days he drove the nostalgic dead-end road and parked below the Lodge. Ostensibly, he came to swim from the little patch of beach his grandfather had made for him one yesteryear, just because he was working on a swimming merit badge. A dozen truckloads of brilliant white sand dumped over the red clay at the water's edge. All that summer, Stubblefield had spent most afternoons there, sunning and training and reading. He had dreamed of swimming all the way to town. The lake was supposed to be a mile wide at this point, which hadn't seemed insurmountable back then.

It looked a lot more distant now, though. And not enough warm days left to get in shape. Stubblefield contented himself with trying to go a hundred yards farther up the shoreline each day. Afterward, lie in the sun until his trunks dried, then put his clothes back on. Go up and knock on the door, the real reason for coming. Visit a few minutes with Luce, if she was home. Stay until she got edgy and then leave.

One day, as he came out of the water, he looked toward the Lodge and thought he saw Luce watching him from one of the tall dining room windows. Just a dim shape behind the glass. Still calf-deep, he bent forward and took a low bow. When he looked up, though, the window was empty.

Later, no answer to his knock on the door. He scribbled a note and left it stuck in the crack of the screen door. Nothing clever, just *Hi, S.* An effort to display interest in their free lonesome circumscribed lives.

And he was truly interested. Otherwise, he'd sell all his holdings, despite the theoretical ag-lease potential. Dump the whole mess at fire-sale prices and buy a red Healey and throw the top away. Just use the tonneau and go tropical and live on Sanibel or Key Largo and wear shorts and flip-flops every day of the year and eat a lot of grouper until the money ran out.

At least, that's what he would have done anytime previous. Go pursue what his Florida friends liked to call his rich inner life. Always saying it with a cutting edge of irony. But here was this lovely troubling woman Stubblefield had felt all kinds of idiotic things for at seventeen. Hard at the moment to let those go and move on. Though that's certainly what smart people would do.

If he were one of those, Stubblefield would have worked harder to keep his former fiancée happy. And now he would be wearing a navy blazer with gold buttons, selling Coupe de Villes on the island and waiting for her father to hurry up and die so he'd be running the dealership. Or would that be Coupes de Ville?

Also, look at Luce, a young hermit. And look too at what he had learned about her messed-up family. Mother, a long-gone runaway. Father, a crazy-ass violent lawman. Sister, a murder victim. Niece and nephew, pyromaniac part-time mutes who had burned his homeplace to the ground.

What would smart people do?

Run away, that's what.

But Stubblefield went to Maddie and tried to buy her mare to please Luce, since she'd gone on and on about how the pony had made the children so calm and undestructive for a minute or two and had caused them to speak a few words.

LUCE WORKED THE SLING blade in rampant weeds growing beside the thread of water running from the spring. The children sat cross-legged on the back porch with a colorful indented circle of Chinese checkers between them. The game was percussive. They moved their marbles rapidly and banged them down on the hollow metal board without clear relation to each other, so that they appeared to be playing their own individual games simultaneously rather than playing against each other to a common conclusion, a winner and a loser.

Stubblefield came around the side of the Lodge from his car. Said, right off, I talked to Maddie.

Luce stopped slinging. She squared off against Stubblefield, her jeans stained green to the knee with weed bits.

—What for? she said.

—Because I like her and want to get to know her better and wish I'd known her when I was a kid. And because of that Sally horse you told me about.

Luce said, She's a pony.

—I thought that meant a young horse.

—Of course you did.

—Point is, I was trying to buy her for you. For the kids, really.

Luce turned away and started swinging the scallop-edged blade in the ragweed and jewelweed like it was either that or yell at him. As far as Stubblefield was concerned, there was entirely too much whacking around here.

—It seemed like a way I could be helpful, he said.

Luce stopped what she was doing and looked at him, all tight and pursed up. Tired around the eyes.

She said, You don't be buying me things. No gifts at all. Not even a box of candy or a jar of honey.

Stubblefield wanted to ask, Why so pissed off? Instead, he turned his palms up in the universal gesture of What the hell have I done now? Luce had been all alight with enthusiasm by the calm interest the children had shown in the horse and, especially, by the single word Dolores and Frank had uttered. Sally, Sally, Sally. So why not let him buy the horse? Or pony, apparently. It seemed like a good thing. A help. Old worn-out pony ought to cost next to nothing. A lot of people would give one to you, if you promised to feed it and not sell it to become dog food or steaks for Frenchmen. But clearly, he'd thought wrong all the way around. Maybe what he needed was a pocket-sized list of rules in minuscule print to consult moment by moment.

Maybe a little bitter in his tone, Stubblefield said, Well, whatever. Maddie wouldn't sell Sally at any price.

Luce said, Oh, was I rude?

Stubblefield looked for a word. Not *vehement*. And *passionate* was out of the question. He said, Emphatic?

Luce made a slight expression. A hint of eye roll or twitch of mouth. She said, Mr. Polite.

Stubblefield said, Would *sharp* or *curt* have been better? Or *ungracious?*

As soon as the words left his mouth, Stubblefield wished he could pull them back, like he expected to be tossed on his ear from his own property. Instead, Luce looked off to the side, clearly struggling to keep her face blank, not laugh. He saw her take a deep breath.

She said, Let's leave it that maybe a jar of honey would be fine, but that's the upper limit. Flowers, if you pick them yourself. But no ponies, no jewelry.

—Well, Stubblefield said, Maddie told me the kids can ride every day if they want to, but they have to come to her place to do it. I think she's lonely and would like having them around. And you too.

—Better that way, Luce said.

—Hey, Stubblefield said to the world at large. How about let's go ride that Sally pony?

Two pair of dark eyes cut everywhere around the porch and yard except Stubblefield's direction.

—We walking or driving? Stubblefield said.

The children glanced toward the Hawk, and then away.

Luce said, Let's walk. It's nice out, and they're always happier if they're worn out at the end of the day. Me too.

On the way down the two-track dirt road, the children ran ahead. Stubblefield and Luce walked on either side of the weedy middle hump. Stubblefield said, So, a jar of honey and maybe, someday in the future, a movie? A ticket, a bag of popcorn, and a Coke. Nothing more.

—That's not what I said. But possibly. If Maddie could keep the children for a few hours.

—Saturday night's a double feature. *Creature from the Black Lagoon* and something involving a big spider or lizard.

—I used to live beside the theater. I've seen all the monster movies.

—A week from Friday, *Light in the Piazza*.

—I liked that book. So, maybe.

SALLY STOOD THREE-LEGGED, getting a hind hoof picked. When Maddie finished, she knocked the crud against a fence rail and rose from her stoop, grunting deep from her diaphragm like an old man lifting from his armchair. Dolores and Frank crowded so close around Sally that they nearly got their feet stepped on. They held brushes, impatient to start grooming.

Maddie couldn't convince them to go with the lay of hair. They scrubbed at Sally's sides like scraping a wall for painting. With less provocation, for two decades, Sally had nipped many purple bruises into the arms and thighs and necks and scalps of farriers and vets and even people getting too insistent about putting a blanket on her for a frigid night. But she stood still for the children, lowering her head, ears up.

Maddie called out to Luce and Stubblefield on the porch: If all you are is ignorant, Sally gives you a pass.

As they groomed, Maddie sang "Back in the Saddle Again." Mostly joking with herself, barely louder than a hum. But the second time the chorus rolled around, Dolores and Frank came in very faintly on the Whoopi-ty-aye-ohs. Voices thin and high like ordinary children's, except their pitch was perfect.

Maddie stopped and said, Didn't know you two could sing.

They both shut up and worked the brushes.

Sally switched her tail at them when they came in range of her hindquarters. Swept so lightly across the face by Sally's thin tail, the children almost danced with the sensation. Frank's hands rose above his shoulders, fluttering like bird wings, as if the power of flight could be the only possible enhancement to the moment.

When Maddie figured Sally couldn't take much more grooming, she swung the children up by their armpits and put the reins in Dolores's hands and said slowly, one word at a time, Don't pull on these. Let 'em droop. Look where you want to go and squeeze with your legs. She'll go that way, if she feels like it. Curve with the fence, so look left.

Dolores looked at Maddie and then turned her head to the right like she was trying to see what was over her shoulder, which was Frank.

Maddie said, Other left.

Dolores kept looking over her shoulder at Frank, and Maddie snapped her fingers to get Dolores's attention and made a leftward-curving motion with her hand.

Dolores looked where she needed to, and Frank touched Sally's sides with his heels. At a slow walk, she went forward, following the fence line of the paddock.

Maddie unhooked the gate chain and went to the porch and very deliberately sat in the space between Stubblefield and Luce, knees drawn up nearly to her chin and the skirt of her cotton print dress stretched tight between the bony joints. They all watched the children ride with high interest. Goldenrod and joe-pye weed and ironweed rose above the top boards of the fence, and the autumn colors of their blooms worked well with one another and with the dry blue sky.

The children came back around to the gate, and when Sally started to slow down, Frank gave her a nudge to keep her moving. She made a slight effort toward a jog, but when the children started bouncing she settled back to an eager walk, with her ears forward. And around they went. It was a great success. Like Dolores and Frank might quit being little glum reavers out to wreck their world.

Luce said, That's a happy sight.

Maddie witnessed a rare occurrence, Luce's unedited smiling face. Then Maddie looked at Stubblefield, who was looking at Luce and smiling too.

—How long have you known her? Maddie asked Stubblefield.

—Couple or three weeks, Luce said real quick. She held up three fingers. Preemptive in case Stubblefield wanted to start talking about his teenage memories.

Maddie said, Three whole weeks? Her tone was actorish, pitched to an audience not currently in attendance except inside her head, and meant to convey, at minimum, a couple of things at the same time.

—Yup, Stubblefield said.

Maddie said, I've known your family way back. When I was a little girl, I knew a Stubblefield who still had a minié ball in his leg from Antietam. Old beardy man that liked to get you to touch his scar and feel that ball move around under your finger.

Stubblefield said, Yeah, well. So you probably knew the cowboy, then?

—I remember him. We were in school together. He was a couple of years older. Wouldn't strike a lick at a snake. Grew up and sat around all day listening to records and drinking. Entertaining as hell in a conversation, but you couldn't count on him for one damn thing. Ask him the time of day, you better look up and check the sun for confirmation.

—My grandfather always said I was a lot like him.

Maddie studied Stubblefield, as if for the first time. Said, You look something alike. He was a tall good-looking fool too.

Luce bumped Maddie with her shoulder. In a whisper, Luce said, Go easy.

Maddie turned to Luce and started to say something, but she read Luce's face and stopped. Instead she turned back to Stubblefield, and in the same whisper said, If you're not careful with her, you'll answer to me.

STUBBLEFIELD DROVE SLOW down a single-lane farm road. On either side, three strands of rusty barbwire drooped between grey locust posts, enclosing weedy pastures in need of cows. He hooked past an unused barn and parked near the back door of a big farmhouse from the previous century. Carved ornaments in the angles of the gables and white paint flaking big as butterfly wings on the clapboards. He started to open his door, and Luce said, No. Either sit here or drive around for thirty minutes.

Stubblefield turned his hands up. Whatever. No hurt feelings.

Not much of a date anyway, since Luce just needed a ride. Though, on the way to pick her up, Stubblefield had stopped at a roadside stand and bought a jar of honey and presented it to her after they dropped the kids off at Maddie's. Saying, Correct me if I am wrong, but I think this was on the list of acceptables.

Luce had held the jar to the light and studied the legs and wings suspended in the nearly coffee-colored goo, and the pale comb lurking barely visible through the murk. At which point Stubblefield said, I'm starting to think it looks like the cat-head baby in the carnival freak show, floating in the jar of dirty formaldehyde.

—Yeah, maybe. But thanks anyway.

Now Luce wondered about herself. An afternoon without the kids, and all she wanted to do was visit her old primary school teachers. She could tell Stubblefield wondered why. But he seemed to sense how anxious she was and went along without question. He felt under the seat and randomly pulled out one book from the several. *Franny and Zooey*, with a linty butterscotch Life Saver sticking to the white cover.

—Take your time, he said.

Luce climbed three steps to the back door and tapped her middle knuckle twice on the frame of the screen door and disappeared inside the dim kitchen.

The teachers were angular bright-eyed sisters of a certain age, wielding sharp intellects. Each deeply read in the smart dead Englishmen of past centuries and also a very select few of the elders among American penmen.

While most of their fellow teachers went by Miss, leaving the impression that teachers swore a vow against men as powerful as any nun's, these three rebels were all Mrs. Among themselves, they had figured out how to go about marriage so as to accomplish the least damage. The husbands lived two hours away, in directions that thirded the compass like a generously cut pie, and none of the men ever visited except on the rarest of occasions, as if a demilitarized zone that they dare not enter had been drawn with a protractor around the women at its center. Nobody even knew exactly what kinds of jobs these men did. On Friday afternoons at three o'clock, the sisters got in their Hudsons, which differed only in color, and drove to their husbands for the weekend. Slightly longer stretches of time for the major holidays, and a couple or three weeks in the summertime. They had no children of their own but had spent decades with the children of others.

Luce was shown into the parlor by one sister while another charged the percolator with grounds and set it to boil on the stove. The third sister, the youngest, already sat in the parlor near a window, reading. Luce hadn't been there since childhood, and yet not even the placement of the candy jar on the mantel had changed. The kind of place where antimacassars draped the backrests of purple velvet chairs, the seat cushions buffed to a pale silver nub by many decades of buttocks dating back nearly to the Grant administration. Bookcases everywhere, filled with leather Miltons and Burnses and Tennysons inscribed on the endpapers with the beautiful looping handwriting of dead people. One of the sisters could recite "Thanatopsis" all the way through without missing a word, and another could do "Snowbound," and the youngest could declaim "The Masque of the Red Death" with utter conviction, though it was not even a poem at all, and thus she was suspected of paraphrasing. So, imagine the festive evenings of January, a crackling fire and a big bowl of popcorn cooked with a strip of bacon.

Luce had all three of the sisters for classes in the early grades, and because of their family resemblance, they blended together in her memory. Also, because they all three praised her extravagantly and urged her forward in life like no adults had ever done before or since. Each one of them had held her tight by the shoulders at the end of the year and looked into her eyes and said, You can be whatever you want to be.

Strange, now, to find herself grown up and face-to-face with them again, being who she had become.

When the coffee was ready, the sisters rowed themselves opposite Luce on the settee. Each one downing half a cup at one go and then firing up a smoke. Three different brands.

The unaccustomed caffeine came on like a vibration in Luce's back teeth and frizzed static into her thoughts.

She blurted out some of what she'd come prepared to say. I've been thinking a lot about when I was in school, and about the care of children. Lily's girl and boy live with me now. My mother wasn't a model for anything but crazy. And it's not like I'm thinking back and trying to force any of you into being sweet ladies. You had hard expectations. If we were called upon, you made us step up and answer for ourselves. These children aren't easy.

The eldest sister cracked two notes of smoker's laughter, indistinguishable from a TB cough. Said, You want us to tell you how to be a mother? If so, you've come to the wrong place.

And then they started talking all at once, lapping over one another and completing one another's sentences as they had done for half a century. Their tone like an argument, except they were all arguing the same point.

The jist was, there's a big difference between teacher and mother. A teacher has six hours a day for nine months of one year. And thirty children to deal with at a time. You do your best, and you expect the same of them. Then you pass them to the next grade and hope to do better with another bunch.

—How analogous is that to your situation? the younger sister said.

Luce felt like she had fallen back into one of the brutal flash-card battles. She said, Not at all?

—Wrong answer, the eldest said. Or at least incomplete.

Luce revised. She said, Not analogous, except for the part about doing your best and expecting them to do theirs?

—Yes, the youngest said.

The middle sister said, Still a quick learner.

Luce started to say her thanks and leave. But then she said, Well, that's all fine, but not much help when I get up mornings not knowing where to start. Or when I go to bed afraid I've failed them. They fight with each other and set fire to things and kill chickens. Sometimes they're mean, but mostly they're scared of the whole world. There's something wrong with them, and I think Lily's husband damaged them. They won't let me give them baths. They don't like to touch or be touched. I can't tell if they can be fixed. Or, if they can, how much.

The youngest sister said, You think we've never come up against a child some man had been using because they're the only thing in his world weaker than he is? And not have any way to prove it?

The eldest sister said, It won't ever go away.

The middle sister, Luce's first-grade teacher with the flashing glasses and violets pinned to her lapel, leaned to set her empty cup into its saucer. She said, Luce, when you were a little girl, you weren't afraid of anything. It's what first caught my attention about you. Probably because I never have been that way. First day of school every year, even now, I look out at those little faces, every one needing something from me, and I start feeling like I can't breathe thinking about the hundred and eighty days ahead. I've learned to remember there will be good days and bad days. For me and for them. Many rivers to cross between fall and spring.

WHEN LUCE GOT BACK out to the car, Stubblefield held up his book. He said, Forty pages, and I'm feeling calm and melancholy. Like meditating, if I had the time to stick with it.

Inside the car, Luce felt her mood lighten a shade or two. She believed she wanted to ride a little more, take back roads and stretch the trip home even longer than it was.

—The kids will be fine with Maddie, Luce said. Something about the way she talks to them, same tone she uses with Sally. Like everybody is all fine and serene, and nobody requires anything from you except to enjoy a big dinner together. Today was going to be white bean soup with lots of ham, and a skillet of cornbread.

Stubblefield drove below the dam and followed the river through the valley. The farm country beginning to wrap up operations for the summer, cornstalks waiting to be cut for fodder and broad tobacco leaves bundled and hanging upside down in open barns to dry, waiting for auction. Long rows of cabbages, the dusty green outer leaves veined like the back of an old man's hand. Beyond the fields, wooded slopes pitched upward to the ridges and peaks, the foliage shading toward yellow and orange and red.

Luce looked at Stubblefield and then back out the window. She said, I'm trying to help the children get better if they can. They were learning to talk when they were two or three. Lily wrote me letters about the words they knew. They stopped, and now they're starting again. I read to them, take them for walks and try to teach them about where they are. Flowers and history. Music. I try not to feel sorry for them. They don't seem to want it, and I think it would be bad for them. Start feeling sorry and coddling them and having no expectations, they'll be like this forever. And maybe they will be anyway. They've killed a couple of roosters, which for a little child is a pretty fierce undertaking. Go look at a big rooster and picture being about three feet tall with one of those wild bastards standing chest-high, spreading his neck feathers and glaring and hooking his yellow beak at you. They'll flog you, claw you, peck your face. I don't really know how they did it with no weapons except maybe sticks.

—So, you admire them? Stubblefield said.

—I'm just making a point about them improving. After that incident at the corner of the Lodge, which was mainly a singe, they've been better about setting fires.

—You counting my grandparents' farmhouse in there, or what?

—That's a possibility, not a fact, Luce said.

—Sort of a dark charcoal-grey area?

—Well, if you want to get sarcastic about it, of course they did it. I just didn't witness it. And you've been swell about that, by the way.

—Glad you noticed.

When they made the turn onto the dirt road that led around the back side of the lake, Luce reached over and took Stubblefield's hand for a moment and held it and then gave it back to him, like an experiment by a thirteen-year-old girl on a first date. And Luce hoped he had enough sense not to make anything of it, except within himself.

CHAPTER 5

GREY-DARK, AND LIT HAD already pulled on the headlights when a spotted hog scooted across the road, traveling low to
the ground at desperate speed, streaming black blood from a head
wound. At the white line on the far side of the pavement, its joints
buckled and it fell forward in a long skid into the weeds.

Bud said, The hell?

Lit braked and got out. Off in the distance, men whooped like greyboys before Pickett's Charge and other epic misjudgments.

Lit looked at the slumped animal. An escapee from a slaughtering.
Had to be. No longer hog, but not yet transformed into pork.

Bud opened his door to get out, but Lit said, Sit still. This won't
take but a minute.

Lit reached through the open door and cut the lights to the black-
and-white but left the engine idling. Set his beer on the roof and rattled in a box of rusty tools in the trunk and drew out a hand axe. He
went to the hog and prodded it with his foot. Nothing but dead flab.

Drunks off in the woods hollered nearer, saying, They damn, and
other expressions of utter amazement.

Lit worked with the axe like limbing a felled tree to section and
split. But only so far as to free the hams. Fuck that other peasant food.
Tripe, ears, fatback, and snout. And all that headcheese mess. He carried the hams by their two feet and swung them and the dripping
maniac axe into the trunk and drove on with the lights out, leaving the

hillbillies to sort out the mystery for themselves when they arrived momentarily to claim their runaway hog.

Around the first curve, Lit hit the gas, and the forgotten half-full bottle fell back across the trunk and to the pavement, shattering with spewing concussion. Bud held his empty out the window and lofted it back over the car to join its fellow in festive breakage.

NIGHT DRIVING. THIS NIGHT, like so many lately, drinking long-necks and listening to the radio, sharing their dope and their hopes and dreams. The dashboard lights casting green shadows on their faces and Luckies drooping from their lips, except when they flicked ash out the windows.

They rode a long way from town. Way out. Not a light to be seen in the indigo night but their own yellow headlights and the tiny white orbs of the heavens, which, because of a fortunate mixture of pills, took on a slight pinwheel effect when they looked up through the windshield for longer than a glance. Lit drove quick, steering with the wrist of his right hand over the wheel and his left elbow resting on the windowsill. Chill damp mountain air streaming in, but balanced by the blast of heat from the firewall. The first fallen yellow poplar leaves resting like upturned hands on the dark pavement.

The narrow road climbed alongside a white-water creek toward a gap, twisting in correspondence with the path of the water. One turn coming hard after the other in a rhythm of shifting car weight, the performance springs and shocks of the cruiser crouching only slightly on the inside and hardly lifting on the outside. No more than a shoulder shrug one way or the other. They crossed narrow one-lane wooden bridges, the timbers painted metallic silver to give the reassuring impression of steel girders. Passed through tunnels of trees vaulting overhead, and the road so slim that two cars meeting would have to scoot over with their right wheels into the grass. But at this time of night, that was mostly theoretical.

Two turns more, and what they had been driving toward stretched in front of them out of the twisty mountain roads. An anomalous straight, longer than the reach of the headlights. Some philanthropist with a paintbrush had measured a quarter mile and swiped a messy slash of white across the pavement at beginning and end. Barely enough space left over at the end for braking before the next hard left-hand curve.

Lit stopped at the line, downshifted, and floored it. The cruiser squatted on its hind wheels and howled, laying two long trails of rubber in first and again at the upshift to second. Even chirping going into fourth, at which point the red speedometer needle quivered past a hundred. Neither of the men said anything during the run.

When they passed the second stripe, Bud said, I counted thirteen. Lit said, It was twelve.

FOGGY AND CHILLY, midnight, they discovered a dozen high school kids drinking beer and dancing to music from a car radio, warming themselves with a roaring fire of burning truck tires on the tenth green of the golf course, the fire centered on the cup. Bud stayed in the car, waiting to observe an epic ass-kicking. But Lit walked to the fire and warmed his hands, said hello to a tall slim blond girl like he knew her. Then pulled a couple of beers out of the kids' cooler and informed them that what they were doing was all kinds of illegal. Guessing at the charges, he'd say trespassing and vandalism, if not arson. Also public consumption and, for most of them, underage drinking. And that's before anybody gets mouthy or breaks to run down the fairway, which would add some version of resisting arrest. Oh, what deep shit they have fallen into.

Lit asked, Does anybody know what the term *mitigating circumstances* means? Raise your hand if you think you know the answer.

Nobody said anything, and Lit said, Right this minute, it means every grey-headed golfer that ever played this hole would trade everything he has if he could swap places with you right now. So I'll just say good night. I ought, at least, to add, tomorrow's a school day, but what the fuck.

Lit got in the cruiser and handed Bud the second beer and rolled on.

LATER, THEY SAT BEHIND the Roadhouse, finishing their current beers before going inside to order a couple more. Before Lit saw him coming, a big drunk with a face like one of the raw hams in the trunk had his head stuck all the way inside Lit's open window, yelling proclamations of anger.

—You remember me? You blackjacked me, you fuck. For nothing but back-talking when you tried to arrest me for breaking and entering. All I stole was a worn-out TV.

—I didn't *try* to arrest you, Lit said. I *did* arrest you.

—I still can't feel my fingers sometimes. But now you ain't got your uniform on. You're off duty and that means you're not different from any other citizen, you little shit. I'm gonna drag your ass out of that car and kick you all over the parking lot.

Real quick, so that it was done before Bud could take it in, Lit cranked the window up to trap the man's neck, and then hit him in the mouth over and over, so fast Bud couldn't count the blows. Lit rolled the window down, and the drunk's face slid below the windowsill.

Lit shoved his door open and got out. The man rose to his feet, blood dripping off his chin, but ready to go again. He acted like he was in a boxing match and squared up for right crosses and uppercuts, old sporting shit. Like maybe a ref in a white shirt and bow tie stood at his elbow to call infractions.

Not nearly so romantic, Lit grabbed a tire iron from under the front seat and with one hard swing, parallel to the ground, ended the thing.

The man lay in the gravel, trying to coil his body around his shattered knee. Cursing Lit and God equally.

—Nobody to blame but yourself, Lit said. You didn't have to bring that down on you, but you did. Free will's a bitch.

Fights came with the job. Bud had witnessed a half dozen already. Some idiot with a load on starts believing he can fight the law, exactly like his Rebel great-granddaddy. Always instructive for Bud to watch the outcome.

Wet from a dunking in the lake, Lit might go one thirty-five. But wiry and high-strung for the express purpose of amazing quickness. When he went man-to-man, he worked his little keen fists in a deeply destructive fashion, probing toward a spleen that needed rupturing bad. The actions of Lit's hands had no common internal wiring to his face, which stayed as blank as the bottom of an empty bucket. He'd be sweating all over during a fight, but his expression remained mild as Jesus in his sunbeam amid the youngster animals. Drunks and criminals could be trying to head-butt him or shove up close, nose-to-nose, spitting out vile epithets, yet the look in Lit's eye remained as if he were peering into another green and peaceful world entirely.

STUBBLEFIELD COULDN'T BELIEVE HIS LIFE. It felt like wiring into some science-fiction time machine or downing a new drug and being jolted back to a lost highlight of life where you'd failed badly. But now you've been given an unexpected second chance. This time be bolder, smarter, funnier, wiser, not a teenage fool, cramped on all sides by pride and shame and fear. Be better all around, knowing more of life and having read more books and listened to more music. Yet how to connect seventeen to the unexpected now?

Stubblefield decided to play interviewer. Out walking the children or sitting on the porch, he drew fragments of Luce's past from her with surprising delicacy, at least surprising to him. He watched and listened closely, asked questions only up to a line beyond which he sensed she'd spook away from him. Mostly, she had to be coaxed, and then sometimes she didn't. He felt like a Depression-era WPA writer interviewing a reticent ninety-year-old about the great flood of 1873 and, at the same time, some half-folkloric riverboat race where a boiler blew and dozens were scalded to death by the steam. Get a little bit of one story and then a little bit of the other, and never be entirely sure how much to believe of either.

WHEN STUBBLEFIELD ASKED why Luce had taken the job at the Lodge, she said she wanted to get far from town, and the lake was beautiful. Old Stubblefield had been kind to her and an interesting man to work for, if you could call what she did work.

And that would have ended it if Stubblefield hadn't kept probing. When he returned to the topic, she said she took the job at a point where she was of a mind to get over thinking about hopes and fears and desires. They didn't help a bit when it came to voyaging safely through a day. Just live every one as it came and not let people intrude on you. Shut up and hope everybody else did the same. Strive for whole uneventful weeks where the weather was about all that changed. She pointed out that weather was plenty interesting to watch as it passed over you, and it had entertained people for many thousands of years. And not just immediate weather but also the larger movements of the seasons. You had to learn how to feel the long flow and not get hung up on the day-to-day. Big swellings and recedings, upturned and downturned sweeps linked in slow rhythms built from millions of tiny parts—animal, vegetable, mineral—not just temperature and length of daylight. For example, the way a rhododendron changed through-out the year, month by month. She claimed she had observed and learned nearly a hundred such parts of the local world. She said, Imag-ine holding every bit of it in your head at one time, this whole place, down to what the salamanders are doing every month of the four sea-sons. She put the bunched tips of her fingers to each temple and said, Boom. Then spread her fingers and lifted her hands in a gesture of explosion.

WHEN STUBBLEFIELD ASKED about vanity—Luce's cheerleader beauty-contest days—she was surprisingly forthcoming. Right now she was about as pretty as she cared to be, considering that being pretty drew little but trouble. She wore no makeup, ever, and went many happy days in a row without glancing in a mirror. She cut her own hair, both for economy and preference. When it grew much below her shoulders, she whacked the ends off. She said, It looks just fine that way. Not fashionable, but with an actual style, mainly from it not mattering what you think looks good right this second in the history of hairdos.

When Luce did look in the mirror, she thought she might still be sort of pretty, if you went by what most people thought was pretty. And if that's the way you went, you had your own problems. It wasn't like being pretty was an accomplishment, and it would go away in time. So it would be a mistake to get too hung up on it. At which point she looked Stubblefield in the eye.

As for clothes, only two stores in town sold women's apparel, little of which she could afford. The sewing shop—with its bolts of cascading fabric stacked one above another almost to the ceiling, its bins of translucent Butterick and Simplicity patterns folded in their tight envelopes with optimistic pastel illustrations of wasp-waisted women, its notions case filled with dimpled thimbles and bright needles ranked precise behind the cellophane windows of their packets, each one piercing the matte black paper twice—might as well not exist as far as Luce was concerned. Sewing a button back on was all the seamstress she ever cared to be.

So, with scant money, she wore confusing clothes, owned for years. In summer, she alternated her jeans and loafers with pink or black pedal pushers and white or blue button-down oxford shirts and white Keds or scuffed Capezios from her life before the Lodge. Come fall, baggy turtlenecks and pointed black ankle boots. Everything always clean and pressed crisp, so you didn't know whether she had a couple of such outfits or a dozen. Which to Stubblefield sounded nothing but delightful. He imagined that her change of attire happened on a schedule determined by what the trees were doing or some other minute cyclic marker of one season giving way to the next. The flowering of ironweed or a specific downward pitch of evening sunlight.

IN REGARD TO ECONOMICS, all Luce cared to say was that she got by. Didn't care to talk about money any more than religion or politics.

Eventually, though, Stubblefield got her talking about her stipend and its limitations. What a nice touch of old Stubblefield's to use that delicate term, she said. She became enthusiastic telling how she sometimes supplemented her cash by selling worked flints and clay pipe bowls turned up in plowed fields in the spring and after heavy rains year-round. Bird points and spearheads and scrapers from an earlier world. Down in the bowl of a good pipe, you could often see a crust of burnt tobacco and imagine some original inhabitant taking a smoke at the end of day. The roadside tourist shops bought them, along with ginseng roots. They sold the artifacts to tourists, and the roots mostly got shipped around the world to China, as had been the case for a couple of centuries. For gentleman problems, Luce explained.

Also, as a cash crop, she had tried growing a patch of tobacco, but her allotment was so small you could nearly spit across it. The government said that's all she could grow, and sent a man and a boy around with a spool of measuring tape to enforce its area down to the square foot. After a summer of work, she barely broke even, and after that she gave up on commercial agriculture. During fishing season, anglers sometimes stopped by the Lodge to buy rock bait, stick bait, nightcrawlers.

Stubblefield learned, to his confusion, that Luce had limited use for cash money. Most of what it bought she didn't want. She was happy without modern conveniences, her desires being mostly impractical and lacking monetary value.

Luce said, What I want most is the ability to whistle the song of every bird in the area.

At which point Stubblefield thought he detected humor going on at his expense.

He said, What about television? That's something money can buy. You might like Paladin. He can be really dry too.

Luce said, I've got radio.

Besides, she told him, you start wanting things too much and you need more and more money. She said she tried as much as possible to live free from the bad idea of money. Otherwise, when you took a job, you inevitably sold your time to someone who valued it lowly. Luce, however, valued her time highly. Luce had it all figured out. Live out of sight from the bullshit of everyday commerce. Use money as little as possible.

But the children threatened Luce's economics. They would need shoes and clothes, and they went through food faster than a pair of bear dogs. Her garden wouldn't hold up three cold months under their hunger. By deep winter, the root cellar would be cleaned out of potatoes and cabbages and turnips and acorn squash, and all the colorful mason jars of tomatoes and green beans would empty out and be clear shapes of air lined on a shelf.

When the children went to school, then what? The State said they had to go, but Luce worried that they might harm the other students. She worried about them being cooped up inside a yellow bus for the long ride into town. All that gasoline in the tank. They were getting better, but maybe not fast enough.

WHEN STUBBLEFIELD ASKED if Luce got lonely—living mostly outside of communication with the world, no phone, wasps nesting in the mailbox—Luce said sure she got lonely, but there had been many reimbursements. Animals, for example. Amazing that anything as big as deer and bear survived the bloodthirsty bygones when we snuffed out everything else of size. Bison gone before 1800, elk not long after, wolves before 1900, and panthers shortly after World War I. Dates verified by Maddie and old Stubblefield and other elders. No more left in these mountains or anywhere else for at least a thousand miles. Complete erasure. Except Luce, out walking at sunrise one morning last fall, saw something at the upper end of old Stubblefield's hay field, something big and pale moving against the dark of the wood's edge. It went along the fence line, and its sand-colored body and long tail didn't lack much of reaching from post to post, which Luce later paced off to be eight feet. And the animal moved like no big dun-colored dog or deer ever did. It went smooth and low and soft-footed in the long grass that in the dawn light was close to the color of the cat. If she had not been alone, she would never have seen the panther or felt the hope it spread into the world like rings around the splash of a rock thrown into a still lake.

When Stubblefield came back around to the topic of loneliness, Luce got insistent about the reimbursements. A great deal of pleasure to be found in the growth of vegetables. And in the fall, birds passing over in waves, their calls singing of distance and other landscapes and the weird tones of Maddie's folklore songs from back in an older America. Or a younger one, depending on your perspective. Also, the sadness and bravery of new doomed sprouts growing from dead blighted chestnut trees. At night, you could walk outside and look anywhere except straight across the lake to the town and not see a light, just shapes of black mountains against the charcoal sky and the brilliant stars overhead. Except sometimes in summer when fishermen went out on the lake in their little boats and shined big flashlights into the water to draw bass. Plus, recently, the hateful satellites whizzing over, marring the constellations.

And the obvious freedom of living alone could not to be discounted. Sample days from Luce's pre-children life included summer afternoons swinging in an army-surplus jungle hammock she had bought for a dollar fifty. It smelled of mildew and had a canvas roof and mosquito-netting sidewalls. She strung it between two hemlocks, and it was like a pup tent levitating. Inside, she could float and look out at the garden and the woods, all misty through the netting, and read books from the lobby shelves. *Seventeen* by Booth Tarkington. Volumes of the outdated Britannica. The usual afternoon temperate-rainforest shower fell on the hammock roof and then passed and the sun came back out. Come autumn, build a late-afternoon campfire in the yard and sit in a striped canvas campaign chair and watch the night come on and drink a scant glass of the old important liquor from the basement. Watch the sun and moon and planets fall one after another down the same curved path to the horizon.

Stubblefield said, So you're happy out walking alone at dawn seeing extinct animals? What about before that? Two in the morning kind of lonely?

Luce said that was pretty bad, no denying it. Sometimes, maybe she felt like a piece of her that used to be there was gone. But she had figured out a shape that days needed to take so that she hardly noticed whether she was happy or not. Keeping your mind on every day as it came was part of it. The garden, the chickens, firewood, cooking. The four seasons. Late summer, the last small watermelons and tired to-mato plants putting out just one or two smallish fruits before shutting down for good. Then pumpkins turning bright, and the last apples in the old orchard little and misshapen but sharp and clean-tasting, with just the right balance of sweet and tart to be good either as eating apples or cooking apples. Autumn collards still small and reaching for the slanted light, and waiting for the first frost to come into their own.

CONCERNING HER CHILDHOOD, all Luce wanted to talk about was a lanky dark-haired girl named Myrtle from tribal land across the nearest ridge from town. The girl spoke almost nothing but Cherokee. They were both free to wander, and sometimes they met at the ridge-line. Luce would have been happy to sit with her all day, smiling and hardly saying a word, making whole villages out of sticks in the dirt of the woods floor. But Myrtle could stay only so long before she needed to head home to help shuck corn or shell peas or whatever other chore the season dictated. The only English the girl knew was the phrase Get, damn hogs. Useful mainly when the neighbors' hogs got loose in the garden. But also a lot of fun to shout on random occasions.

Stubblefield asked what it was like after Lola left, and Luce said, Better. She remembered that some people in town speculated pretty urgently, with no evidence whatsoever, that Lit had killed Lola and buried her up on the mountain. And of course kids heard it from their parents and couldn't get enough of talking about it at school. When

Luce went home confused and full of questions, Lit didn't sugarcoat it. He told third-grade Luce and second-grade Lily that their mother had run off with a man from Shithole, Florida, and that the man had soon dumped her, so probably Lola was walking the streets of Tampa.

Young Luce had been out west as far as the county seat, twenty miles away, but except for having a marble courthouse with a green copper dome, it was not noticeably different than the lake town, except that it had two of everything. Even two barbershops with identical red-and-white poles spiraling to infinity inside glass cylinders. Yet, sadly, only one library per town. Even with the doubling, walking the streets took a matter of minutes. Up one side and down the other, a few blocks each way, and then you were done. So it was not clear to young Luce what walking the streets of Tampa might mean.

However, one of several benefits from her mother's absence came immediately. Lit seemed somewhat less high-pitched every day. He quit drinking liquor and switched to beer and mostly confined himself to one or two on workdays. Also the house rested a whole lot quieter without all the quarreling. Lola couldn't hardly scramble an egg, so the food didn't change noticeably. Luce and Lily mainly lived off bologna-and-cheese sandwiches and boiled hot dogs except when Lit brought home sirloins and fried them up in a skillet with sliced potatoes.

—Did you miss anything about her? Stubblefield said.

—No. And that's my last word, no matter how many times you ask.

Except when Stubblefield tried again, Luce said she remembered something from way back in childhood. Lily being sick. Colic or cholera or something. Lily wailing and Lola holding her, walking the living room floor back and forth, saying, Baby, baby, baby.

Stubblefield said, So a sweet memory?

—Yeah, sweet. I was scared that Lily was so sick she might die and leave me by myself with them. I started crying and Lola put Lily on the sofa and grabbed me by the wrist and yanked me to the kitchen and backed me against the refrigerator. Bent down right in my face, yelling about how weak I was. Didn't even take the cigarette out of the corner of her mouth. I remember how it glowed and wagged up and down while she yelled.

AT SOME POINT, Stubblefield wondered how much he was really learning about Luce. She would talk freely about dress patterns, the daily details of gardening, his grandfather. But Stubblefield kept feeling like he was watching a cardsharp shuffle the deck, all the fine subtle movements to misdirect your attention, and at the end, a reassuring spread of hands to hide the pit opening under her life.

Stubblefield liked to read mountaineering books about Hillary and Smythe and Mallory. There was a term that expressed how high you were, how far the drop below your feet, how bad the weather. All the cumulative danger of the world you had entered. The word was *exposure*. At some far degree, if you lose a glove, you lose your hand. You fall, you die. Stubblefield became convinced that Luce was pretty badly exposed. But if she believed she had succeeded in paring her life down to essentials and reimbursements, he needed to figure out which category he might best fit himself into.

TAKE PINBALL, FOR EXAMPLE. Especially on a wood-rail Gottlieb *Cyclone* or *Harbor Lites* table. Night after night, Lit's reflexes allowed him to play a single quarter on and on until he got bored. His touch against the spring to launch the chrome ball into play was art. After that, carefully judged nudges and checks with hands and hips and knees guided the ball in regard to bumpers and kickers and chutes without tilting the table. Flipper work too subtle to comprehend. You could go to college and study mechanical engineering and physics for ten years and not understand it.

Psychic and saintly was the way Bud viewed it. The air disturbed by a leaf falling to the parking lot played a role in how Lit's fingers twitched. Each second, Lit did two dozen different things at once, attending fully to the present moment but with a disinterested look on his face. Every machine in the county displayed his high score.

Tonight went the usual way. Lights flashing behind the backglass, bells ringing, numbers in their hundreds of thousands and free games spinning the wheels until Lit wanted beer. Usually that was when he collected his money. Instead, he handed the table over to Bud. Said, Keep it warm for me, I'm coming back.

Before Lit finished his second can, Bud had burned through all the accumulated credits. Every penny of a thirty-five-dollar cash-out thrown away.

Before the machine finished dying its loud sad death, Lit was out the door.

Bud caught him in the parking lot. Lit already in the cruiser with the engine rumbling and the lights on.

—You leaving? Bud said.

—Not leaving, I'm gone.

Lit sprayed gravel, and soon his two red taillights faded to nothing down the road. Leaving Bud standing alone.

No big deal. By tomorrow everything would be fine. And no long dark walk home, either. A man in Bud's position had many new friends to count on. He went back to the bar and started talking up a ride to town. Acting cheerful, though pissed inside.

But it was a slow night, and late. The few drinkers were pros, planning to stay put until closing time. Bud held up a ten, dollar a mile. But no takers. Finally, the offer of a twenty, more than any of these idiots had ever made in a day, got him a ride in a panel van full of cabbages. The driver, drunk and mute, rarely drove faster than fifteen or twenty, but it was white-knuckle anyway. Lake close on the passenger side and the wheels dropping off the pavement over and over. Bud rolled his window down in case they fell over the edge and sank to the bottom. Swim through the window and up the black water. Rise into moonlight.

He rode holding the armrest and bracing his feet against the firewall, wondering with considerable bitterness why this was the best he could do. Bootlegging had made Bud a man of consequence. An eminence, much to his amazement. But there was no glamour to it. He was just a delivery boy, and it was making him soft. His lost money swirled constantly, bright and desirable, in his head. Brooding, too, about the injustice of being taken for a sidekick, even though Bud liked Lit an awful lot, even when he was high-strung. For Bud, the relationship felt part like brethren on a football team without all the ass patting and showering together, and part like boy crushes where you don't so much want to be *in love* with the other boy as to *be* him.

But apart from that, just sticking to the practicalities, getting close to the law was not bad strategy in case complications arose in regard to Bud's new profession. And possibly helpful if he got caught prowling up at the Lodge.

On Main Street, Bud climbed out of the van, thanking the spirits of commerce that he hadn't been foolish enough to pay in advance. He stretched a five through the window, and the driver was too far gone to notice the difference. Bud walked the dark streets home trying, all at once, to focus his mind on his money and the lessons of the teenager-prison counselor. Be patient. Defer gratification and wait for rewards to pour down. Not part of the lesson, though, was how long you were supposed to wait. Bud's patience had a fuse, and you could hold up thumb and forefinger of one hand to depict its length.

A FTER A WEEK OF INDIAN SUMMER, skies deep blue and leaves beginning to turn yellow and red, a cold front blew through. Chilly rain fell out of a pewter sky for two days. Stubblefield became animated and nostalgic about the northern Gulf of Mexico in the warm days of October. And at first, Luce enjoyed hearing him describe a place she'd never been. How most of the shore was muddy, and you had to know where to go if you wanted white sand and clear water. But he knew exactly where. Plus, epic bouts of fishing to be accomplished, whether casting from shore or boat. Little cheap rental cabanas on stilts at the edge of the water. And white clapboard bars set in crushed-shell parking lots under live oaks, where the beer was ice-cold and the oysters hadn't been out of the Gulf more than a few hours, and they handed you a zinc bucket overflowing with them, and one brown leather glove and a thick-bladed knife. You twisted the shells open and gave the live oyster three spurts of Tabasco and watched it quiver and then tipped your head back and slid it from the shell into your mouth, and chased it with cold beer. Maybe a saltine or two, depending on your attitude toward the texture of a raw oyster. And then dancing to a neon Wurlitzer full of beach music unknown in other quarters of the country. One bare light bulb swinging from its ceiling cord, pitching dancers' shadows crazy against the walls. Later, after midnight, swimming out half drunk into the black water and not caring how damn deep the bottom might be beneath your white wiggling feet nor what big-mouthed fishes might be gliding almost between your legs.

By the time he finished talking, Luce felt like she was sinking from him, going down slow. Him still treading water in the moonlight up above. She sat quiet a long time. He had been delicate, hardly hinting at an invitation, but what she found herself wanting to say was, Let's do that, baby. Go be careless and young. Get sunburned and drunk. Eat too much and dance too much and go night swimming. Do something entirely new. It had been so long since she had even wanted to.

Until recently, it had been theoretically possible to throw clothes in a bag and get in the car and go. By tomorrow, be sitting on the beach at sunset drinking a beer. In the new reality, though, the children.

She said, Down at the Gulf, it's like the ocean?

—Well, it looks a lot the same. Water as far as you can see.

—No trees on the other side? No towns?

—None whatsoever.

A week later, James Brown and the Famous Flames were playing over in Tennessee, and Stubblefield asked Luce to go with him. A long dark way across many mountains on winding roads, and there wouldn't be two dozen white faces in the whole place. And damn, James Brown, one of Luce's favorites. What an adventure.

—Can't, Luce said.

—People will be dancing in the aisles, Stubblefield said. I know you want to see him led off the stage totally beat, sweating and barely conscious, and then throwing the cape off and dancing back to the mike for one last time. And then doing it again five or six more times after that.

—The children.

—Please, please, please, Stubblefield said. We'd be back by dawn, and maybe the kids could stay with Maddie.

—I can't leave them that long. But go and do. I'm not your warden.

—I don't think you're my warden. Just, it wouldn't be any fun without you.

—See, I'm supposed to be flattered, but I'm not. Get over thinking I'm your vehicle like that. All you'll end up is disappointed and mad at me. You need to quit thinking I'm your perfect girlfriend. I never was, and I never will be.

Stubblefield acted like he hadn't heard those last bits and said, Seeing James Brown would be like going to church and speaking in tongues. But I don't want to quarrel about it.

—Oh, did I miss something? Luce said. Should I get out my diary? October ninth. Our first quarrel. I am devastated.

IN THE FOLLOWING DAYS, having passed on the spectacular dates, Luce tried to think of reimbursements. Breathe an autumn afternoon's crisp breath, tilt your face up to yellow sunshine, observe ragged blue mountains lying in five folds to the sky, receive the faint daily joy that's offered. Such as, for a couple of weeks, a tortoise with bright yellow concentric rectangles on its brown shell had walked west to east across the lawn shortly after dawn. Or that during the same period, wild hen turkeys, usually five, had come at dusk and launched themselves, one by one, into a big oak down by the lake, where they roosted to keep away from night dangers, especially all the predatory mammals that liked to eat them. And though Luce fell into that category, she wished this particular bunch luck, no matter how good one of them might taste roasted in a hickory-fired oven, with six strips of bacon draped over the breast and an apple, an orange, and an onion shoved up inside the cavity.

Perfect attendance, that was the goal. Try to get enough quiet so your mind lined up right, and you found out new things about yourself. The Gulf and James Brown would, no doubt, be splendid and powerful. Climactic experiences. And staying home with Dolores and Frank would be frustrating and confining and inconclusive. To little effect beyond the awful dailyness of life. The dismal failures and rare moments of minor victory. And it wasn't even as if love factored much. Luce didn't expect to love the children, and she sure didn't expect them to love her ever. That was a lot to ask in either direction. But there was something she was feeling toward them, and it had to do with their survival. Damaged and scathed, they sure were. But they had lived through a ruinous encroachment. And, yet, they hadn't become withered and tender children. They could be little fierce savages when they wanted to. Much of the time, they didn't give two shits for your particular world and could endure pain, whether yours or theirs, as stoic as an Apache. And when they saw an opportunity, they avenged themselves against the reality they occupied. Strike a match and score a point toward getting even. Some days they seemed nearly fatal and exhausted as elderly Geronimo photographed in his later years, blank-faced but still watchful out of beady sharp eyes. Whatever feeling Luce was starting to have toward Dolores and Frank, she hadn't yet figured out the name for. But it resided in the same family as respect.

Still, those dates would have been grand. And really, for short periods, Maddie made a perfect babysitter. Cocked and loaded every day of her life, the double-barrel always close. A plaited blackjack and chrome pistol in her purse. Armed and fierce and ready to charge the jaws of death to save little ones. Plus, she was isolate enough in her thinking to find Dolores and Frank lovable.

Even without the dates, Stubblefield had begun making it clearer every day that he was in for the long run, if that's what Luce wanted. The kids didn't spook him, and he didn't spook them. He hadn't fled from her life, which probably he should have done. At which point, Luce spun off briefly, wondering what defects he must have to be so interested in her. And none of it really mattered. She was too overwhelmed with the newness and strangeness of the kids, her life suddenly feeling out of control every day, and the responsibility likely to be hers from now on. So, bad timing when it came to romance.

Something about Stubblefield, though, kept working at her. Just flashes at night, lying half awake. The planes of his face, the angles of his eyes. Maybe simple geometry could explain the unwelcome attraction. Too, so much of her late-night music was about love or desire. Hard not to be swayed by it.

But she couldn't dismiss easily his light touch with her. No pushing or pressing, none of that herding and corralling bullshit, unlike any of her old boyfriends. And maybe who you fell for and who you eventually loved wasn't rational, no matter how hard you tried to list pros and cons and sum the results. You couldn't think your way through it, not all the way. Maybe just the scent of somebody carried more weight than everything else put together. She remembered watching him swim. Surprised by how much more at ease he was in the water than on land. Suddenly graceful. The movements of his arms and back and legs, the long muscles under the skin, looked effortless, almost languid. But measure his speed by landmarks along the shoreline, and he was flying.

THE KIDS. They were such a hard fact, at least in their physical presence. No matter how much Stubblefield tried to send out sensitive feelers, hoping to connect with them somehow, and thus become essential to Luce, he failed. All his waves of hope kept being met with mighty currents of dark undertow, and his first concrete attempt at making a connection was a total bust.

Stubblefield tried to engage them in basic conversation. Just chattering, really. Something about how you're not from here and neither am I. We're all three here because of ancestors. So this place is strange and familiar at the same time, but in a way, maybe this is where we belong, at least for now. The children eased away toward safe space. Not running or backing off, just sidling slow and retreating steady. No direct eye contact, but always keeping him in their peripheral view.

The next time Stubblefield came to the Lodge, he had devoted some time to thinking. How it was mostly by nouns that the kids reached into the world and touched it provisionally, like a tap with the tip of one finger. So, touch back with equal delicacy. When he got out of the car, the children were squatting on the porch, knees to chins, playing the kindling game. Didn't even look up. Stubblefield climbed the steps and set an unopened cellophane sleeve of cookies down near their competing shapes of imaginary fire. He said, Fig Newton. Didn't say another word or wait for a reaction. He walked through the screen door and let the spring slam it behind him. Cool as cool could be.

When he saw them again, it was raining. The trunks of hemlocks streaked vertical black, and the lake flat and dark. The children rocked so hard in the porch chairs that on the backswing they banged the knobs at the tops of the spindles against the siding behind them. And going forward, they held the ends of the arm rails white-knuckled until the chairs almost stood on the tips of the runners and nearly flung them off the porch and into the boxwoods. Their heeling and pitching was both asynchronous and rhythmic in the banging against the siding and the rattling of the curved runners against the cupped floorboards. A percussion song. At the bottom of the steps, Stubblefield said, Good rocking, and made a little one-finger eyebrow salute. Dolores and Frank let up, and by the time he climbed to the porch, they had slowed down enough to salute back, though if you were in a critical frame of mind, the way they did it might have seemed ironic, if not sarcastic. Which suited Stubblefield fine. All he wanted right now was for his existence in their lives to be acknowledged. He wasn't planning on going anywhere. With luck, they'd have to deal with each other's peculiarities for a long time.

Next visit, the children were playing in the yard. They both had pie pans, identically black from many excursions into the oven. A rich history of peach and rhubarb and blackberry and apple and pecan and sweet potato and pumpkin pies dating to the previous century. Separately, the children explored the joys to be had from banging the pans against various hard objects. Spinning them away with the sweep of hand and wrist and arm. Watching them float briefly on air and sink to the grass, becoming a circle of shadow set into a field of green. When Stubblefield got out of the Hawk and walked near, Dolores said, Stubblefield. She didn't look directly at him, just said his name. No different than saying *tree* or *rock*. Then she and Frank began running away. Like they expected him to come after them. But Stubblefield let them run, remembering the old Irish sheepherding wisdom his grandmother had applied to her late-life failures of memory. Don't chase it, and it will come back to you. Barely loud enough for them to hear, Stubblefield said, Dolores and Frank. Not like he was calling them, just stating their names. They ran to the edge of the woods and stopped and looked back. Stubblefield did the one-finger salute, and the kids saluted back. As he walked to the Lodge, he saw Luce standing grey and ghostly behind the screen door, watching him. When he went to the door, she opened it and leaned to him and gave him a rough, awkward, slightly clashing kiss. He stood and touched his tongue to his front teeth, checking for chips, and then he said, What was that for?

—Thank you.

—For what?

—You know.

—No, I don't. I kind of need you to say a word or two here.

He expected her to balk, but she said, Well, for not being afraid.

STUBBLEFIELD TAPPED ON the snowflake translucent glass of the door and walked in. The lawyer glanced up from a pile of papers, raising his big fountain pen higher than necessary to indicate he'd been interrupted in mid-thought. The still blades of the ceiling fan reflected an X off his brown pate. He said, Sit.

Stubblefield sat. Said, I've been thinking about those ag leases you mentioned.

The lawyer studied his calendar, one of those page-a-day deals fanned on a chrome stand, a chunky red number on each perforated sheet. He flipped through the recent past, making a show of how long it had been since they last talked. As he got back to the final day of each month, he enunciated the name as if he were calling out words for a third-grade spelling bee. October, September, August. Then he slowed down for a few pages before finally stopping.

—Ah, he said. Here we are.

He dug in a file drawer for a yellow pad and turned to a page of big blue figures.

He said, So, you've had plenty of time for deep thoughts.

—I'll think of some clever comeback tonight and drop you a postcard tomorrow, Stubblefield said. Right now, thing is, I'm going to be here for a good while, and it's not just me now.

The lawyer said, Hum. He raised his eyebrows, casting waves of wrinkles up his forehead and over the dome of his head.

He said, The back taxes haven't gone away.

—Sell the Roadhouse, if we can find a buyer, Stubblefield said.

—Oh, I've had a name or two in mind.

—And those leases sound good. Same deal we talked about, if you're set to go.

—*Je suis prest.*

—I took Spanish.

—I'll draw up the papers. You can come by tomorrow and sign.

Stubblefield sat within himself a few beats. He said, I thought you old boys worked off a smile and a handshake.

—We do, when we go into business with each other.

Stubblefield stood and said, I'm trying not to get insulted, but if you want a deal, this is it. I'm not signing any papers.

He reached his hand across the desktop.

The lawyer looked at Stubblefield and then down at his yellow pad of numbers all the way to the bottom line. He grinned and stood and took the offered hand. Hell, he said, I guess you only live the one time.

CHAPTER 9

*P*OOL HALL.

Said so twice on the blacked-out glass of the windows on either side of the door. Same angular gold script as the *Citizens' Bank* a block up Main Street. Some probably dead dude from the twenties with good handwriting must have passed through town and made a couple of quick tens. Still a lot of casual business to be conducted here, such as taking orders for jugs of cheap vodka and grain alcohol tinted brown to become Scotch. On non-traveling days, the pool hall was like Bud's office from afternoon until night, when he shifted to the Roadhouse.

Inside, festive odors of stale spilled bootleg beer and tobacco in its many forms. Dark as midnight, except that each of the five tables occupied its own circle of yellow light descending in a smoky cone from a shaded hanging fixture. Men moved about the room, entering and exiting the bright circles like Jimmy Durante saying good night at the end of every week's show.

At a back table, a game of eight ball. Bud hunched in concentration, the nap of green felt around the head spot rubbed to a bare greasy brown like a tanned hide. His stick twitched a fraction back and forth behind the dingy cue ball while he waited for his opponent, who took pride in a tight rack, to finish jiggling the triangle of balls. Bud set the butt of his cue down on the floor and said, Shit or get off the pot.

The break, when it finally happened, offered an awful lot of flourish, but after the balls settled down, Bud found himself with no shape at all. He eventually lost a tall stack of quarters and kept on losing, game after game, until he quit in disgust and walked outside to cool off, blinking against the brilliant blue-and-yellow October day. The air so lacking in haze that after his eyes adjusted, he could make out the cross members on the Juala Bald fire tower.

Bud sat on the bench with three old men in sweat-stained grey felt hats and white shirts and soft pale blue overalls. Also, the former dime store bandit with his air of distraction and pink forehead dent. The men went right on without pause, swapping watches and knives and telling elaborate nasty stories of their younger years, which most would call lies, the main elements being women and fighting. But the old tellers more than balanced out their lack of fact with truth of desire.

One of them delivered an antique joke of stunning dirtiness, very deadpan. The other men sniffed back their sinuses and made other hawking noises in lieu of laughter.

Lit passed down Main Street in his black-and-white. Raised a forefinger to the bench sitters and kept going.

One of the elders said, Sad shit there.

Bud's ears pricked. Sad why?

—Everything. His wife and his girls. He's a lonesome man. Luce is all the relation he's got in the world anymore.

—Say what? Bud said.

—They don't speak when they pass on the street. Treat each other like they're both dead.

It took Bud a few seconds to let that sink in. And then all of a sudden, it hit him like a big fat-ass epiphany.

He said aloud, Goddamn. And then he caught himself in time to avoid blurting, So Lit's Lily's father too.

Bud, without even a parting witticism, walked to his truck and drove down the lakeshore, past the dam, and through the valley on the river road, thinking and panicking. Breathing fast and shallow until he got dizzy and pulled over to hang his head out the window to heave a little.

Being Lit's former son-in-law hardly seemed promising, no matter how you looked at it. Lily hadn't liked to talk about her people, and when she did, Bud wasn't usually listening. If she called her daddy anything at all, it was Daddy. That's the best Bud could remember. And what kind of name was Lit, anyway? Not a person's name Bud ever heard. Or else it slid right on by while he was thinking about something else.

It was like falling into some game with rules everybody knows but you. Such as that business about not flushing with your foot. And because you don't know the rules, you keep stepping on your own crank while lesser people jump ahead. Exactly like life in general.

Bud clutched his shark-tooth necklace in his fist. Then he cut a deep diagonal slice across the pad of his middle finger with the serrations millions of years old. When the blood domed out, he put the finger in his mouth to taste the iron.

Bud closed his eyes and blew air through pursed lips like a silent whistle. He counted to fifty. When he got his breathing under control, he went through the pertinent facts about his identity.

What signs could they possibly know him by? Bud was a nickname, and to the best of his recollection, it never came up in his various court matters. As for Johnson, it was one of the three most common names in the country. No way would Lit or Luce know he was John Gary Johnson, neither from the trial nor the marriage. Lily always called him Johnny. And nobody up here had even seen a picture of him.

Bud and Lily's wedding had been a sudden JP thing in South Carolina, a state that didn't give two shits for blood tests and those sorts of delaying tactics. Down there, they believed getting married should be totally unpremeditated, if that's the way you wanted it. Five minutes, in street clothes. Quicker than you could get a driver's license. So not exactly the kind of ceremony where you hired a photographer. And Lily wasn't much interested in her family back then. She was too happy to get away from home and too hot for Bud to worry about her people, such as they were. She hadn't even bothered to send a post-card from their Myrtle Beach honeymoon, a largely drunken forty-eight hours, limited only by Lily's beautician buddy, who had agreed to keep the kids but had put a two-day limit on the whole af-fair. No grace period whatsoever. Bud had taken the attitude, So what if we're late and some hairdresser gets mad? Like she's going to set babies out on the curb. Lily argued that you don't do friends that way, and Bud said, Test her on it, that's what friends are for. Nevertheless, Lily prevailed, and they drove home so fast and full of beer to meet the deadline that when Bud stepped out of the car for a roadside piss, he didn't care who saw. When a state trooper wearing his Smokey Bear hat passed by, Bud didn't even try to turn his back to the road. He just switched hands to salute. And for once, good luck prevailed. No lights flashing, no wail of siren to accompany a squealing one-eighty. Smokey drove on. Must have awarded extra points for entertainment value.

All of which added up to a compelling argument for Bud's ano-nymity in this town, even with the sad remainders of Lily's messed-up family. Unless he'd slipped up sometime.

Bud raked back into the past and only reached last week before a bell rang. A vague memory. Waking up one morning—or, rather, afternoon—all cotton-mouthed and feeling queasy. Preemptively rushing to the bathroom and kneeling at the porcelain with his head bowed for a long time.

He wondered now if he might have run his mouth that night play-ing cards with a few of his high-volume customers. Get a load on among impressionable ears and start being the big man, telling all kinds of tales about how damn cool you are. Wouldn't be unimaginable to have dropped some comment about a murder charge and a bitch wife. Little towns like this, shit got around, and Lit always had his antenna up.

Bud felt panic rising again in his chest, like the first surge up a percolator tube. He took a deep breath to damp it down. Told himself,

If you're not who you want to be, at least act like who you want to be. Form a clear picture in your mind of a bastard nobody wants to mess with, and then become that picture. Get on with it. Find the money and move on down the line. Go to Brownsville, or all the way to Havana and live with the bearded rebels.

Something swirling and tropical pushed heavy air up from the Gulf, the remains of an end-of-season hurricane. Weather hit the wall of mountains and stalled. Wet roads and rain falling out of a blank low sky. Early dark, and every indicator saying summer is long dead. Cold times ahead. Every glint of headlight from dead leaves on wet pavement pointing the way down Lonely Street.

—A slow tenor-sax kind of night, Stubblefield said. Or maybe a Chet trumpet solo with an equal ratio of silence to music. Gloomy and sensitive.

—Movies, Luce said.

Beads of raindrops on the windshield bled together into a sheet of water between wiper passes. A last bunch of purple coneflowers and goldenrod shed their petals on the seat between Stubblefield and Luce.

Bad night for a real first date. And also unwelcome that Luce needed to announce a three-hour deadline for how long the kids could stay with Maddie. This despite Maddie making some winking, embarrassing comment about the kids being welcome to stay for breakfast. A happy surprise, though, as far as Luce's attire. A vintage cotton print dress, cornflower blue with yellow wisps of viney figures. The bodice and waist snug, and the skirt somewhat full and a little faded from the wash. No raincoat or umbrella, only a white cotton sweater over her arm for later when the fog rose. Dark hair loose at the shoulders. Her look not at all in the current style. More from another time, a former life, back when she wanted to be beautiful and thoughtless. Not have any ripples ringing the pool of her perfect life.

Devastating was more the first word Stubblefield came up with, no matter the current fashion. And dangerous, possibly, to assume the outfit was not worn somewhat ironically.

INSIDE THE ROADHOUSE, all was murk. Light mostly from three neon beer signs over the ancient oaken bar. The puncheons squeaked against their pegs as footsteps fell upon them, and they swagged between the stout joists where gravity and decay and all the other evil shit time wreaks against material things had dragged them downward. Stubblefield led Luce through the dancers to a back booth, the tabletop pale yellow Formica patterned with overlapping black outlines of boomerangs. Not as jolly a place as Luce had guessed, though she had nothing to guess upon but scenes from black-and-white movies where nightspots were pretty glamorous and existed somewhere far away from here.

They were barely seated when two tall rum and Cokes magically appeared. Luce looked at them and then at Stubblefield.

—*El patrón*, he said. At least for now.

A three-piece band played on a raw plywood flat barely six inches higher than the floor, hammering out "Baby Blue" from meager materials. A guitar, a bass, a drum kit. And the guitarist's urgent hog-calling vocalizations, the kind where you can't understand a single word but the message is unmistakable. The drummer was maybe a little eager with his rolls and cymbal crashes. The guitarist pushed his picking and singing through a tweed Fender Bassman amp the size of a suitcase. The volume cranked so high that tubes blew regularly enough that he kept a cardboard box of 12AX7s beside the amp like a janitor with his light bulbs. He played a black lacquered guitar, shining with points of light from the neon.

Stubblefield asked if Luce would like to dance, and she said, Not yet.

The band's covers were mostly the kinds of songs people wrote in the past when everybody took songs more seriously. Back a couple or three years, when Gene Vincent and Charlie Feathers and Groovey Joe Poovey were having hits. Guitar licks falling like little ball-peen hammers beating on roof tin, and some young man at the edge of sanity shouting all his yearning and anger for the world to hear, keening it out mad in the manner of old battlefield Celts. Two and a quarter minutes of urgent utterance broadcast mostly over radio stations you couldn't pick up until dark.

At some point, the band tuned endlessly and then played an original composition, made up by the singer-guitarist himself. He had drawn various ideas from circuit-rider hymnals, Stephen Foster, Uncle Dave Macon, many elder bluesmen. Also George Gershwin, Allen Ginsberg, and Elvis. It was the history of America filtered through the mind of a handsome self-educated country crackpot with a pompadour and a Telecaster. The dancers all sat down. For the last lines of the song, the singer fell to one prayerful knee, and the job of making eye contact with the audience rested entirely on the band, for the singer pitched his crazed unblinking gaze toward higher things, a better world where desire prevailed beyond understanding.

At the end of the song, the band took a break and the composer came over and scooted next to Luce across the burgundy vinyl. A courtesy call on the new owner. A round of three rum and Cokes materialized. The guitarist's greased hair was a shade of Superman black that never grew out of any earthling's head. Also, he sported a mustache and a tuft of growth beneath his lower lip the same absurd color. Some hillbilly hipster reimagining himself as Nathan Bedford Forrest or Jeb Stuart.

—Hey, man, the guitarist said.

Stubblefield said nothing. He put out a look of mild expectation, mainly by way of upraised eyebrows.

The guitarist said, What?

Stubblefield said, I liked that last one. Maybe some other time we can talk about all your references. Like, you could do an annotated version.

—But?

—I'm just saying a fact. I liked it, but that's me. Some people want to dance. Well, first they want to drink, and then they want to dance. Some of them, if they're drunk enough to dance, they're drunk enough to puke in their loafers. So all I'm saying, sometimes a break is good. They sit down and order more drinks. Rule number one, you can't force everybody to think.

—Shit, the guitarist said.

—That was a compliment. If people sit down, don't take it personal. If all they do is dance, nobody makes any money.

Luce said, I never heard anything exactly like it.

The guitarist said, Is that good or what?

—Good for me, Luce said. I'd hear it again anytime, if it was on a record and if it would play on my record player.

—If?

—It's got a crank and a big brass horn, Stubblefield said.

—Well, we've not got a record.

The guitarist downed his drink and slid out of the booth and walked back toward the stage. Stubblefield went right into something else more pressing, made so by Luce's nostalgic dress.

He said, Hard to believe we're sitting here together now, all these years later. Back at the pool, the announcer said your name, and for days afterward, that's all I could think about.

—How do you think about a name? Luce said. You can't think about a name. Not for more than two seconds. There's nothing to think about.

—It focused my feelings.

—All you saw of me was that minute it took to walk around the pool with a bunch of pretty girls.

—It was an awfully full minute.

—And my name summed it up for you, then?

Stubblefield shrugged.

—I don't even like it, Luce said. But it's that or Lucinda. And from here on out, if you want to talk about beauty shows that I can't really remember too well, then I've got a headache and need to go home.

—Sure, Stubblefield said. He made the riverboat-gambler spreading-hand gesture of the lawyer. He said, From this second forward, I'm all about the present moment. Be here now. Not back then.

Luce made a scoffing laugh of unbelief, then too late put her hand to her mouth like suppressing a sneeze. Stubblefield began to think she was having a good time. From what he could tell of her recent life, there might not have been much flirting in it.

The band fired back up with several sarcastic slow-dance favorites for Stubblefield's benefit. He drew Luce, only half unwilling, onto the floor for twangy Ventures and Santo & Johnny arrangements of "A Summer Place" and "Mr. Blue" and "Sleep Walk" and "Where the Boys Are."

LUCE HADN'T DANCED in a long time, but you can always hold each other and sway. It felt good, though she couldn't help wondering how long it had been since a man had held her, and then it was back to midnight in the switching room. She stepped away from Stubblefield and he followed her to their dark booth and fresh magic rum and Cokes.

—What? Stubblefield said, across the boomerang Formica.

—Nothing. I can't dance anymore. I used to be good at it, but not anymore.

—We don't have to dance.

—It's okay. We can try again later. Be back in a minute, Luce said.

She got up and walked across the room, and as she passed the bar, a man brushed the back of his hand against her ass. Accidental, but not. Luce didn't make eye contact, just kept walking, not feeling him drop his cigarette and follow her until it was too late. As she opened the door to the ladies' and stepped in, the man put his foot out to stop it. He gripped her shoulder and turned her around.

His face right in hers and his breath all Scotched up, Bud said, Luce, why's that boyfriend of yours been asking around about me?

Luce didn't know what he was talking about, but one look at him and she knew who he was. Bud still blinked from the bright light over the bathroom sink, and also his surprise that she wasn't cowering in fear but shouting right in his face. So when she let up from her first outburst, he seemed confused with her reasoning. But he got the drift, which had to do with him being a murderer. Which took him a few seconds to begin acting cool about.

He said, Pretty girl, you're free to have an opinion, but the court saw it my way and let me go. And now I'm here.

—You were born guilty, and we both know you killed my sister, and the children saw you do it. You did something to them, too.

Luce watched his focus fade, and a moment where he started to get twitchy. Then, like an actor momentarily losing the thread of his character and suddenly grasping it back, he got confident again. He said, Now, why do you want to get going in that direction? Listening to those little bastards' lies.

—They can't hardly talk.

—Big surprise. I never knew the natural daddy, but their mama was not the sharpest knife in the drawer. So, what do you expect?

—What I don't know is why anybody would marry you. But I know Lily was sweet and trusting, and I'm not. I can figure the things you did by how they act.

—You're letting your private imagination run wild in bad directions. But go ahead on and make up whatever mean stories get you fired up. Nothing to do with me.

Just angry, not really thinking or planning, Luce said, I'm going to get back at you.

—Back at me? Bud said. What does that mean?

—What do you think?

—Well, let's see. Could mean several things, such as kill me.

—You'd have it coming.

—Now, I'm no lawyer, but you probably crossed the line into con-

veying threats. Which is how they'll put it when I go to a magistrate
to get a restraining order. Probably be your daddy to serve it.

Luce was caught wrong-footed by the unexpected threat of law
and her father against her, and couldn't come up with anything to
say.

Bud went riffing forward without hardly drawing breath. He said,
And by the way, pretty girl, who are you to threaten me? You're not
such hot shit around here anymore. Used to be a cheerleader way long
time ago. Which I've done some imagining about. A lot more whole-
some than whatever trash you've made up about me. Just saddle shoes
and bobby sox and pleated skirts. Wool sweaters with the name of the
team animal spelled out across the titties. Red underpants for when
you turned cartwheels in front of the crowd. Back here in the sticks, a
cheerleader must be about like being a movie star for a couple of years.
But then what? All downhill from there. Now you're living up yonder
at the ass end of nowhere, as you hillbillies say. In that old ruin by the
lake. All by yourself, except for those retard kids. Real dark lonesome
nights, way down that rough dirt road.

Luce's breathing went shallow and quick. She realized her mouth
was partly open. She closed it and drew a breath from deep down and
said, How do you know where I live? What I wore back then? How do
you know anything about me?

—Public knowledge. Which is simply a bullshit mix of facts and
opinions. Not threats. And they can't do anything to you in this country for stating facts and opinions. Not yet.

—You burned the uniform, didn't you? Luce said. You've been
where I live.

—Calm down. All I did was look through some yellow newspapers
at the library. You were a tight little piece in those old Friday night
pictures.

A SONG PASSED BY and Stubblefield got up and drifted toward the
bar looking for Luce. When he got to the back hall, a man stood in the

door to the ladies', and Stubblefield saw the top of Luce's hair over his shoulder.

—What the hell? Stubblefield said.

Bud turned and grabbed Stubblefield by the front of his shirt and wheeled and shoved him hard inside. The mirror broke. Then all three of them were there with the door closed. Bud clicked the lock behind him.

In the cramped space, Luce and Stubblefield crowded up against the toilet. One bare bulb over the sink, its light fragmented by the spider-webbed mirror. A machine for sanitary napkins to match the rubber machine screwed to the same stud on the other side of the wall, in the men's. A loop of cotton toweling hanging from a white dispenser.

—It's Johnson, Luce said to Stubblefield.

Bud squared his shoulders against Stubblefield and studied him and said, So you're the asswipe asking about me?

Stubblefield said, I was checking rumors.

Bud shook his head sorrowfully. Fuck me twice, he said. Makes me feel dirty that my business is anything of yours.

Stubblefield said, I wanted to know what you're doing here.

—Well, as the philosophers say, everybody's got to be somewhere. And even Sister Luce agrees I'm free to live wherever I want to.

—What is it you're after? Luce said.

—I don't guess you happen to have any money squirreled away in a clever place? Bud said. You don't live like you do. But I heard your boyfriend might have some.

—So is that it?

—Be way simpler if it was. I'm just after what's mine.

—The children, then? Luce said.

Bud made an incredulous expression. He turned to Stubblefield and said, She's sure pretty, but if she's as big a whore and pain in the ass as her sister, and even half as ignorant, you have my tenderest sympathies.

Stubblefield swung a misconceived roundhouse toward Bud's mouth. It took a great deal of time to come around, plenty enough for Bud to cock his head to the side so that Stubblefield's fist barely glanced off the brow and dwindled most of its energy into nothing.

By the time Stubblefield collected himself, Bud had reached into the cuff of his railroad boot. He came out flashing a black-and-silver switchblade with little imitation quillons like on a sword. He tripped the button, and the blade sprang from the handle into life. It had a blood gutter running partway down its cheap chrome length, and it cast jagged reflections from its angled faces.

Bud sank into a knife-fighter crouch and his eyes got all concentrated. He said, Legal tip. Looks bad in court when you throw the first fist. Way it stands, you brought on what happens next.

Stubblefield raised his arms to shoulder level and pushed out flat palms in a gesture like a traffic cop whoaing up approaching cars. Bud flicked the blade and cut the palm of the left hand into the meat.

Bud danced in place, three little steps like a boxer, and watched Stubblefield's face blanch and his hand start bleeding down his arm. Luce had never screamed in her life, and she didn't scream now.

Dark blood splattered on the dingy white linoleum near the base of the white toilet. Stubblefield tried to swing another blow, but Bud smacked it away with his empty hand. Stubblefield bent double and grabbed his cut hand with his good hand and pressed them both between his knees. His face was turning the color of the linoleum.

Bud stood straight and dismissed Stubblefield without further comment, like his pain and fear didn't factor at all. He looked at Luce and slowly wiped the blade's two faces on the thigh of his jeans and pressed the button with his thumb to release the spring and folded the blade slowly back into place with the forefinger of his left hand. Very fast he said, You better figure this out before somebody gets hurt. I don't give two shits about your whore sister's bastards. I'm glad to be shut of them. All they ever did was gag up dinner or crap their britches at bad times and keep me from getting up on her whenever I wanted, which was all she was good for.

—You asshole, she kept you in groceries, Luce said.

—Stupid bitch thinks I won't cut her too, Bud said, in the direction of Stubblefield. Y'all need to go on about your own lives and leave me alone. And if you take this to the law, I'm really going to bear down on you heavy. This right here is nothing. I wasn't trying to go deep. He'll heal.

—But why are you here? Luce said to his back as he went out the door.

Bud turned back around. He said, We were talking about facts and opinions. Here comes another one. Way I see it, up there by the lake, if somebody was to holler, nobody would hear it.

It took a pretty major effort not to look off, but Luce kept her eyes straight at Bud's and said all in a rush, You ever come around my place and those kids, I *will* kill you. And you can go straight to Lit with that, and I'll own it under oath.

Bud grinned and said, Correct me if I am wrong, but besides being the word for scream, holler's also local talk for a sort of narrow valley, ain't it?

He slammed the door shut behind him.

Stubblefield was still bent around his wound. Blood dripping into a pool at his feet. Luce straightened him up and made him hold his cut hand under the faucet. Somebody started to come in the door, but Luce put out her foot and blocked it.

—Later, she said, and flipped the lock.

She pulled at the roll of towels, but it was at the end. All the used droop looked grubby. She lifted her skirt and stepped out of her half-slip underneath. It was the color and sheen of mercury with lace at the hem, and she didn't even try to rip it into strips of bandage. She wound the whole thing tight as she could around Stubblefield's hand. They went out the back door, the way to the stables in the day of horses.

LUCE DROVE THE HAWK, headlights dim in fog, probing forty feet out and then fading into the grainy dark. Stubblefield hunched forward pale-faced with his clammy forehead almost on the dash, his bleeding hand clamped between his knees. He rocked in his seat, saying, Shit, shit, shit.

Stubblefield twisted and thumbed on the dome light with his right hand. He unwound the bloody wad of silver slip from his cut hand and held his wound to the light. Blood began running down the inside of his forearm and dripping off his elbow. Stubblefield tipped his head down and studied his bloody sign. On his black shirt it looked like a grease mark, and puddled on the upholstery it looked exactly like what it was. He switched the light right back off.

Luce said, You need stitches.

—I look like a damn autopsy victim.

—Your hand's cut. We'll get it fixed.

—I saw bones, he said. I thought they would be white. They're sort of blue.

—Tendons, Luce said. They're bluish.

—Bones, Stubblefield said.

—Move your fingers. Touch each one to your thumb.

Stubblefield did so, and everything worked right. The bleeding, though, still bad.

—Wrap it back tight, Luce said. You need a bunch of stitches.

—No shit. But not the hospital.

—That's where I'm headed.

—No, Stubblefield said.

Luce turned and looked a quick question at him.

—Because if we do, Lit will hear of it. Your father keeps up with everything.

—And then, so what? Luce said.

—And then that could be bad. What I heard, he and that man are tight. Buys uppers from him. And you heard what he said back there. I'm not leaving you that exposed.

—Shit, shit, shit.

LUCE PARKED WITH the headlights aimed through fog at Maddie's house, amid its tangle of wildflowers. Half-dead brown stems and stalks and canes arcing toward winter, the tangle cut through by a narrow footpath to the steps. No light showing on the porch or in the windows.

Not wanting to startle Maddie, with her shotgun hanging over the door on two hooks cut from forks of tree limbs, Luce said, Maybe we'll sit here a minute with the lights on and then toot the horn.

Stubblefield reached with his good hand to the horn ring and held it down for a long blast.

A yellow light came on in the window to the right of the front door. Almost at the same time, Maddie opened the door and stepped out into the headlights. She had on a pale nightgown that fell to her bare feet. Her white hair fanned across her shoulders, and she held the shotgun at an angle slightly below parallel.

Luce opened her door and got out and shouted, Maddie, it's Luce. We need your help.

Maddie dropped the twin muzzles to rest on the porch boards and visored her free hand against the light. She said, Shut out those god-damn lights and come on in the house. You'll wake up the kids.

The fire had burned to a bed of hot coals, and Maddie threw on a dry split of red oak and it blazed up in seconds. Stubblefield sat at the dinner table at the end of the kitchen, and Maddie switched on the light and cleaned his hand with peroxide and looked at the cut.

She said, You'll live. It's not all that damn deep. I guess there's a reason this couldn't have been done at the hospital?

—Yeah, Stubblefield said. One day when it gets to be a good story, I'll tell it to you.

Maddie struck a match and burned a needle. Licked the end of black thread to sharpen it and aimed through the needle's eye dead steady and drew about a foot from the spool and scissored it and paired the wet end with the dry and knotted them. She pressed the back of Stubblefield's hand firm against the table and told him to keep it still. The cut gapped and didn't want to go back together, and Maddie's pressing and yanking on his hand caused Stubblefield to make a noise like a high-pitched cough.

Maddie said, Need a stick to gnaw on, like in cowboy movies?

Stubblefield said, Go on.

Maddie made the best sense she could of the bleeding slash and sewed a baker's dozen of tight quick stitches, angling from the pad of meat at the base of the thumb toward the little finger. Then she slowly tilted the brown bottle and poured the remainder of the peroxide over his hand. Pink foam rose along the puckered line of stitches, and the blood on the tabletop washed into the woodgrain.

—From now on, palm readers won't be able to make shit sense out of your future, Maddie said. Look at that ragged new love line. This is going to throw everything off.

—Ha ha, Stubblefield said, looking down at his mangled hand.

—The children? Luce said.

—Let 'em sleep, Maddie said. Get him home before he passes out on me.

MIDDLE OF THE NIGHT, Stubblefield sat at his breakfast table, holding his cut hand higher than his heart in a failed attempt to keep it from throbbing. Grouped on the white Formica like a modern still life, a half-empty fifth of Smirnoff stood beside a full Davy Crockett jelly glass sitting in a pink plasmatic puddle. Stubblefield angled his hurt hand into the light. Still oozing. The black thread looking damn bad against the waxen skin, even paler than the tabletop.

Luce slumped in the armchair. She had set the radio to her late-night music. Lightning somebody. Smokestack something. So many of the musicians seemed to be either little or blind. Then an ad for a record store and Royal Crown hair dressing.

—He's white, you know, Luce said.

—Who's white?

—The DJ. I've seen a picture of him. He sounds black, but he's white as they come. His voice is an expression of his state of mind because he loves the music so much.

She paused and said, You didn't tell me.

—What?

—That he was here.

—Rumors. I had to drive an hour to a library that takes downstate papers to find out he'd been let go. I didn't want to worry you until I knew for sure.

—Future reference, don't ever leave me out again.

Couple of songs went by, and the phone rang. It squatted dense and black on the table at the end of the sofa. Luce answered immediately. Old habit.

Bud's voice, pitched thin over the wire as cricket song, said, They're not your damn children, Lucinda. Go live your life, and forget about me. Do it and don't look back. And remember what I said about keeping your mouth shut, because I meant it.

Luce said, How did you know to call here? But the line went dead after her first word.

She put the phone back on the hook and looked at Stubblefield.

He said, Him?

AN HOUR LATER, Luce sprawled on the sofa, asleep, her head pillowed on her right arm, her shoes kicked off. The girlfriend dress twisted around her, bloodstained.

The line of her hip and thigh and calf hit Stubblefield as painfully pretty, and somehow consonant with the heartbeat throb in his hand. He sat at the table way into the early morning with his vodka and Luce's powerful radio music, watching her sleep. Holding up his cut hand like swearing an oath, and imagining the remote borders he might be willing to cross on her behalf.

OUT OF FEAR AND ALSO making assumptions like he would do if he were dealing with normal people, Stubblefield placed a couple of phone calls. Within a day, a guy he knew in Jacksonville had an address for Luce's mother.

You need a safe place far away to hide, what's more normal than over the river and through the woods to grandmother's Florida beach house? That was as close as he had to a plan. Get Luce and the kids gone from Bud's orbit. Get Lola to keep them for a couple of weeks. Let him go back and try to get Lit or the sheriff or somebody to pay attention. Get Bud out of their lives.

Luce probably should have known it was a mistake from the start, but she was scared, and wanted to believe that something as simple as distance might protect the children. Also, Stubblefield's argument for normal was pretty compelling. When you're up against it, family is who most people turn to.

STUBBLEFIELD CARRIED a musty kapok daybed mattress from the sleeping porch to the Hawk and pressed it to fill the entire backseat area. Luce cooked popcorn on the woodstove, enough to fill a brown paper grocery bag and leave dark butter stains on the bottom third. They set out driving south in the late afternoon, the children alert and eating corn by the fistfuls, studying the passing landscape with their eyes pinpointed by the low sun. And then, soon after dark, the children burrowed under a quilt and slept as deep and innocent as the dead.

Luce spent a great deal of time twisting the knob on the radio, which drew strange new stations, such as one from a town with a bus station big enough to advertise both its own newsstand and its restaurant, said to be known far and wide for T-bones and chili dogs and banana splits.

—Living in this car wouldn't be all that bad, Luce said. Hard to hit a moving target.

They were way far from home, driving down into the flatlands of Georgia, a waxing half-moon in the sky. Supper had been a while back. Cheeseburgers and fries and vanilla shakes ordered over a speaker at a drive-in and arriving on an aluminum tray that stood levered from Stubblefield's half-open window. Luce had never had food served in such a novel manner. The children didn't even wake up, but there was a box of Cheerios and a few cans of corned beef hash if they got hungry. They were happy to eat cereal without milk, and their favorite way to eat the hash was cold. Open both ends of the can and push one lid against the grey cylinder until it plopped out, with its impress of ridges intact, and then chop it into two exact portions with the other of the sharp-edged lids. To make up for the bad nutrition, Luce figured she'd cook a big stew of kale and white beans and tomatoes and smoked sausage the next chance she got.

They drove through the middle of Milledgeville as the second showing of the evening movie was letting out. *The Defiant Ones.*

—I saw that, Stubblefield said.

—How was it? Luce said.

—About what you'd think. He nodded toward the one-sheets in their lighted glass frames on either side of the box office. Tony Curtis and Sidney Poitier chained together and getting ready to fistfight each other.

—Sort of a county-fair three-legged-race kind of story? Luce said.

—Yeah. Pretty much.

Then, for lack of anything else to say, Stubblefield announced, State crazy house is in this town. Also, the man that wrote Brer Rabbit lived near here. Some time ago.

Luce failed to say anything at all in admiration of his knowledge, and in a minute Stubblefield said, There was a historical marker back there.

—Saw it.

They went out the bottom end of town, into dark country. Luce twiddled the radio to mostly hissing static with intermittent fading snatches of music. Far into the dark flatwoods, out of nowhere Luce said, You fetch up to our age, still single, people start wondering what's wrong with you. Like you owe them an accounting of your love life. Most people are married by now. Why aren't you?

—I almost got married one time.

—Almost, like engaged?

—Briefly, Stubblefield said. It's a boring story.

—Yeah, but tell it anyway.

Stubblefield pitched it as a comedy, youthful idiocy way back a couple of years ago. Though it hurt a good bit at the time. His almost wife was the daughter of the owner of the Cadillac dealership, which in a small town made you nearly royalty. Her name was Alice, and she got intense about Stubblefield shortly after he moved to the island, when he was still the mysterious stranger come to town. Alice was fairly pretty, with swoopy reddish hair and good legs. Freckles across her nose and shoulders in a tempting spray. She featured herself special, to the point that she was at the end of youth and still uncommitted and prone to get attracted to somebody new flashing into her life.

All her previous boyfriends had worn nothing but frat-boy khakis and Izods, like they were in some pathetic paramilitary unit that got their asses kicked all the time. Back then, Stubblefield was still getting over his brief beatnik motorcycle phase. Still immersed in his little square black-and-white books of poetry with alarming titles, and sometimes sporting a goatee and a black turtleneck and black leather pants. His garb caused a woman on Centre Sreet one day to ask him what it was he liked so much about his unusual leather pants. Stubblefield said, You don't have to wash 'em, you just wipe 'em down.

It was all thoughtless romance with Alice, and could have been the start of several decades of bitter misery, except that a month before the wedding day Alice's heart changed directions. A better boyfriend came along. Not a passing whim, like Stubblefield, but somebody solid. Some old high school beau or golfer suck-up to her father. She informed Stubblefield all distant over the phone.

The diamond, though, was returned in person. To be exact, Alice flung it in Stubblefield's face as if he were the spurner. It hit him at the brow and bounced onto the concrete stoop outside his front door. Then it angled off into the shrubbery, sparkling all the way.

The harsh tone there at the end was surely the idea of the new boyfriend, who struck Stubblefield as high-minded and adamant about his sensitivities. He wanted no trace left behind to remind him that he was not the first explorer to plant his flag on that pale frontier.

A week later, Stubblefield took out a classified ad in the local paper. *For Sale: One (1) engagement ring w. 1.5-carat diamond. Fair-to-poor condition. Also matching wedding band. Excellent condition. Diamonds are forever, but the heartbreak has passed. $1 ea.*

Which sealed his fate on ever getting a good deal on a new Caddie, but also made him more than a few friends around town. For a week, many Tanqueray tonics were bought for him down at the waterside bar. Drinkers young and old raised toasts welcoming him to his new fraternity of dumped lovers.

After Stubblefield finished his answer to her question, Luce said, Pale frontier?

—Figure of speech.

WAY INTO THE NIGHT, Luce got head-bobbing sleepy, and Stubblefield reached to her far shoulder with his good hand and slouched her over in the seat toward him until her head lay tipped against his leg and her dark hair spread over his lap.

He drove down an empty road into the tree-farm pine barrens that led to Florida, feeling happy and as if, right this minute, everything matched his expectations of how life ought to be. The Hawk was dark as a piece of night, except for its dash lights and the overlapping beams of headlights. In the foggy late-night hours, Stubblefield pulled over at a wayside picnic spot and slept an hour or two with his right hand tangled in Luce's hair, and then he went on driving. At the first thin rim of dawn the children's eyes rose into the rearview. All bright with interest in the sudden new landscape.

They skirted the Okefenokee in early-morning fog, the wet air coming in the wind wings rich and urgent. Luce opened her eyes for a minute and said, What's that smell?

Stubblefield said, Alligators.

She said, Good, and settled her head back on his leg while Stubblefield explained to her about the culture and history of Florida. For example, they've got snake farms. Imagine setting out on purpose to grow snakes. Florida was the Wild West before there was a Wild West. It was nothing but Indians and Spaniards, and then it went straight to cowboy gunmen like John Wesley Hardin. And it still is wild, or at least lawless. Good God, you can get away with all kinds of shit down here. The politicians are all criminals. Granted, that is only a distinction from everywhere else in that they're so blatant about it that they often end up in federal prison.

Around about there, Luce drifted back to sleep.

DOWN AT FLAGLER, Lola lived in a shady cinder-block cottage three streets from the beach. Dead live-oak leaves spilling over the gutters and a rusty red Olds Rocket 88 with all the good driven out of it parked in the sand yard.

Stubblefield went to the door and knocked. Luce and Dolores and Frank stayed in the Hawk.

Lola answered, wearing a floral-print beach wrap hanging open over a shimmering teal bathing suit. Barefoot, and her toenails painted pink. Freckled cleavage tanned to a line and then an inch of pale cream visible below that. Her hair wet and tumbling to her shoulders. A cigarette between her lips.

Stubblefield thought he must have come to the wrong place. This was not the grandmother he had imagined. He said who he was, and who he had with him. Her daughter Luce and the children of her murdered daughter, Lily.

—I do remember their names, Lola said, talking around the cigarette and very dry in her tone. How did you find me?

—Made a call.

—Not like I was hiding out or anything.

—She needs your help, Stubblefield said.

Lola said, Huh?

IN THE CAR, Luce studied the woman. Her mother. The word called up nothing but dim memories of shouting. Rough hugs. A face shoved close, breathing Wild Turkey and planting sloppy kisses on her forehead, leaving candy-apple-red smears.

And something failed to sum. Her mother must be, what? Old, at the very least. Luce did some fast head arithmetic, and the surprise total was not far past forty. And, even so, Lola looked years younger, for she had been damn handsome to begin with and had undergone production of only the two accidental girls spaced close together in her final teenage years. Plus, she had successfully skipped most of the wear and tear of raising them. So she had low miles on her, and what she had were apparently road miles. Adding the youthful effect of breasts and tousled hair and beach clothing, she could probably pass for Luce's older sister in any light more flattering than the glare of midday sun. Though, actually, this was midday.

Luce got out of the car and leaned the seatback forward. The children climbed from the back and began exploring their new world.

Lapsing into their water-witch manner, following invisible lines of force across the yard, quartering the space, doubling back, feeling for something with senses other than the usual five. They finally settled ten feet apart and seemed not to be looking at anything in particular, but still alert.

Not much in the way of greeting between mother and daughter. A hug was too much, a handshake out of the question. Lola tipped her head back and blew smoke out the corner of her mouth, and Luce got straight to business.

—Lily's husband, Bud. He hurt the children. And then he killed her. He's come to town, making threats. And Lit won't do anything about it because he's buying dope from him.

Lola said, Golly, I wonder why I ever left?

STUBBLEFIELD'S SWADDLED cut hand throbbed. He looked at all four of them, the way some bloodline thing connected the wings of their noses, their eye slants. Nevertheless, Lola and the children didn't care to own each other. They wouldn't look her way, like she was some ghost wavering before them in a dimension they took a pass on sensing.

—I wasn't made for a grandmother, Lola said.

—Or a mother, Luce said.

—News flash, Luce. Neither were you. We're a lot the same. Lily was the one different.

—You don't know anything about me, Luce said. I'm not the same as you. And if I ever was, I've changed.

—People don't change, Lola said. Maybe you're still young enough to pretend that's not true. People are who they are, and everybody around them has to take it or go somewhere else.

—I didn't go anywhere. None of us did.

—But I did. I couldn't take any of you one day more.

Stubblefield had been standing off to the side saying nothing, but now he said, Great God.

Lola glanced at him like she hadn't even noticed he was still there.

—Here's the final word, Lola said. I can't help you out. Sounds like you're maybe exaggerating some. I heard he got off. Sometimes, juries get it right. And that doesn't mean I'm not sad about Lily. But when I left, I left. I'm not looking back. And I'm not looking for a family. I'll fix you some ham sandwiches and let you talk about the good old days if you care to. And then pretty soon, it will be time for all of you to get in the car and head out home.

Luce said, Hell, we can eat a hamburger on the road without having to listen to another word of your shit.

—Well, Stubblefield said, I guess that about says it. Dolores and Frank, go give your granny a big goodbye hug.

The children didn't attend to the suggestion in any way other than to flick each other a glance.

Lola took a final lungful of her Kool and flipped the sparking butt at Stubblefield and went into the house. The butt bounced off Stubblefield's chest, and the screen door bounced off Lola's still-fetching ass before clapping shut.

And yet, before they could load up and drive away, Lola stuck her head out the screen door and shouted, I never loved a damn one of you.

ON THE WAY BACK NORTH, Stubblefield took A1A, to let Luce and the kids see the ocean. He hadn't slept but a few snatches in days, and he was all drained of adrenaline and had switched to take-out coffee. His vision and hearing and thoughts seemed kind of gritty.

Somewhere after St. Augustine, he pulled Luce across the seat to him and said, That was all my mistake. I thought it would be a safe place. It's not how I expected it to go.

—It's what I ought to have expected. But I let myself start hoping. That was the mistake.

Stubblefield drove awhile, Atlantic on the right and palmetto scrub on the left, and tried to line his thoughts up. He said, There's a kind of person that wants you to carry their trouble. If they can, they heap it every bit on you and walk away without a guilty look back. And if they can't do that, they lighten their own load by handing off a piece of woe to anybody who'll take it. You two girls didn't have a choice but to take what your mother dished out. All the rest were fools that let themselves get altered in their thinking by the prettiness of her.

—She is, isn't she?

—You had to get it somewhere.

They crossed the St. Johns on the ferry and went up Little Talbot and then across the inlet to Amelia, flying fish leaping almost as high into the air as the car windows as they drove over the low wood bridge.

Stubblefield checked his wallet and did some figuring. They could stay awhile at his old beach town with the fort and the lighthouse and the shrimp boats. It wouldn't be quite like the dream date on the Gulf he had imagined. No beer-joint oysters or beach-music jukebox dancing or night swimming. No being young and free. Mostly being scared and not knowing what to do about it.

But, through a stretch of beautiful autumn weather, they rested and walked on the beach. The children ran up and down and threw shells at each other and waded in the cool water until they flopped in the sand exhausted and happy. For brief moments, they let Luce wrap them in towels and sneak in a hug before they squirmed away.

One afternoon, near sunset, Stubblefield built a small driftwood fire, which delighted the children. They sat calmly, watching the flames. In a while, Dolores got up and collected dead dune grass from the beach and came to Stubblefield, sitting at the fire with Luce. Dolores bundled four long stalks in her hand, and lightly whacked him on each shoulder. Very ceremonial, like a knighting. Then she threw them in the fire and backed away, her dark eyes looking just over his shoulder. She stopped and stood, waiting for something to happen next.

Stubblefield went to the tide line and collected ribbons of seaweed and twisted and plaited them, using old Boy Scout rope-making skills. He knotted the ends to form a small circle and set it on Dolores's head. She immediately shook it off, but then picked it up and put it back in place and wandered in the direction of a few sanderlings quickstep-ping at the edge of the water. Frank sat near the fire and watched the whole process, and then he came over and stood at Luce's shoulder.

She said, If you want one, say please.

Frank said, One say please.

So Stubblefield made him a wreath too.

Each evening during their time there, they ate shrimp, a new food to Luce, and she could not get enough of it. The children went to bed early, exhausted, and slept until dawn to the drowsy wave sounds ris-ing from the beach. Way late, Luce and Stubblefield sat on the sofa of the beach cottage and listened to the radio and held each other, kissing like teenagers. Every song some variant of *oh baby baby*. But if Stubble-field went beyond a certain line, Luce was off to the bedroom to sleep with the children. Sweet about it, and sort of regretful, but off. Leav-ing Stubblefield to read and try to feel sort of gallant until he fell asleep.

Except one night, toward the end, she came back. Stubblefield dozed on the sofa with a paperback from his car library. He woke to Luce's hand on his face, and then sliding down past the collar of his shirt to his shoulder. She gripped him at the muscle above the collar-bone, and pulled him to her, which kind of hurt. Kissed him deep and said, One of these days it could be so good.

Before Stubblefield even roused awake, she was gone again. The door already closing behind her before he thought to say, Wait. After-ward, a restless late night for Stubblefield, with only the thin substi-tutes of poetry and Top 40 tunes on the radio.

Day by day, the money ran out. The last night, on the sofa before bedtime, Stubblefield told Luce a fairy tale about how they wouldn't ever go back to the lake. Just start driving, and before you know it, be blasting westward at dawn down two-lane Nebraska blacktop. A pale moon setting up ahead and a bright yellow sun rising behind. Drink-ing truck-stop coffee and sharing a box of doughnuts for breakfast, three apiece. Listening to a radio station out of Red Cloud reporting wheat prices, and then Spade Cooley followed by the Sons of the Pioneers so as to capture in just two songs the exuberance and melancholy of the famed lone prairie with its match-strike daylight and night skies deep as the mind of God. You the tallest thing standing for miles across the sweeps of grass. And to let the place enter their dream lives, camp on blankets in a wheat field and watch stars and planets move westward across the slopes of convex space until they all fell asleep.

—Great, Luce said. Let's do that, baby. Someday.

THEY WAITED UNTIL late afternoon to leave. By the time they were driving back through the dismal pine forests at the state line, it was dark. The kids slept on the backseat mattress, exhausted from another day on the beach. Luce spun the radio dial up through the frequencies and back down, over and over. Fractional blips of voice or music phasing in and out, interrupting the overall hiss and warp of interference. She wouldn't say a word. She didn't cry, but with every mile they drove north, dread filled the car like floodwater rising.

Stubblefield tried to draw her close. She felt like one solid muscle resisting the pull. But as soon as he took his hand away from her shoulder, she let go, quit clutching into herself, and leaned to him.

Luce said, I asked why you're not married, but you didn't ask me.

—I've been too glad about it.

—Yeah, well. There's probably about twenty reasons, but do you want to know one of them?

—If you want to tell me.

—I'm not talking about what I want. Do you want to know?

—Yes, I do.

So Luce gave him the story in brief. The room over the drugstore beside the movie theater. The library with the tiny librarian. The telephone office in the former hotel with the dark hallways. The wall of Bakelite plugs, the cot, and the quilt. Mr. Stewart and the Saint Christopher medallion. No anger, no emotion. Just the facts.

By way of conclusion, Luce said, I lived through it, so if you can't stand to hear it, you can take me home and go to hell. Men get so damn strange sometimes.

Stubblefield kept driving, trying to think of the right thing to say. Like a magic spell in a story. A few perfect words that make your wishes true. But they wouldn't come. He said, all at once, I'm sorry, I love you, I'll kill that bastard.

—He's moved on, Luce said.

—I found Lola. I could find him.

—Nice offer, but that's all long gone.

She fiddled the radio up and down again and then switched it off and twisted in the seat until she was lying on her back, her head in Stubblefield's lap, looking up at a full moon above pine trees, flowing bright and dark through the windshield until she fell asleep.

CHAPTER 12

Should have been a night drive like any other, but as soon as the beer and pills kicked in and the stars started jittering and pinwheeling, Lit set in on the same questions he had asked in the summertime when he came sniffing around for uppers. The difference was, now the trees were nearly bare and back then he hadn't really cared about the answers.

Lit couldn't possibly have a concrete clue to go on, Bud thought, only pool hall rumors and bullshit lawman instinct, thus far clouded by his need for pills. And the suspicions were the consequences of Bud's own actions, primarily getting drunk and running his mouth to the wrong people. Nobody to blame but himself, except possibly Lily's bitch sister, if she ignored his warning and set a fire under Lit's skinny ass, either getting him all sentimental about his little baby girl from the way back years or the idiot grandchildren. Which gave Bud pause, since he'd never entirely clarified that last relationship to himself. Lit a granddaddy. Nevertheless, a deep disappointment for Bud that even his best friend had started acting strange.

Lit probed on and on into Bud's past, but he didn't mention Lily. Or Luce's suspicions about the kids. But they were back there in the history Lit wondered about. However evasive Bud tried to be, however hard he squirmed to change the subject, Lit kept circling around. Every question had to do with Bud's identity. What was Bud's full name? Where all exactly had he lived in his life? Had he ever been married? In his previous life, had he ever encountered anybody who grew up here?

Bud felt a little glazed from trying to stay even with Lit on the uppers and beer, and he floated various lies and evasions that never rose above fair to middling. He could see where this was all heading. Lit penning him in. No way Bud could keep a string of lies consistent forever. In a few days, Lit would be right back at him, and Bud would have forgotten many details of his answers. His new lies would mismatch the old ones, which was exactly the way they trapped you. Then you went down.

Bud said, Come on, fuck this shit. What do you care about history? I thought we were friends.

—I guess we are, Lit said. You know a lot about me and my habits, but I don't know much about you. Right now, I need you to be straight with me.

Sounded kind of self-serving to Bud. Lit mainly starting to get sad about the cutoff of Benzedrine if his questions ended up leading them both to a bad place.

—That's what you're needing? Bud said. Me being straight? And here I was having a good time. I thought what buddies did was ride around and tell each other lies, and drink some beers and take some pills.

—That too. But I'm getting some pressure about you, and I need the truth.

Bud said, Don't pull that tired mess. I learned a long time ago, when somebody starts talking all sincere about truth, they're usually getting ready to fuck you. Truth isn't in your own self, and it sure isn't in theirs. Whatever you tell me or I tell you, and call it truth, is nothing but convenient feelings and asswipe opinions. Real truth is way beyond people. Our brains weren't tuned to get but a glimpse of it off in the distance.

—No. That's not the way it is.

—Yeah, that is the way it is. People love the word, but all they use it for is like a club to beat you with. If we ever had truth in our heads, we couldn't live with it. But because we're friends, I'm happy to hear about your feelings and opinions, and maybe tell a few of my own, as long as we agree to call things by their right names.

Bud shut up and stared out the window at an impossibly big moon. He kept his head straight and the panic in his stomach damped down by wondering what it would cost to bring the white-haired lawyer up here. Eat these rubes alive in court. In two hours, that old boy would burn them all a new one.

Lit kept on driving deeper into the mountains. One beer later, he started again on places and dates and surnames. Said, What if I made a call down to the capital asking if they have a sheet on a man named John Gary Johnson? Put whatever they have in the mail. Particularly a photo. Be here in a few days. What would I find? I'm not out to get you, but don't leave me hanging. People are talking.

—What people? Your crazy girl with her made-up stories?

—No.

And then, it hit Bud through the haze. What was he so scared of? He'd gone through one trial without getting put down. And last time on the phone, the lawyer had said the State boys had their tails tucked between their legs from the beating he had administered, and they probably wouldn't retry without new evidence. So, Luce could hold whatever opinions about him she cared to, as long as the kids couldn't witness against him. Bud had been feeling like the surface of a pot of water right before coming to a boil. Quivering. But now he went calm and collected his suavity back.

He said, Suppose you and the gossips around town are right about me. Your problem would be that a court of law let me go.

Lit drove awhile, and then glanced sideways, his face perfectly blank. Half illuminated by the greenish lights of the dash, and the other half shadowed.

He said, Not a problem for me. I'm not talking about law. No judges and juries. No lawyers. I'm talking about making somebody pay.

Possibly, running more lines of bullshit might have served Bud's purposes much better, but he panicked at the expression on Lit's face.

He'd seen plenty of Lit's work. And Bud knew from bitter experience that the hand-to-hand was seldom his best choice. He couldn't stand up to Lit unless he got awfully lucky. And luck mostly ran against him.

So, be the first one to go bad. Claim the high ground. Ancient wisdom passed down from old Stonewall. Some situation where he was outnumbered and outgunned against a mess of Yankees, as usual. An underling asked what they were to do, and Stonewall said, Kill them all. According to the mythology, he seemed sort of sad about it.

Which is how Bud felt when, with no prelude, he put his knife into Lit all the way to the quillons as they cruised up the road toward the quarter-mile slashes. He probed deep into Lit's side where essential organs lay greasy and dark against one another. Every thrust opened the wound wider and dug deeper.

Lit's concentration on driving wavered. The car went tacking up the road.

Bud leaned and took the wheel one-handed. He threw a leg over the drivetrain hump and kicked Lit's foot from the pedals. The car stalled and rolled to a stop. Then it rolled slowly backward, jerking and grinding against the transmission until Bud stomped around and found the emergency-brake pedal left-footed.

They sat nearly sideways in the middle of the steep black road with the headlights skewed toward the trees. Lit lived, but not in good shape. His hands gripped his cut middle, trying to hold himself in. His head not entirely under control.

—How could you do me this way? Bud said.

Lit bled out between his fingers. White in the face. He said, What?

—I thought we were friends.

Lit worked his mouth, but nothing got said.

—I better drive, Bud said.

He climbed out the passenger door and walked around the front of the car.

Lit's last moment of consciousness, a full moon blazing above the treetops and then Bud crossing the windshield, bleached by the headlights.

Bud shoved Lit across the bench seat until his head leaned against the passenger armrest. Bud cranked up and drove on across the gap. Somewhere along the way, Lit passed.

Way around the back side of the lake, up a narrow dirt road, Bud pulled Lit out of the car and dragged him far off into the dark woods. Wilderness. Maybe some grizzled hunter in the distant future of flying cars would come upon chalky mystery bones gnawed by porcupines and woodrats.

Bud drove the patrol car back around to the end of the lake where the water backed up deep behind the dam. He found a steep slope of bank and rolled it into the lake. Windows down, hood and trunk lid up. Great silver moonlit bubbles broke the black water. Then the long walk home. Many miles, keeping an eye out for approaching headlights, but of course there were none in the middle of the night. In town, the three stoplights flashed yellow, streets empty. Bud, trying to prove to himself how fearlessness worked, walked right down the sidewalk.

CHAPTER 13

Y OU NEED TO LOOK at that bootlegger, Luce said.

The sheriff, behind his desk, said, Look at who for what?

—Johnson. Killed my sister, and now probably Lit too. And I'm afraid for Lily's children, if I can't stop him. Bootlegs for most of the county, but you don't know who he is?

—I know who the bootlegger is, but I've never heard Johnson. People call him Bud. And I appreciate your suggestions, but there are facts here. Do you want your back patted or do you want straight talk?

—Oh, sure. Straight talk.

—So then, fact is, the murder charge didn't stick. And we don't even know Lit's dead yet. We know he's missing. Which might be his way of resigning and moving to someplace like Florida or Maine. He's not the type to give two weeks' notice. Plus, Lit had enemies in four or five counties. But you know all this.

Luce felt weary. She said, I know Bud did it. And he hurt the children pretty bad.

The sheriff formed a look on his face like being indulgent wasn't entirely beneath him. He said, And you know this how, Luce?

—I've lived with them. They've been hurt.

—They said it?

Luce was about to say, Not in so many words. And then she knew immediately that it was not the moment to be terribly precise in telling the truth. She shut up and looked the sheriff in the eye.

He paused, like an actor pretending to think, and then he said, I'm keeping an eye on Johnson, and I want to find Lit as bad as anybody. But the main thing is, I'm sorry for you. I've seen you around town since you were a little dark-headed girl whose mother ran off. You got a bad deal there. Now you've lost your sister, and you've had a pair of messed-up kids loaded on you. And Lit's missing, and never was much of a father. It's natural to look for somebody to blame. But life is mostly shit, and it heaps on more when you're already so loaded down you think you can't go on. Putting one foot in front of the other and keeping going is about all the pleasure you get in life after you quit being young.

—Going for what?

—For no reason. Stop looking for reasons. Lit's never given up wanting every day fired up like he was eighteen, and that's a lot of what keeps him in trouble. Don't make that same mistake.

LUCE RIFLED THROUGH the few items of her previous life until she found her last birthday gift from Lit, a handsome fatherly present for a sweet-sixteen daughter. A slim straight razor with a shimmery pearl handle. The blade was a long rectangle of rippled blue steel with a crook at the end to flick it open by, an edge so keen you'd damage it by sharpening on the finest grit of whetstone. A thick oiled leather strop was the only way to go.

—Happy birthday, Lit had said. Cut a man anywhere with that, he'll have a hard time quitting bleeding. With the least stroke, it seeks bone.

Teenage Luce had thought the gift of a straight razor stupid beyond belief, and her father an idiot. She hadn't taken his message to heart, the dangers congregating all around. What a wonderful, peaceful world she thought she lived in back then.

So Luce had left the razor at the bottom of a shoe box where she collected purse droppings. Lipstick nubs, broken tortoiseshell barrettes, single earrings, stretched-out ponytail elastics, packets of Clove with one brittle stick left, worn-out emery boards, a rusty church key, a yellow plastic whorl that adapted a fat 45 hole to a skinny LP spindle, a quarterback boyfriend's class ring that she had worn on a chain around her neck for a month.

But if she had taken her father's gift as it was intended and carried it on her person at all times, Luce could have cut Mr. Stewart's throat. Blood leaping into the air and covering his white shirtfront and tweed lapels. Horny, thrusting Mr. Stewart trying fruitlessly to suck air through a windpipe hanging out his neck like the end of a garden hose. Lay him wide open.

So, in retrospect, maybe Lit had known a thing or two after all. It was one of those timeless patterns. Children rediscover their parents' wisdom when they finally become adults themselves. If *wisdom* is the right word for going relentlessly armed with a blade honed so microscopically keen that when you cut somebody, they never stop bleeding.

STUBBLEFIELD WAS THE owner of a nostalgic pistol. Early days after the fire, he had looked around the outbuildings of the old place for something to remember it by. In the smokehouse, he'd found his grandfather's .32–20 rusting in a wooden box along with other tools. The head of a hand axe, an awl, various sizes of chisels, a plane. All Stubblefield remembered the pistol ever being used for was shooting snakes in the yard and weasels or foxes trying to kill the chickens. So it made sense that it had ended up in the toolbox. His grandfather hadn't made a symbol of manhood out of it, and it wasn't fancy. No nickel and pearl, merely a plain Colt, all the blue gone and the grip chipped. But, of course, it was the pistol and not the plane that Stubblefield decided to take with him as a memento. He had cleaned it and oiled it and displayed it beside his record player, like a smart-ass objet d'art. Now Stubblefield went to the Western Auto to see if they carried .32–20 loads.

Man behind the counter said, Sure we do. Old boys up the coves still use them. So Stubblefield bought a box of Remingtons, and then on the way out the door changed his mind and bought three more.

—What you planning, going to war? the man behind the counter said.

Back at his cottage, Stubblefield decided to move in at the Lodge whether Luce liked it or not. He grabbed up the essentials. Some clothes for the cold weather to come, the record player, *Kind of Blue*, the pistol.

When he got to the Lodge and began unpacking his things from the trunk of the Hawk, there wasn't any discussion. Even the kids helped carry a load.

That night, they all slept together in the main room. The children on their bed near the fire. Stubblefield and Luce half-reclined on a settle with their feet on an ottoman, Stubblefield's good hand in her hair. The fire burning low and the radio low too, so they could hear sounds from outside. The pistol within reach and the doors locked.

FIRST A DAY OF blowing cold and even a skift of snow high on the peaks as the front arrived. Then a clear cold night followed by a morning where, even two hours after dawn, real shadows gone, strange frost-shadows cast crazy brilliant interpretations of the angles of Lodge and smokehouse and springhouse glittering across the lawn. By late afternoon, the day had become warm enough to sit on the porch in the weathered rockers.

Luce poured two glasses of red wine from a basement bottle with a mildewed French label. Old and awfully good and autumnal in the November sundown with brown frost-bit apples still hanging from bare limbs in the orchard and a fingernail radius of yellow moon following the sun to the horizon. Leaves covered the grass. Something yet trilled in the woods, a final katydid or frog. A bite in the air, and not a cloud in the sky. Bands of soft color glowed above the westward peaks. Peach and apricot and sepia, fading in pretty degrees to blue and finally indigo straight up. Expressed as art, the colors would lay on canvas entirely unnatural and sentimental, and yet they were a genuine manifestation of place many evenings in fall.

At the end of the porch, the children played the kindling game, improvising a new rule where the palms of the losing player got whacked three times each with a stick of kindling. Which worked only until somebody hit too hard and Luce went over and shut the game down and aimed the kids toward the record player.

Back in her rocker, Luce reached her hand to Stubblefield. The wine had put her in a mood. It was just a feeling, but she had become certain Lit was dead. She was not grief-stricken at all. They hadn't ever been much at all to each other, but she was swept over with post-funeral numbness. Except, no funeral because no body.

When the wine was gone, Stubblefield let go of her hand and fetched two short glasses of Scotch dating back to the age of silent movies.

He said, I didn't know him beyond two conversations where he set me up to act a fool. I can't guess what you're thinking about.

—The war. It was the center of his life.

In memoriam, Luce told Stubblefield how, when she was little, not many of the men around town wanted to talk about the war in any detail. They wanted to shut up about it and bask in victory and have a family and a good job and own a house and drive a new car all the time without having to smell a previous owner's hair oil in the headliner ever again. Lit, though, wanted to talk about it. Luce and Lily composed his audience, for Lola classed every one of his stories as lies and left the room when he got going.

But Lit told the little girls all about the many bad scrapes he had fallen into. D-Day, for starters. But after that spectacle, things soon broke down into countless little brutal skirmishes, not at all like something involving generals in the background making big plans with an overview. Lots of blood all the time, in graphic detail. Days and days with hardly any sleep or food. Small bunches of half-lost men with their faces blank from exhaustion and fear. France was nothing but footslogging and gunfights. Way later, far eastward, the final movement of Lit's tale began with getting shot at by a Nazi tank in a frozen turnip field.

Lit and a dozen hungry men trying to eat half-frozen turnips like apples, raw with the skin still on and not bothering to more than brush at the black dirt clinging to them. Dug them up with their hands clawed and stiff. Grey sky, snow imminent, a bitter wind. Such had been the weather for weeks. A boy named Codfelter, subject of much amusement, and not just for his name, had come up with an enormous turnip. Right then, a round from the tank's cannon hit beside Codfelter and all but took his leg off at the middle thigh, though a flap of skin kept it attached. The force of the round wrapped the lower leg around a strand of fence wire. Several rotations. The boy tried to crawl away, bleeding heavy. But the band of skin held him back.

In some versions of the story, Lit shot Codfelter to put him out of his misery. In others he cut the rope of skin with his knife and improvised a tourniquet and helped Codfelter elude the tanks only to watch him die in a hedgerow, all bled out and white-faced. Sometimes Lit was captured in that tragic vegetable patch, and sometimes it was days later. The only parts that never changed were the weather, the field and its black dirt, the tank, and Codfelter's awful leg.

The capture always led to the story of being liberated from the German prison camp near war's end. Knowing the Russians were coming with overwhelming force, the commandant lined up all the prisoners and the German guards in the yard. Two lines, face-to-face. Lit figured they were about to be machine-gunned. Yet when the Russians topped the closest hill, the commandant pulled out his Luger and shot himself through the roof of his mouth and out the top of his head. It was quick Lit who dashed and grabbed the pistol before it hit the ground. And then, he claimed, all the stunned and defeated Nazis put their weapons down so that moments later, when the Russians came rolling in to liberate the camp, Lit was in charge.

There were endless addenda to the story, adventures involving being taken farther east with the Russians. And then the war ended. That night, sitting around a campfire, everybody got good and drunk on vodka. Come hungover dawn, the Russians gave Lit a handshake and a hearty fare-thee-well, for they were heading in opposite directions. Lit did not even know what country he was in. They all seemed an awful lot alike after a while. He spent weeks and weeks wandering westward across ravaged Europe with all its viciousness and culture, to make his way back to American troops. Along the way, lots of young eastern European women, recently widowed. Sad and needy, and ready to take him in for a few days. He could go on and on about their charity and their peasant charms. Their skill with a pot of water, a pinch of salt, and a potato.

When she finished the story, Luce wasn't even close to getting weepy about her dead daddy. He wasn't that kind of daddy, and she wasn't that kind of daughter.

III

A COOL NOVEMBER DAY, blue sky and sunlight thin and angling, even at noon. Leaves entirely off most trees, but still hanging tough and reddish brown on the oaks.

Luce says, Good day for a pony ride.

Stubblefield makes an expression, eyebrows up. A question.

—We can't live indoors forever, Luce says. And since you're going to be here awhile, drop us off at Maddie's and go to town. Get the rest of your things. We'll all be back before dark. She turns to the kids and says, Pack your lunch. We don't want to go with our hands out, riding Maddie's pony and begging dinner at the same time.

Stubblefield tries to find a place to carry his pistol. Sticking it down the waistband of his pants seems treacherous, so he puts it in his jacket pocket. But its weight pulls that side down uncomfortably, so he loads a book in the other pocket for balance.

The children plunder through the kitchen, and Luce tries to let them do what they want, or at least what they can. She's long since stopped getting judgmental about what a meal ought to be. Simply watch them and say the names of the things they choose and get them to repeat after her. If most of what they put in the lunch bag is edible, that's enough for now. So, leftovers of last night's mashed potatoes and this morning's home fries, Luce lets it go. After all, she doesn't really think of mushy white potatoes and crisp brown potatoes as being the same thing either. Maybe a little harder to be cool when they seem to believe lunch should be bread-and-butter pickles and ketchup. Or a jar of beets to share. But Luce takes the attitude, when you start fretting the day-by-day you lose track of the long view. And the long view is, they need to learn to speak for themselves and do the best they can. For now, if they bag their own lunch and it's pickles and prunes and they say the words, all you do is put both thumbs up and say, Good job.

THE SHADOWS BENEATH the big pines near the shore fall darker than under other trees. The deep pine straw smells sharp and clean. Astringent. It's what those half-moon evergreen urinal cakes are going for but miss by a mile.

Bud waits and watches. Lights the next Lucky off the butt of the one before. This is what? The third or fourth time he's been here the past month? He's beginning to worry that his money is no different from Blackbeard's buried treasure. Once real, now imaginary.

In time, Luce and the kids and the boyfriend walk to the car and drive down the road. Ten minutes later, Bud goes to the door. No more summertime latched screens with their simple hooks. The big wood door is locked tight. He had guessed it would be. So, a small hammer and a thin chisel. A few educated taps, and the door opens.

Bud entertains no plans, no list of places to look. He's given up trying to guess what either of the two sister bitches would consider clever. Whatever idea strikes at the moment is what he goes with. He checks the back sides of framed artwork. Lifts the corners of wool rugs. Lies on his back and looks at the undersides of coffee tables and end tables and settles. Feels up into the bases of mica-shaded hammered-brass table lamps and down into the cavities of many big shapes of useless pottery.

Upstairs, walking the halls lined with identical doors to the many guest rooms is no different from gambling. Bud sends out feelers of hope and waits for mysterious powers to cough up rewards. He enters rooms that call to him. Tarnished brass numbers relating to his birth date or to some year less shitty than most of the others. Inside 218, he opens bureau drawers, lifts corners of the mattress, blue stripes over cream, a big mysterious brown stain featuring waterlines like the lakeshore out the window. Bud lies down. His theory is, get calm and let the power of money speak and tell its whereabouts.

He falls asleep, which is fine at first, because he dreams immediately of the money. A vague sense of it fleeing from him, first down these very hallways, and then down walkways between rows of barred cells stretching into the distance. Down a bright tunnel of headlight beams through black night. Nothing but trees, the trunks rowed and leading onward into the dark. The dream goes on forever, but no message is delivered.

Bud wakes to the sound of the kitchen door banging closed, people moving around downstairs. The door bangs again, and then an armload of stovewood from the pile on the back porch thumps onto the floor. In time, the sounds settle. Bud walks down the hall and waits at the top of the stairs, listening. All the rattling comes from the kitchen. He creeps down the stairs and across the room toward the front door. Almost there, he sees the children sitting together on one of the faded rugs, playing with kindling, forming shapes like they're getting ready to burn the place down. Their heads lowered in quiet concentration. Frank placing his sticks to build a strict combustible cone. Dolores free-forming an imaginary geometry, many pieces and angles and spaces, perfect airflow. Bud takes two more steps toward the door, his hand reaching for the knob, and a floorboard creaks against a nail. The kids look straight at him.

—Hey, Bud whispers. I'll let myself out.

Dolores stands, pulling Frank with her. They begin backing slowly into dimmer light. Looking at Bud dead-eyed. No screaming or crying. They get to the door frame to the dining room, and Dolores, real flat, repeats her mother's words. I'll fucking kill you if it's the last fucking thing I do. Frank echoing a second behind her.

They run up the steps, and they keep running, thumping feet growing distant.

Bud runs, too. Out the front door, down the lawn to the lakeshore, and around to where his truck is parked. Panic rises in him like a bad dinner. He can't draw breath. He twists the key in the ignition and pats his foot so fast on the accelerator that he floods the carb and has to wait for it to clear. And then he has to vomit and doesn't even have time to get the door all the way open before his insides spray out bitter onto dead poplar leaves.

He wipes his mouth and gasps for air, seized up all through his center. Heart attack is Bud's first thought. So bring it on, then. Check out right now. Fuck everybody and fuck tomorrow too.

Bud waits and waits, and fails to die.

Turns the key, and the engine fires. He floors it, and before long, he's flying crazy down the gravel road. Three curves along, partway into a tight left, the empty back end of the pickup gets loose and begins coming around, skittering across the gravel in slow motion. He stomps on the brake, and that makes things worse. The truck swaps ends and comes to a stop in a cloud of dirt.

He sits in the road and tries to breathe. Grabs his necklace and cuts his thumb deep on the serrations and then tastes the blood. Memory is so damn harsh when it grabs you tight. The little bastards remember, and they are talking.

BY THE TIME LUCE comes from the kitchen, Bud is gone down the lawn and into the trees, just another flicker of dark shape silhouetted against the bright metallic light of the water. Luce goes looking for the kids, calling their names, knowing they won't answer unless they really want to. She makes a quick pass through the ground floor and becomes convinced they've gone outside, though they've lately had an understanding about that. She finds the front door unlocked and begins running.

In front and out back, no children and no smoke signals rising in the near distance. She runs the lakeshore a couple of hundred yards in either direction and then back to the Lodge. Looks harder this time, calling their names as she checks the sleeping rooms of the second floor and down into the cellar and then up into the eaves, opening doors and saying their names in a tone that means business. She gives up and heads straight for Maddie's place, running as long as she can and then walking.

But Maddie hasn't seen them. They're both thinking Bud but not exactly saying it. Maddie starts down the road to the phone at the country store to call the law, for whatever that's worth. Luce goes back home, shouting for the children constantly. Alternately walking and jogging in the thin angular light of late fall, the lake blue with tiny waves breaking against the shore rocks.

EVERYTHING QUIET and empty up in the windowless, claustrophobic warren of servants' quarters, the halls shoulder-wide, the rooms like closets, the tiered bunks narrow as coffins. They press together in the dark, as far under a bottom bunk as they can get. When everything stays quiet and empty for a long time, they come out wary and slip down the two flights of stairs and start packing for a long journey. They wrap a fist of matches in wax paper. The splits of fatwood kindling they've used for their game and a leather thong for making a fire bow, if it should come to that. They put great faith in their feel for the various materials necessary for fire, how to light them up. The difference between dry kindling on a clear day and damp kindling in a drizzle. How moisture fights you and wants material things to rot slow over long years, whereas you want them to blaze away right now.

They pack a red box of raisins, a cylinder of red-skinned bologna, and a yellow wedge of cheese. Canned peaches and green beans and okra and tomatoes. A jar of peanut butter. Flesh-colored sleeves of Ritz crackers and a jar of dark honey with a chunk of comb in it.

Also, out on the back porch, a red gallon of kerosene used for lighting the woodstove. Less than half full, a heavy slosh in the bottom of the can. Oh so dangerous, according to Luce. Keep away. But they take it anyhow.

Then to the smokehouse, the box of Lily's things. Frank buries his face in one of the flat foxes from the stole and takes a long inbreath of Lily's scent, and then puts it back in the box. It's the bundles of dry tinder they're needing. Finally, a pat of pockets to make sure the lightning buckeyes are on board.

They know to stay away from roads exposed to the world. Woods are the place for escapees. Each carrying a tow sack of goods, they walk over the ridge to Maddie's place and sit still in the dead weeds outside the paddock and watch the windows of the house for movement. They sneak to the shed and get the bridle and scoop grain into their sacks, and open the gate and go in. Sally walks over to meet them, and when Dolores holds out the bridle, Sally puts her head down and takes the bit of her own accord and Dolores slips the headstall over her ears and buckles the throatlatch. Using the fence rails like a ladder, they mount up and fit themselves into the curve of Sally's back and ride out the gate.

Their only idea about where to go is farther away from people, deeper into the mountains, up to the highest peaks. So they look where they want to go and grip Sally with their legs. She steps out eager, ears forward. They enter the edge of pines and fade into shadows.

IT'S NOT UNTIL after a few beers in the dim calm of the pool hall that Bud begins lining his thoughts into proper order. He let himself lose the picture in his mind of who he wants to be. And way back then, in the children's memory, is somebody he'd like to forget, even if they haven't. One sure thing: getting puking scared is not at all what needs doing right now, not with witnesses running loose.

Shit piles fast and deep when you act on one bad idea right after another. No going back, though. You can't fix the past. It's broken beyond repair, not worth thinking about. And there's no predicting the future, at least beyond the knowledge that you can't expect any mercy whatsoever from it. Anything you try to do to shape it in your favor is likely to rain down a deluge on all your hopes. So what to do right here, right now? Maybe be patient, play a few games of eight ball, and see if an idea arises.

And it does. Late afternoon, one of the regulars comes in talking about the volunteer rescue squad loading gear into their trucks in the parking lot behind the sheriff's office. Off to look for a couple of kids missing around the other side of the lake. Possibly with a pony. The fellow worked himself up in the telling, pretty excited and fraught as he went on about the wild country over there, the lost little ones. The cold death they'll die for sure up on the high mountain.

People can get so sentimental about a couple of stray youngsters. But the little bastards lighting out offers new possibilities. What a blessing it would be if they passed. How long, though, since blessings got bestowed? Long time.

So, what are the chances that a couple of frigid morns up on the ridges will lay the kids down for good. Slim to none. Bud figures they might need helping along to the next world. And if they're never found, nobody will think anything but that they died in a rock crevasse or deep in a laurel hell.

Sundown, Bud drives around to his best clients, letting them know he'll be taking a few weeks' vacation, maybe as high as a month. So they better order big for his next run. Full payment in front like always. Except prices are up. No explanations or excuses, gas going up or whatever. Life can get fucked up fast when you try to be a pleaser. Because people won't ever be pleased, not even if you drop them ass-first into paradise. They like bitching too much.

By the time he's done with his rounds, Bud has a couple of rolls that should let him drive until there's no more road to ride. Wipe the board clean and start over. New places, new people. Nobody to witness against you. Let the past be what it is. Gone, gone, gone. Drive until you hit water too wide to cross. California, maybe. Or South Florida, the drain at the end of America's bathtub. Mexico, that's where cowboy outlaws used to go. Live another life under palm trees at land's end like a new-minted soul.

So who's standing in the way of clearing the tracks for good and heading out? Two, is all. Or four, if things turn real messy. And one thing Bud knows for sure, it's blood washes things clean.

WHEN STUBBLEFIELD gets back to the Lodge from bringing more clothes and records and books from his garage apartment and buying sacks of groceries, the sun is falling to the ridges. It's not dim enough for headlights, though the sky to the west is forming sunset bands of violet and iron. Around the last bend in the road, he sees the door standing open. Through the windows, every electric bulb in the Lodge blazes. He drives across the lawn to the steps and runs inside, calling for Luce. No answer, and when he stops in the lobby and listens, he knows right away the place is empty. Back out on the porch, he gets still and hears Luce, way up the lakeshore, calling for Dolores and Frank. Her voice thin and frantic.

Stubblefield grabs the flashlight from its place by the back door. Runs to the car and reaches the .32–20 from under the seat, and an extra handful of cartridges from one of the boxes, destroying the precise grid. He stuffs the pistol into his pocket and runs along the shore, stopping over and over to listen for Luce's voice. When he catches up with her, she stands dazed and numb at the edge of the water.

He holds her, and she falls into him briefly, like he's her last shelter. And then she squirms to get out of his arms to do what needs to be done. Searching. Blaming herself.

—What? You ought to have tied them down? Stubblefield says, as they walk up the lakeshore.

A WATCHER WOULD think Sally knew hidden paths through the dark woods. But she is just aware of her riders, and steps slow and steady to balance the load. Not fooled by the thick layer of new-fallen leaves, feeling for the hidden slick rocks underneath. And not going straight at all. Going the way the land requires, so that curves are the shortest distance between two points.

They climb a steep damp trail along the bold creek of a cove. A canopy of hemlocks and maples all the way, black as midnight underneath. Then they contour around a dry shoulder of mountain with oaks and hickories, their limbs bare enough to show stars and the slice of moon scooting along in the breaks between clouds. Look up and glimpse Orion and his dangling sword, the Seven Sisters fleeing before him.

They keep contouring, bending back into another identical cove with its own canopy of maples and hemlocks and its creek, and then around to another shoulder. Over and over, that slow sinuous movement into wet dark and out to dry bright. But all the time, climbing.

Dolores and Frank rock along for hours, warm from pressing against each other and also from Sally, who steams in the moonlight. They doze a little but stay awake a lot, because of the importance of looking where they want to go. Up and far away.

LUCE AND STUBBLEFIELD find a blue-and-white De Soto coupe pulled off the dirt road at the edge of the lake. The water flat, and the same shade as the night sky. The car windows are fogged opaque, but it is a known vehicle to Luce. Inside will be the artistic man who teaches music at several mountain schools many miles apart on twisting roads. Like a Methodist circuit rider from two centuries previous, roaming the revolutionary hills on a weary gelding. Presumably, the musician has an actual place to live at a less remote radius of his circuit. Low pay from the State, though, sometimes requires that he overnight in his car near the lake, sharing the backseat with his wardrobe of two suits, navy and charcoal, three whitish shirts, and one red necktie. Also his professional clutter. Envelopes of sax reeds, little vials of oil to lubricate the pistons and slides of brass, white plastic flutophones for teaching younger kids the basics of fingering, crushed packets of Viceroys, and several bottles of cheap Scotch at various degrees of empty.

Luce raps a knuckle at the driver's window and then steps back.

The teacher rolls down a rear window and sticks his head into the night. All that shows clear is his dark hair and his blinking eyes.

—Yes? he says, with the precise pitch of annoyance due someone whose telephone has jangled at midnight.

—Little kids, Luce says. A girl and a boy. Yea high.

She makes a leveling motion with her hand at her hip.

—Sort of blond-headed, she says. Maybe with a pony mare. Seen them?

—With a what?

—A blackish pony mare. White socks in front.

—Seen them when?

—Anytime from afternoon to right now.

—Not at all, he says. No children seen whatsoever.

—How long have you been parked here?

Instead of gesturing his response with a middle finger, he flicks three fingertips under his salt-and-pepper chin whiskers with great aplomb. When he rolls the window up, the sweeps leave parallel tracks in condensation on the inner side of the glass.

After that, Luce and Stubblefield wander for what seems like hours in the night, flashing their feeble light on black trunks and humped stones, startling small animals, which skitter through the downed leaves. Luce singing out Dolores's name in three rising syllables every minute, and in between, Stubblefield barking Frank. And at some point in the night, they hear off in the coves and along the ridges other searchers calling too, echoing out the same two words like simple-minded spirit voices of the green world. In the silences, floating thin in the air from a great distance, coon dogs bay as they work the high mountains on an entirely different mission.

TOWN DARK AND EMPTY, the three streetlights flashing yellow, Bud creeps alleyways. Trying to work some imaginary juju shit to guess which townsfolk might be hunters and fishers and summertime campers. When he needs to see, he clicks the flashlight with his fin-

gers over the lens, so that about all the shine he gets is bloody glow
through skin.

Luck strikes at only the third garage. He finds an army-surplus
pup tent and a down mummy bag rolled tight and smelling like poultry and must. A brown greasy World War II knapsack collapsed onto
itself like the carcass of a goat or small deer left to the elements for a
couple of seasons. Also a damn unexpected prize, a jungle machete,
rusty from tang to tip. All of which goes to show what great rewards
come from pausing to plan.

That afternoon, when Bud started figuring he needed gear for the
journey up the mountain, he headed first to the grocery, and then the
Western Auto. Buy a fat warm sleeping bag and an assload of matches
and one of those wonderful little nesting cooking kits no bigger than
a baby moon hubcap that, when unpacked, reveals a half dozen shiny
vessels for boiling and frying and poaching. And, at the center, a precious metal cup with folding wire handles to drink your coffee from.
All fine, until the thought emerged from the general milling inside his
head that there might be bad backwash from such a shopping trip.
This time, unlike the fishing rod deal, he very much shouldn't want to
call attention to himself as a novice mountaineer. So, how to satisfy his
needs anonymously? It took but a second to come up with the correct
answer, and yet he wondered how slack-minded bootlegging had made
him. Why hadn't pilfering been his first idea?

Back home, Bud stuffs the stolen knapsack with his food and gear.
Best if his truck stays in town, so he dodges alleyways and empty lots
to the shoreline. Keeping to the trees, he walks until he finds an un-
chained canoe. Paddles on and on across the spooky black lake to a
narrow cove. Starts walking up the mountain.

Survival. That's what it comes down to. Like, in *Argosy* and *True*.
Every month, along with swimsuit girls, some story tells about how
you're lost in the Arctic or the Amazon, and a polar bear or a jaguar
rears up out of nowhere and opens its monster jaws to crunch your
skull like a mouthful of popcorn. But real quick, you push the muzzle
of your .45 deep into its pink mouth and pull the trigger, and red stuff

blows out the back of its head onto the snow or the litter of the jungle floor. Or it could be coral reef and great white shark and some kind of underwater sling gun. All the same difference.

It's cold and dry here. Dead leaves everywhere. Dark too, at the moment. But these bears are well known to nap all winter. As do snakes. After the first frost, the woods are safe as church. Which Bud rethinks immediately. Surely safer than church. Lifeless as these woods are now, all the blood must flow in summertime, whereas Jesus's blood covers the world every day of the year.

The trail pitches hard upward, and it being the middle of the night, Bud soon stops and tries to camp. The woods become so expansive in total darkness, yet Bud goes fireless by choice. At least in the sense that he chooses to quit burning up his too small supply of matches trying to light sticks that don't want to burn. Best save at least enough to equal the number of cigarettes he's brought along. And forget about trying to set up the tent. Without wasting his batteries, he can't hardly see the palm of his hand waved in front of his face. He sits in the dark and eats half a pack of cold red Valleydale wieners and puts the rest in his knapsack for breakfast.

When he lies down to sleep, every distant sound amplifies and warps. Wind in the trees and creek water over rocks. Voices mumble conspiracy against him. Bud huddles in his bag on the cold ground and feels it trying to pull at him. The heat of his body soaking into the earth like water.

How did fucking life reach this fucking pitch? Not even stars to offer light, and his legs crunched together by the mummy shape of the bag till he feels constricted like a deceased elder in his coffin.

TWO IN THE MORNING, a stand of tall red oaks in a peninsula of forest interrupting a big hay field. Unexpected light rises under the trees. A Coleman lantern hanging by its bail from a tree limb projects a harsh white dome across the ground and up the tree trunks and into the brown dead leaves overhead. A group of men stand together in the

blaring light like actors on a stage, their eyes dark under hat brims. The
shadows of the people and of the trees stretch long across the ground.

Luce stands apart, gathered into herself and fatal.

Stubblefield is with the group of men. They're looking at a green
canvas tarp covering a small body.

The sheriff says, There's no need for her to look. We have his wallet. It was still in his pocket.

—How was he killed?

—Hard to say at this point. When the searchers found him, it was
already dark. A lot of animals around here. Plenty of wear and tear.
We'll get him out in the morning and see what the coroner says.

Stubblefield holds his cut hand to catch the light, looks at the bandage. He says, I'm betting knife wound.

—We'll see. Like I told her, there's a lot more than one suspect.
Need to keep an open mind.

—Have you talked to him since Lit's been missing?

—Of course. He seemed pretty broken up. Said they were tight.
Never had such a good friend in his whole life. Said he didn't believe
for a minute that Lit had taken off on his own without a word. Something bad must have happened. I believed him.

—You believed him? The end?

—I'm not as big an idiot as Luce thinks. He has an alibi for the
night Lit went missing. A couple of men saw him at the Roadhouse
until late.

—Two drunks hanging at a beer joint can't remember one night
from the next.

The Sheriff says, Everything doesn't have to be connected. Most of
the time, something happens and then some other things happen.
Usually the simple answer is the right one. I'm keeping an eye on this
guy. But it'll turn out to be somebody with a grudge against Lit.
There's plenty of those around. It won't be a friend. And, by the way,
I don't think of it as *a* beer joint. I think of it as *your* beer joint.

Luce looks up and comes fuming over. Says, Lit's dead. He's been
dead. The children might not be yet. Why are we all standing around?

Luce and Stubblefield ride in the backseat of the patrol car like criminals. A smell of Pine-Sol and vomit. Back at the Lodge, dawn is still a ways off. Maddie waits for them in the kitchen, and to kill the time, she has coffee going, cat-head biscuits browning in the wood-oven, and a pot of grits, yellow with butter and speckled throughout with coarse black pepper. As soon as Luce and Stubblefield and the sheriff come through the door, Maddie scrambles a dozen eggs in a huge iron skillet left over from the days of Lodge hospitality.

Maddie repeats what she said on the phone last afternoon. If the children and the mare are still together, they might be heading for the highlands, the peaks and balds, which Sally might remember from summer grazing in the long grass many years ago.

—Ifs and mights, the sheriff says. My thinking is, if you lose your car keys, the best place to start looking is on the kitchen counter and in your coat pockets before you head up a foot trail to the top of a mountain. Might be coincidence that your mare wandered off the same day as the children.

—I doubt she'd have carried her bridle with her, Maddie says.

—Well, I'll keep that in mind, and we might find ourselves up there eventually, if we don't get results down here. Normally, we find lost kids in the first six or eight hours. This time of year, by the second night out in the cold, we're just trying to find something for the parents to bury.

—Good Lord, Maddie says.

—Luce likes straight talk, the sheriff says.

BY THE TIME the partial moon slides down the sky and disappears, they are far up, pretty high. Creeks becoming thin enough for Sally to step over without getting her feet wet. The woods have slowly quit being jungle and have started to become alpine. Firs and balsams, and heathery stands of flame azalea and huckleberry.

Later, they stop and get off and stand bleary and disoriented in a bald place at the top of a mountain. All around, ghostly frosted clump grass.

Sally collapses her knees and then her hind end, an awkward fore-and-aft jerk, to lie down. She blows three deep breaths and falls asleep. Dolores and Frank use her side as a backrest and lie canted toward the sky, eating raisins and watching the stars fade out toward dawn.

They sleep a brief while and wake high above the world to silver bands of light illuminating valley fog so deep and broad that only the tallest peaks rise dark and solid from it, like islands in a pale sea. As if the island they occupy is theirs alone, a place where they hold the only power to be reckoned with.

But as the sun climbs above the east ridges, the sea draws into the ground until only a distant small shape of elongated fog remains between ridges, underneath which lies the lake. The landscape reconnects all its parts, and the children on their pinnacle are not any kind of power anywhere.

Below them, a hawk floats on a cushion of air, and the children look down on it, studying the novelty of sunlight glinting off the tops of its spread wings, the brown feathers like bronze. With two strokes, it rises and sweeps over them, close enough that they hear the sound of its wings cutting the air, a faint rattle of feathers.

Sally stands and walks stiff-legged a few yards across the bald and begins cropping long grass, dead brown and lapped over by frost in smooth striated waveforms. The children each take fists of grain from the bag. Much tingling and laughter at the velvet sensation as she lips it out of their palms.

Neither reasoning nor planning for the day ahead, and hardly consulting each other except, perhaps, by glances and gestures and thought waves said to be shared exclusively by twins, one thing becomes clear. No going back. Ahead, mountains and woods and creeks, endless by the look of them. Follow old wagon roads, cart tracks, footpaths, animal trails. Go the way the sun goes, as far away as you can. Don't worry about what happens next until it happens.

Bud's life has been such that he hasn't witnessed the beauty of dawn in some time. And yet, now, peering out at it from the hole in the mummy bag, how disappointing. Everything grainy and unformed. A new damp chill in the air, and the low sky the color of cold bacon grease.

A fat granddaddy bear, not yet settled into his winter den, waddles from the trees and begins rooting around in the knapsack. He's scarred around the head from various fights in the past and sort of dusty-looking under the long glossy black hairs of his outer coat. Very casual. A pro. A few motions of the wide forepaws, with their long curved claws, and the knapsack and tent become ribbons and Bud's stuff is scattered all over the ground.

The bear is first drawn to the wieners, which scent the air for hundreds of yards into the woods. In three bites, he eats a full loaf of bread, including the cellophane wrapper. The bear sits up on his round ass and sucks down all Bud's uncanned food like a cartoon glutton. Then he gets interested in anything else falling even vaguely into the category of edible. Such as Bud's suede gloves with the sheepskin linings.

Bud, with just his face from eyebrow to lower lip out the hole of his bag, watches and figures maybe he's next. He tries to sit up and find the zipper at the same time, but his fingers jitter. The inside pull eludes him, and he can't squeeze his hand out the face hole to get to it from the other side. He jerks himself vertical and tries to hop away from the bear, but he falls onto his side. Breath won't draw right, and his dia-phragm burns. The bear walks near, sniffs and blinks tiny brown eyes, huffs from deep in his chest, the breath steaming in the cold air. He shies away and disappears into a laurel thicket.

After a while of calming himself and fiddling with the zipper, Bud squirms out of the bag like an extrusion, then eats some of the canned stuff leftover from the bear's breakfast. Anchovies and Vienna sau-sages and Red Devil potted meat. His campsite looks like a plane crash.

Before he starts walking, he has to decide which way to go. He wants to turn around and go home, and has to give himself a pep talk about going forward and doing the necessary. Get it over. Put the past where it belongs and start the new.

He squats beside the creek and scrubs the rust from the machete with glittery grit from the water's edge. He tries to sharpen it on a smooth creek rock, spitting on the rock and then stroking the long edge back and forth in the lubrication. Spitting again and swapping sides. All he knows about knife sharpening is that you hold the blade at such angle as to mimic taking a thin slice out of the stone. He rubs and rubs, and his breath clouds around his head. Thinking, when I'm done up here, I'll bury this son-of-a-bitch deep deep in the ground and it will rust away year by year. When I'm an old man, it probably won't be anything but a reddish stain in the soil.

A BUNCH OF MIDDLE-AGED MEN in the cold light of morning, all bleary-eyed and uneager to get moving and continue the search. Happy to keep stoking the fire and spiking their mugs of coffee with Wild Turkey and Black Jack that they mostly either bought direct from Bud or at one remove. One of the men looks at the sky and sniffs. Says the air smells like snow.

The sheriff looks especially busted up by his few hours of sleep on the ground. But voters have a way of holding it against you if you go home instead of sacrificing a night in bed to find two lost kids. Now his hair hurts when he tries to smooth it down. He keeps taking his hat off and rubbing his head and looking into the hat like the band is what's causing his trouble.

They've not made it into the woods more than shouting distance from where their vehicles are parked along the lake's back road. Partly out of laziness, and also because they cannot imagine two children, even if they are riding a worn-out mare, going far before they give out. Like when they, themselves, go hunting in November. And also, the mountain gets weird and dangerous and scary when you climb way up on it, especially if you're the manager of the grocery or the guy that works the recap machine at the tire store.

The sheriff finally says maybe everybody ought to get off their asses and start finding the poor kids. And then he and his number one suckass, Carl, bid the others adios and head back to their black-and-white. Can't everybody be out in the woods at the same time.

The sheriff and Carl ride around in the patrol car. Stopping at houses at the edge of the deep woods. Carl sits in the car listening to the radio while the sheriff knocks on doors, takes his hat off, walks in, and asks, Seen two retarded kids wandering loose? Might have a horse with them?

Late morning, the sheriff swings back by the Lodge to check if the kids have come home, see if there is any cooking going on. See how Luce acts.

Not like he hasn't given it a passing thought that she and the boyfriend might be behind the children's disappearance. He doesn't believe it, but that's where you look first, close to home. A wife disappears, you look to the husband. And maybe Luce inherited some of her father's crazy streak. There isn't a lawman rule book to learn this stuff from, and the sheriff hasn't been to police school. Being an elected official means you don't need any training or qualifications. Nor even common sense. All he really knows how to do is build roads on padded State contracts. Also how to make voters feel comfortable or uncomfortable, peaceful or excited, whichever is more useful at the moment.

After eating a big plate of Maddie's pinto beans and cornbread and collards, the sheriff hasn't come up with any clues. Luce seems genu-

inely broken up by the disappearance of the children, and the boyfriend isn't any kind of killer. The sheriff tells them to be patient, let
the professionals do their jobs. Everybody is doing everything they
can to bring the children home safe. Stay by the phone.

Luce says the obvious: I don't have one. So she gives Stubblefield's
number, and the one at the little store down the road.

—But we're mostly going to be out hunting for them, Stubblefield
says.

—I'll be here, Maddie says.

WHEN THEY'RE ALONE, Stubblefield tries to convince Luce to come
back to town with him to wait at his place, let the sheriff and his people work. All of which lasts about five seconds.

—It's mainly a bunch of deer hunters looking for them, she says.

—Then they know the woods.

As they put on their jackets and head out across the lawn and along
the lakeshore to search, Luce sets him straight, talking fast and bitter
and distracted about deer hunters. Nothing but drunks with
high-powered rifles and a two-dollar paper license issued by the State.
Coon hunters are nocturnal, and bear hunters go deeper in the mountains. You hear their dogs baying miles away. But deer hunters, they're
the scary ones. Hiding in camouflage, mostly two by two in deer
stands, little tree houses the size of a double bed, above spots they've
been baiting with corn and salt blocks for weeks, about as sporting as
shooting a hog with its head down in the trough. They huddle together, whispering to one another and sipping Jack and Coke all day,
waiting for something to move. Late afternoon, half drunk and nothing to show for the day, they get twitchy. Pop a shot at falling leaves
and cloud shadows moving on the ground. No court ever convicts
them for a hunting accident. How could they have known that some
woman walking through the woods alone was not a deer? But, Luce
says, she never worries much once she's at least a mile out from the
nearest dirt road. They rarely get far from their trucks, because that's

where the beer cooler is. Which explains why jacklighting is so popular. That way, sometimes they don't even have to get out of the truck,
just roll down the window and pull the trigger. So what they know of
the woods is nothing but a thin band stretching from the roadways
only as far as they'd care to drag a field-dressed doe.

When she's run her thoughts all the way to the end, Stubblefield
says, I stand corrected. Luce makes a fist and swings it roundhouse,
slow-motion, and glances his brow.

They spend both halves of the midday searching on foot again near
the lake and along the old railroad bed. They go back to the Lodge and
drive to Maddie's to see if Sally might have come back, then down to
the store to check for messages. Followed by hours of driving fire
roads, stopping frequently to blow the horn and shout into the woods
and listen for some response.

IT'S DEAD WINTER up on the ridges, all the bare sticks of trees like
weather-beaten skeletons broken into forearms and hands, rib cages,
shins and feet. Some resigned to horizontal death and some still trying to reach upward. They ride the cold ridges deeper and deeper into
the mountains, but with less urgency now that they're high above the
world.

They stop often to rest and eat, and they light a fire each time.
Break out their materials and use their skills. Sometimes, small cowboy campfires no bigger around than a pot lid. But also much larger
blazes if the combustibles lie handy. On into the afternoon, a mist
starting to hang in the air, they come upon a dead blown-down balsam, its needles dry and brown on the branches. Once a tree of maj-
esty but now a giant brush pile.

A pyramid of dry sticks and the last cups of their kerosene, and the
balsam soon lights up like a great torch throwing yellow flames thirty
feet into the sky, roaring hoarse and sucking wind upward so that it
pulls their hair forward into their faces. Dolores whoops in the manner of old warriors, whether Cherokee or Rebels at Gettysburg. Sally

goes sideways a few steps and then settles. Frank walks forward with his arms straight ahead and his palms out until he can't stand the heat. He backs up and presses them to his face, and then he does it all over again.

The fire dies as quickly as it kindled, leaving burnt branch tips. Hundreds of little flames like candles at an altar. Soon the flames die away entirely, and hundreds of smoke tendrils rise toward clouds of the same grey.

Dolores and Frank watch from start to finish, like it's their favorite movie. Talking to each other the whole time, if that doesn't have to mean constructing sentences out of generally agreed-upon vocabulary using approximate rules of grammar. Outside the world of people, a category they feel little allegiance to, they talk plenty.

THE TRAIL CLIMBS STEEP, following a creek bank, giving every impression of being a main thoroughfare. Thigh-clenching, ass-cramping climbing through lots of unexpected greenery, even in this dying season. Laurels and hemlocks and those kinds of plants that probably either never die or live a great long while. Like maybe the biggest of the hemlocks were sprouts when Jesus walked the earth. They go on and on the same every day, ignoring the pithy symbolic yearly circle of life and death. Being happy all the time. Happy, happy. Then, probably, one day they fall over dead. What a grand life plan that is compared to oaks and maples and all the other loser trees that die a thousand colorful deaths for our autumn enjoyment. Pleasers never get paid back a fraction commensurate with their effort. Which goes along with one of the main rules of life. Which, unfortunately, has two parts. The *a* is, You got to get paid. A fine idea if it stopped right there. But the cruel *b* part is, You got to pay.

Without his bear-shredded knapsack, Bud carries his remaining gear in the pockets of his pants and leather jacket and inside his sleeping bag, which he sometimes drapes over his shoulders like a fireman with a limp body and sometimes balls in his arms like a mama with her baby. After a long while of slogging upward, Bud's feet hurt. Blisters bubble on the insides of both big toes, and skin peels off both heels in moist white petals. Underneath, weeping new flesh. A lot of good daylight gets spent sitting in the leaves with his boots and socks off, picking at his feet.

Hours into the climb, scenery loses its attraction. It's nothing but ten feet of dirt and leaves in front of his aching feet. Bud is bored and thinking about violence, but trying not to, because violence is best accomplished spur-of-the-moment. Let it happen out of nowhere. Anything else, and you go from being a hothead manslaughterer to nothing but a cold first-degree murderer. Act with great purity—like there's no past and no future, nothing but the red right now—and there's a degree of innocence to it, no matter how heinous and bloody the outcome. And that's not just Bud talking out his ass for his own convenience. The State itself draws the same distinction. Premeditate and they'll fuck you over bad.

It's a legal concept confusingly related to something the counselor in teenager prison liked to drag on about. Deferring gratification. Which you'd think would be a bad thing, or at least awfully dreary. The catch is, in the everyday crap of life, premeditation is a valuable skill. If you learn to do it, you step onto the path to success. Never ever do anything you really want to do at exactly the moment you really want to do it. Always stop to think about the consequences of your actions. Defer all the way to the grave, and you draw a ticket to heaven or something. Yet there's this one amazing exclusion when it comes to rarefied moments of sudden violence. All bets are suddenly off, and there's a happy and unexpected reward for jumping in with both feet and letting anger run bloody buck wild without any thought of future consequences. Who would have guessed?

On up the creek, two or three little branches of trail peel off ignorably. Then after a dazed while of not thinking at all, but just letting the drab repetition of the world overwhelm him, Bud finds himself standing on something that he can't even say for sure is a trail. Everything brown or grey, bare trees as far as he can see, and rain starting to fall in earnest. Dead leaves cover the ground hock-deep like a bad snow. Untracked. Stand still, and all you can hear is rain in the leaves and your own breath.

Bud looks for an empty shape among trunks, a suggestion of a lane. Which all depends on which degree of the three-sixty he whirls to look. In leafless woods, the thousands of trunks stretching into the distance shape themselves to suggest a lane everywhere you look, when you're looking for a lane.

—Fuck if I'm not fucked now, Bud says aloud.

The trouble is, the mountain encompasses so much more territory than Bud would have guessed, never having climbed one before. From town, looking at it way in the distance, flat against the sky, the mountain seemed simple and compact. Not really that big a deal to wander around and cross paths with the kids. On it, though, the mountain encompasses more space and is way more three-dimensional than Bud imagined. The confusing landscape goes every which way. Near-vertical pitches climbing to side ridges and falling into countless coves. Bud lifts his necklace into his mouth, sucks on the tooth, then licks the serrations until he tastes iron. Even an idiot knows that if you need to climb a mountain, the way is up.

Time passes, and Bud persists. At altitude, every kind of bad late-fall weather crosses the sky. Rain, and then freezing rain. Later in the afternoon, sleet hisses against the frozen rain in the trees and the dead icy leaves on the ground. Finally, heavy snow before dark. Big wet flakes falling straight down, an inch an hour.

With neither tent nor campcraft to get him through the night, Bud walks on in the dark, shawled in his wet sleeping bag. It hangs sodden and heavy across his shoulders, and the wet feathers stink. Might as well be carrying a dead body through the aftermath of a flooded henhouse. He casts it aside.

His gear has dwindled mainly to his leather jacket and one wet wool blanket, the machete, and the flashlight. He shivers uncontrollably, and admits to himself he's flat lost. Snow lies ankle-deep and keeps coming.

With his batteries almost spent, Bud decides to walk in the dark five hundred steps, feeling the ground with his feet, wishing and hoping and praying that when he thumbs the flashlight switch he will have stumbled onto a path. He does it over and over, and each time, he stands stunned and confused to see in the beam only blank forest, except for his own receding footsteps rapidly filling with snow. Nothing but random oak and poplar trunks, no sign of track or trail or other mark to indicate way of passage.

Bud's arms fall to his sides, and he stares bewildered at the circle of light puddling around his feet. The symmetry fascinates him, until he notices that the light, which had been white, has turned yellow, giving the snow a quaint look, like old-time photographs. He watches it dim and go dark. Rattling the flashlight does nothing.

One fuckup over the line. You could collapse dead, face in the snow, and nobody know it. Eventually, all that would be left would be some mossy scrag of spine and skull laid out nose down like a shot hog. Thinking this, Bud just hangs his head in the dark, wondering if he has strength left to keep going and find shelter, maybe a rock overhang. Sit huddled all night eating anchovies. Probably that's nothing but hope, and he'll be dead by dawn.

But when Bud looks up, he witnesses a miracle. Way up ahead, at the saddle of a ridge, a tiny spot of light glows through the woods. Thank you, Jesus.

MAKING FIRE FROM sparks is a lovely and fragile art. Of necessity, the early movements are delicate, the materials fine as hair and fingernail clippings, shreds of dry leaves. Whether by bow or flint and steel or even a scant few matches, the second you achieve a spark in tinder, you lean close to it and breathe on it from your throat like a sigh. If you purse your lips and blow, everything goes black.

Done carefully and with luck, maybe a flame no bigger than the tip of a finger lives for a few seconds. Then, when the tinder begins to catch, an old man with his long hair on fire, crumple a few more whole leaves and place twigs above the flame. Nervous as pick-up sticks in reverse. Judge wrong, the sticks collapse and snuff the flame. Do it right, and the flame grows, but still fragile. More twigs and then small broken branches. And when that layer starts to catch, that's when you purse and blow. Do it on and on until, when you look up to the sky, everything is dark and grainy as soot with little silver sparkles dancing in your vision. From there, it's easy. Nothing but the architecture of broken wood. Pick a shape and lay pieces in squares, triangles, cones. Place them close enough to burn one another but not so close as to shut out the air between.

In the cave of a hollow tree, the children crowd together. Right at their feet, the fire they lit at dark needs constant attention. They judge their sticks and limbs to be skimpy for lasting the entire night, and they begin rationing early on. Still snowing hard enough to discourage them from leaving their tree to hunt more wood in the dark. They feed the fire only the least amount to keep it alive.

Close by the fire, Sally locks her knees and sleeps standing. The outer hair of her winter coat lies on her back like a thatched roof. Underneath, a thick layer like boiled wool, so snowmelt runs down her sides and drips off her belly without soaking through. In her time, she's lived through many such nights. Miserable and shivering, icicles hanging in her mane and tail. But she's always been standing come sunrise.

Same for the children. They are not tender babes. They have experienced considerable pain. Cold is more like discomfort, one more thing to take. Shut down, let your breath become shallow, and wait for it to be over. Then go on. No tears, no wishes.

They feed their little fire with twigs hardly bigger than pencils and lean against each other, not thinking forward or backward. Let the night play out, and go on in the morning. Keep running. But it isn't the Lodge and Luce they're running from. The Lodge was a fine weird place to live. And Luce was a little bit like Lily, what they still remember. But they don't expect mama love. What they need is everything even and smooth. Not love or hate, pleasure or pain, hope or fear, safety or danger. Nobody kissing your cheek at bedtime till you tingle with pleasure in your stomach, and nobody making you bleed. Accept one and you have to accept the other, that's the deal. You can't control everything that happens. All you control is your mind. Make it like the lake on a still day. Don't react any more than you can help, not to out-siders. Trust only the two of you all the way. Hoard up your love for each other and state your rage by way of things that want to burn.

And that had been working pretty well for them, until Bud erupted out of nowhere. Then they broke all the rules. Reacted big, let them-selves get scared again. But not just scared. That was no big deal. Fear was every moment. Constant as breath, no matter how hard you tried to tamp it down. What they did was panic. And that was way outside the boundaries of the deal.

BUD FAILS TO ANNOUNCE his presence. Stumbles trembling straight into camp from the dark. Lucky not to get shot. Hunters have many stories of beasts and ghosts that haunt the woods at night, hungry for human blood. As it is, they are mostly too drunk to shoot. So when Bud arrives, one of them raises a toast with his jelly glass.

Nobody gets at all worried about Bud's closeness to death, or even offers a dry blanket. Sit by the fire and take a cup of coffee or a drink of white liquor, is all the concern they muster.

Whereas Bud is convinced he is neck-deep in a life-or-death sur-vival kind of night, here is this clutch of hoary men, on the same mountain in the same weather, yet occupying a whole different reality from his. They're having a party. Cozy as hell in the killing weather. An enormous blaze from chain-sawed lengths of resinous fir and hick-ory and oak. A brown tarp stretched between tree trunks to keep them dry if the snow falls too heavy, but for now they sit out in the open, some of them in shirtsleeves, and let the heat of the big fire sizzle it away before it ever reaches them.

Around the fire, the world draws down to a small beautiful circle. Warmth and light, red coals in a deep bed on the ground, yellow flames leaping high. Sparks shooting up into the black sky, passing white snow falling into the light. An odor of pork cooking. The outer compass of their world marked by faintly lit columns of stout tree trunks gyring away to blackness.

Sleep is not a big part of the old boys' plans. They haven't slept for days except to nap briefly. Plenty of time to sleep when you're dead, or when you get home to the wife. Up on the mountain, they stay awake all night feeding the fire and drinking their handmade raw shine from the recent past, such as a couple of days ago. Telling hunting tales and ghost stories and imaginary stuff about the incredible pussy of yester-year. Many timeless jokes about one another's dicks and dogs, their equal lack of skill. How the baying of any dogs but the speaker's own signifies nothing. Also, religious moments of silence and clarity listening to coondogs singing in the distance.

Hard to find joy in the world so much of the time, but the old boys have found some here. It makes them feel young. A renewal of their powers, if only for the dark hours. Come dawn, a camp of hungover sleepless sixty-five-year-old men will look like a mummy convention. But that is for morning to worry about. Right now it is hardly midnight, and everybody seems magically like they did forty years ago.

Bud pours himself a cup of coffee and squats on his heels so close to the fire that, after a few breaths, he has to waddle back two steps to keep from singeing his eyebrows. No good way to conceal-carry a machete unless you're wearing a long overcoat. Bud has his stuck through his belt, and it hangs below the waistband of his leather jacket and drags the ground as he squats.

One man points to the machete and says, Somebody's been shopping at the Army-Navy and thinks they're beating through the jungle in Borneo.

Then he starts right back where he had left off before Bud's arrival, complaining about his wife's housekeeping. Says, It's so nasty most of the time at my place, I wouldn't even eat a walnut that rolled across the floor.

Pretty soon, Bud's clothes begin raising steam on his front side. He shucks his boots and sets them mouth-first to the heat. Sad little animals with their tongues out. His socks stick to his feet, bloody at heel and toe, and when he gets them off, his heels still peel away layer by layer and weep pink fluid. Little red threads net below the skin, pitiful capillaries ready to burst. Bud stretches his feet to the fire. The two big toenails already blue-black.

The smart-ass with the Borneo comment says, Take my word, those are going to fall off.

Bud finishes his coffee and pours his mug full of white liquor and begins trying to catch up.

Old Jones, the former bootlegger, sits a quarter way around the circle from Bud, keeping within himself, like he's waiting to see if Bud will recognize him.

Which Bud already has, but he keeps cool about it. Not like Jones has much cause to hold a huge grudge. Probably doesn't miss the long drives and the worry about the law. All that *Thunder Road* shit. And way too old to live through a stretch with the Feds. In general, life has probably been pretty good for him lately. Fair to partly cloudy since Bud appropriated his job. Semiregular payments, even though the real percentage is a lot smaller than the figure they agreed on back in the summer.

Yet, maybe, you have some sneering asswipe sit on your front porch lording over you, threatening you out of business, and then later, in a sweet twist of fate, that asswipe lands himself helpless in front of you as a test of your mercy. What do you do? Even Jesus, meek and mild, might give payback a passing thought.

And sure enough, before long, Jones says, Son, what the hell you doing up here?

Bud visors a hand to his brow, acts for the moment like all he sees is one more unknown face out of many in the fire glare.

—Got lost, he says. Nearly died.

Everybody laughs but Bud.

Jones says, No shit, Sherlock. Where were you headed? Making a run to Atlanta?

Everybody laughs again, and then Jones says, Some of you might not have got introduced. This is the new bootlegger.

Silence.

Bud studies the crowd and tips his forefinger to his brow.

Jones, talking to his cohorts, says, I'm wondering something. This mountain's not a good place to sell bonded liquor. We're making our own. So, same question. What the hell is he doing up here?

Bud had been too preoccupied with not freezing to death to have premeditated a good story. He starts riffing grammar however it links up in the moment.

—Seen a couple of kids? he says. Boy and a girl? Blond-headed? I'm part of the search party. The kids have been gone a day or two now. So, probably in this weather, we're looking for bodies.

—Party? the old bootlegger says.

—Got separated from the others some while back. By the lake.

—And you kept on climbing by yourself? For what, six or eight hours?

—I really want to find those kids.

—Yeah, Jones says. That's exactly how you struck me back in the summer sitting on my porch. The kind of fellow would give Jesus a run for his money when it comes to lost lambs.

But the tone Jones tries to set in regard to Bud won't hold. This isn't anything anyone is interested in. They drift back to the night they want.

And Bud is so happy to be suddenly not dying, that he doesn't have room to be worried too much about anything. You fall from the brink of icy death into the warm lap of plenty, you lie back and enjoy.

Doesn't take any time to learn that these old boys have all the shit in the world they need. Everything carried up by several packhorses, now standing at the edge of the circle, each one relaxing with a hind foot tipped. There's food to last a couple of weeks, eating big. Sixteen-inch iron skillets, a refrigerator rack for a cooking grate, a Dutch oven for when biscuits and cornbread become necessary. A chain saw and a maul and splitting wedge to keep the fire fed. Much pork, especially in the form of bacon, but also wonderful sausages and smoked country hams. Syrup in gallon tins. Dozens of eggs sunk down in sacks of flour. Everybody wants pancakes at three in the morning, they're set to go. Plenty of dried white beans to cook with ham hocks if anybody gets to craving vegetables.

Also, theoretically, all the coon and possum the dogs can raise. Except, sadly, little to show in that category of meat. Way deep in the outer reaches of firelight, pinch-waisted hounds shift about hump-backed with self-conscious looks on their faces. Talk of their failure swirls around the fire. Some dude lifting his head and saying something and then somebody else. Faces tipping up to the fire and catching the light and then nodding dark.

Somebody says, I never did confidence your blue tick much.

Jones says, Can we keep the local-color shit to a bare minimum?

And then he says to Bud, Whose kids would those be that you're looking for?

—That Luce girl, Bud says. Trying to adjust his language to the audience.

—Lit's girl, somebody says.

—Not hers. Her sister's kids, somebody else says.

On the far side of the fire circle, a faint voice behind the roar and crackle says, Bad for one family to have so much trouble strike so close together. Lily and Lit and now this.

—Maybe we'll find the kids tomorrow and maybe Lit's gonna show up any day, Bud says, trying to get out ahead. Maybe Lit's been to the beach with one of his women.

—Anyway, somebody says, the kids are retarded or something, so I guess they wandered off.

—Though you got to wonder, Bud says. Maybe she got tired of being substitute mama for messed-up kids. Probably they'll never be found.

Some few of the drunk hunters who have known Luce since she was a child stick up for her, and some who hold Lit in low regard figure it's possible. And then somebody brings up the school burning down when Luce walked out on her job, and they nearly all nod solemnly.

The talk swirls back around to shared memories and other useless bullshit. Baseball games back shortly after World War I, how somebody dropped a fly ball or hit a home run in the ninth inning. Ridicule and glory. Men who weren't in those particular games doze off sitting up, then come back to consciousness. Deep in the night, the snow thins down to just a wet flake or two falling into the circle of light and melting away.

ONE IN THE MORNING and the weather bleak, Stubblefield drives the lakeshore until he hits pavement, then turns in the direction of town. Cold rain falls through the headlights, drizzling forty-weight viscous down the windshield, on the cusp of deciding to freeze.

Luce had been exhausted from lack of sleep and gainless searching, hardly able to speak from calling the children's names into black woods. Both of them frazzled from many cups of Maddie's bitter gritty coffee. At midnight, Stubblefield had led Luce to the settle and calmed her to sleep with her head in his lap. Saying meaningless phrases about how everything was going to be all right. Kneading her shoulders, smoothing his palm down her face from hairline to jaw, fingers through her hair from brow to crown, fingernails on her back under her shirt.

He eased her head onto a throw pillow and covered her with an afghan, put on his jacket with the .32–20 in the pocket, and walked into the kitchen. Maddie sat at the table with a cup of coffee, and she looked a question at him, and he had said, Sleeping.

It suddenly occurred to him that Maddie hadn't been home since the kids disappeared. He said, Where did you stay last night?

Maddie said, Luce's not got but about forty bedrooms and doesn't use a one of them. I made do.

Stubblefield said, Thank you, and headed out the back door, grabbing the flashlight on the way.

Now he drives across the dam and along the shore to town like through a tunnel, a dark wall of woods rising to the left and the lake barely visible to the right, an emptiness behind the rain. Stubblefield is terrified of the next couple of hours, not at all expecting to find the kids and be the hero. But the night at the Roadhouse keeps coming back around. Bud dismissing him as no kind of threat, then slicing him open. Luce scared but glaring Bud straight in the face. The cut hand is still wrapped in windings of muslin bandage, dingy and unchanged for the past two frantic days. Underneath, a wide pink scar and a thin line of brown scab.

If he finds Bud home alone, it probably means the kids are dead. Then what? Stubblefield's first fallout with Bud went poorly, and the terror of that moment still grabs at his breath. But a saying of his grandfather's loops in Stubblefield's head. Ride to the sound of guns. A stirring sentiment, except his grandfather never spent a day in anybody's army, which could serve as an excuse to make a three-point turn and head back toward the Lodge. Yet Stubblefield keeps on aiming the Hawk forward.

For a short while around the black lake, he succeeds in holding a bright image in his mind, a pinpoint of diamond light. Convinced that hope rules us, not fear. But at the city limits sign, the light blinks out. In its place, the blood and darkness he saw down inside his cut hand. Still, he drives on into town and parks. Walks two blocks in the rain. Wet dead leaves on the pavement and windows dark in the bungalows. Bright rings misting around the scallop-shaded streetlamps.

At Bud's place, no light shines. But the green pickup in the driveway casts fresh waves of fear. Stubblefield draws the .32–20 from his coat pocket and goes through the side yard to the back door. Gives the knob a slow twist, to no effect. The lock is nothing much, though, and he's brought a stout wood-handled screwdriver from the Lodge. One yank outward, and the door pops open with a screech of old wood shredding. Stubblefield presses his back to the clapboards of the outside wall and waits. He listens on and on. But nothing. No sound of children, no Bud coming with his knife to check out the noise.

Stubblefield steps inside and switches on the flashlight in quick bursts to orient himself. In the kitchen, dirty dishes in the sink and on the counter. In the living room, a dirty white T-shirt on the floor, a pair of white socks with two red bands around the top. In the bathroom, the medicine cabinet contains one bottle of aspirin.

He enters the bedroom carefully, in case Bud is in there asleep. But only an unmade bed and more dirty clothes. No books, no records. Nothing anywhere to indicate personality or taste, nobody to point his pistol at. The closet is empty except for a pair of new palomino loafers. He begins opening drawers. Not enough clothes to fill a suitcase. But, in a bureau drawer, he finds a rubber-banded roll of bills. And then, in the nightstand drawers and under the mattress, identical rolls. Also a little brown leather pocket notebook.

He takes them into the living room and sits on the sofa and places the rolls upright on the coffee table. Muffles the flashlight with an amber glass ashtray and studies the notebook. Page after page, phone numbers and matching liquor orders. He unbands a roll and counts. Five hundred exactly. He doesn't bother to reband the money or to count the other rolls. Together, the meaning of the book and the cash is simple. Whatever Bud has done the past couple of days, he hasn't run far.

Stubblefield sits in the dark and waits, pistol in hand, trying to bring the diamond light back. If Bud shows up, point the pistol at him and ask some questions. See what happens next.

After two hours, Stubblefield unwinds the dirty bandage and drapes it over the money and the little book displayed on the coffee table. A message. He walks through the front door, and outside, big flakes of wet snow fall and immediately melt everywhere but in the grass. By the time he reaches the dam, snow falls much harder, brilliant and dizzying in the headlights.

At the Lodge, when he steps out of the car, snow falls on his hair, his shoulders, catches in his eyebrows. The lawn is white, and dawn is not even a faint luminosity in the clouds above the eastern ridges. In the kitchen, Maddie still sits at the table, drinking coffee. A pan of biscuits nearby, ready for the oven. She doesn't wait for his question.

Says, She's still asleep. She needed it, but probably she'll be mad if you don't wake her up now.

Hoping to replace the pillow under Luce's head with his leg before he wakes her, Stubblefield eases in. But his weight on the settle cushion does the job, and she reaches a hand to touch his knee and then sits up and finger-combs her hair. Gives him a glancing cheekbone kiss.

—Where have you been?

—What?

—You smell like outside.

—Out looking. But nothing.

She touches his hair, the drops of water.

—Rain?

—Snow.

She turns her palms up and looks at them a long time.

Stubblefield says, Yeah, bad night. Let's eat and get back out.

At DAWN, COLD MIST, pale metal colors. Grey and yellow and blue. Then various degrees of early light as the sun burns through the fog. Each twig and fir needle in its own case of ice. The sun reflecting off the crystals, every which way except the usual. The ground deep in wet snow, and evergreen boughs drooping under the weight. Light bouncing crazy, eye-burning brilliant. Weird and exciting.

Frank lifts his hands above his shoulders and flutters his fingers. Dolores nudges him hard, smiling.

Breakfast is a jar of pickled okra, a bracing start to the morning. They vie to eat the biggest pods, and blink tears from their eyes while they crunch the white seeds between their back teeth. Dolores tips the jar to her mouth and drinks a gulp of the salty green vinegar and reaches it to Frank and he does the same. Both of them laughing at their own puckering and weeping. When they mount up and ride on, Sally's mane dangles festive beads of ice.

Pathfinding would be more difficult if they had ideas of their own about where they are and where they want to go. Being lost means nothing. Especially when being found seems like a thing to avoid. Where they are is fine, so long as they move through it, onward to someplace else. So they keep looking ahead, and Sally keeps going.

Frank loses his hat. His ears become red, and then they get blue. Dolores takes off her ear-flapped toboggan and whacks him on either side of the head with it and puts it down over his hair until it covers his eyes. From then on, they decide by ear color when to swap the hat. That is so delightful that at the next rest stop they strip naked and swap all their clothes. An hour later, they change back.

Snow tastes pretty good a tablespoon at a time, but not more. Birch twigs broken off and frayed at the ends occupy five minutes of taste buds if scrubbed between teeth and gums and against the tongue. A single sprig of balsam is interesting, but study it too long and the symmetry and repetition of the needles makes a pattern that gets as creepy as snake scales if you don't put the brakes on in your head and make it stop vibrating.

At some point, Sally quits paying strict attention to the direction they're looking. Among all the possible turnings, she starts curving back to Maddie's house, making a big circle.

Midmorning, the sun is out strong, and the snow and ice melt fast. Grey-brown everyday floods back. Which is good for travelers. Though a little sad after the brief transformation of the world into something white and brilliant and new. Now mud seems muddier, and Sally's hoofs make sucking sounds, step by step. Whereas before, it had been a clean four-beat rhythm of crunches. Lunchtime, they don't even build a fire. They take turns eating peanut butter two-fingered from the jar.

NOVEMBER MOUNTAIN WEATHER. Without warning, it's snowing and you're about to freeze to death, and then twenty-four hours later, sunshine and your coat thrown over your shoulder. Slogging now, the trail muddy with snowmelt. True, part of any trip is slogging, but you don't have to like it, you just have to get through it. One foot in front of the other.

The old boys had sent Bud on his way with his clothes and blanket dry from the fire, and a hobo bundle of considerable food and a big square of dirty Visqueen and four lengths of nylon rope to make shelter. Also a map drawn on the inside of a flattened cornmeal bag. As-

surances of mild weather for at least three days, and many good wishes
for finding the kids.

They made a halfhearted offer to send some men with him, but Bud
would not hear of it. They'd saved his life, and that was more than
enough. Now he needed to move fast, cover ground. The boys mumbled about backs that hurt and hips and knees that had catches in
them. Get old, no guarantees you won't break down and do more
harm than good. Though what feats of endurance they once accomplished. They said that one of the fellows, back when he was eighteen,
carried a fifty-pound sack of flour on each shoulder over Laurel Gap to
his mama, cut off by spring flooding that had washed out all the roads
to her cabin. Twenty-five miles and thousands of feet of elevation gain
and loss. Took him less than eight hours.

Bud said, Well, hell. I guess that was a walk. And the old man
who'd done it said, I was about crying that last five miles.

Bud keeps going, seeing what he can see. But every step, the mountain expands, like huffing into a balloon, except the balloon's more like
a big sheet of newsprint crumpled into a ball. Nooks and crannies in
every direction. When he's covered a few miles, Bud stops and eats
cold leftover pancakes rolled around cold sausage and dark smears of
apple butter. Sun blazing and the sky blank and blue, but a little snow
still in the cups of leaves and ankle-deep patches in north shade. Bud
isn't sure how to finish his mission anymore. The old boys know him
now. Every one of them could point fingers at him in court.

But so what? Do things right, no bodies and no weapon, and everything will still fall clear. Don't think about that sad Lit business. It got
emotional, and naturally there were flaws. Get feeling betrayed and all
trembling scared, blood to your elbow, you're prone to misjudgment.
Case in point, the depth of the woods around here. Apparently, they go
on and on, and these hillbilly fools wander way into them to a remarkable extent. So bury deep and don't ever deny being up here. Just trying to help, looking for the kids of your sadly deceased wife. Survived
a great snowstorm. Didn't find them, came back brokenhearted. Left
town for greener pastures. End of story.

But for a while after lunch, Bud lets his thoughts wander. Find the kids and take them with him back to town. Get there late night. Leave them standing safe and sound and no more bewildered than usual on empty Main Street with the three lights flashing yellow. Drive west for days to some unimaginable place with no connection to his past whatsoever. Galveston or Gallup. Start fresh. Get a damn job.

Like that would work. He'd be looking over his shoulder from now on.

Bud keeps on through a long afternoon of gloomy walking with no faith in the future. Then there they suddenly are right in front of him. Three inches deep in the muddy ground. Hoofprints. Water half-filling the cup. Easy enough to guess which is the toe and which the heel and start following.

DOLORES BEGINS SINGING "Back in the Saddle Again." She can do all the verses exact, but half the words don't register much beyond their sounds. They are like other notes of music, with no more or less meaning than a finger twitching on a banjo string. Put a banjo in her hands, and Dolores could probably play the song as accurate as singing the words. It's all nothing but a pattern of notes. Hear it once and it sets in the mind. When Maddie sang the song, Frank was fairly preoccupied with the job of grooming Sally, but he attends close now to Dolores, and when she gets back to the chorus, he echoes the words.

Sally keeps bending, contouring along ridgelines, hunting paths. She steps out strong down the trail, and all the children feel is that they are going forward. Through the twists and turns, they lose three thousand feet of elevation during the afternoon. The lake becomes visible again below them, a ragged trail of liquid silver trapped between slate-colored ridges, like mercury cupped in the palm of a hand.

WOODLORE DOESN'T FACTOR big when it comes to tracking a horse over wet ground, where with every few steps it sinks to the ankle. You follow the holes. Bud's railroad boots cling wet to his feet, muddy to the fifth eyelet. Everything inside squishing. He hopes it isn't because his feet are bleeding again. But to look on the sunny side, he's survived beyond all expectation. A puzzler, though. How did those two morons live through that brutal white night on the mountain?

Maybe they didn't. And Bud's following nothing but a lost horse.

He holds that happy thought in his mind for a few miles, until he comes upon the browning core of an apple with little-people teeth marks.

So, probably not dead.

No use getting down about it. Bud wonders where they might be going. Takes out the old boys' cornmeal map and runs his finger over it, trying to place himself among its lines and words. But it makes no sense to him. Pretty different from something you'd buy folded precise as the bellows to an accordion at the Esso station. Meaningless squiggles and place names drawn with a dull carpenter's pencil. Hog Pen Gap, Bear Wallow Branch, Picken's Nose.

Those fucking backwoods morons. If they wanted their real estate to ever be worth anything, instead of its only value being to hold the rest of the world together, they'd use names like Butterfly Ridge, Wildflower Glade. Imaginary places where fairies sip dewdrops from honeysuckle blossoms. Ahead of my time, Bud thinks. But what else is new?

Unseasonably warm in the late afternoon, particularly in contrast to the blizzard. For the novelty of it, Bud sheds his upper wear down to the skin. Let sunshine beat on his pale chest for a few minutes.

He comes to a place where the trail bends to the south, onto great sunny expanses of dark rock scattered with little eroded pockets filled with water. Everything angled to catch the light, becoming warm as summertime. Above the bare flats, patches of intricate moss and stunted pines struggle out of fissures. Below the flats, a sharp edge of rock, and way down at the bottom of an ass-clinching drop, a river runs like a white thread.

As Bud rounds the bend, what does he see on the rock but dozens and dozens of rattlers. Sunbathing, taking the rays. All beside and atop one another, mottled and twined, and not moving or making a sound. Some of their heads spread as broad across the brow as his clenched fist. Fat as his calf in the middle of their bodies.

It hits Bud funny. All those thick slack cylinders of malignant meat. His insides twist up. He thinks he's going to retch. He bends over, but when he does, his sight goes grey except for shimmering particles of light. He sort of sits, sort of falls over. The long machete blade strikes stone like ringing a bell.

At the sound, a few snakes jump like they've been shot. They squirt off over the rocks and down into cracks and off the lips of overhangs. And those forerunners spook the rest of them, and like cattle stampeding, they disappear. An awful fog blowing away, like they were never there at all.

Bud tries to walk on, watching his step. But that doesn't work so good. He gets all wiggly in regard to the plane of the trail. Sits down and draws his thoughts together, trying to get to the point where he can reason again.

THE BED TO A NARROW-GAUGE railway, new slim trees growing where steam engines hauled out monster trees that were saplings in the time before white people. The trail falls contrary to water running down the same slopes. Water tries to go with gravity, straight as possible. The trail follows contours. Not steep, but dropping steady on and on, finding the easy way down. It's all sidehill. The feel of the woods changes over the course of the afternoon. No balsams, more laurels and galax. All those names Luce likes so much.

Sally holds stronger opinions than previous about their pace and which way they go when they get to a turning. Dolores and Frank shift about on her back until they're facing each other, and they play an intricate game of finger signals and coordinated hand slapping. A trailside observer would have trouble figuring the rules and how points are scored and what might be called a good play and what an infraction. The game goes on until the usual conclusion. Somebody hits too hard and the other one retaliates. They shift around, back to back, and ignore each other and watch the passing world for a while, Dolores looking at what's ahead and Frank watching their past spool away behind.

In the west above the high peaks, bands of afternoon light start building in the clear sky. Platinum, bronze.

Way deep in the afternoon, camp time, they see a place they know. An older bent tree with a pointing nose. They get insistent, and Sally gives in and turns where there is no trail. The sun falls low, and the light in the dead brown leaves is momentarily etched and golden. Shadows stretch long across the ground.

An hour later, indigo twilight, and some big yellow planet falls slowly through the treetops. They have a fire near the edge of the hole, the stump to a toppled hickory as the backlog. A pile of downfall scrounged from the woods, and the blaze as tall as themselves. Dry sticks of hemlock for immediate gratification, mixed with bigger limbs of hardwoods for longevity. The light rises upward with the smoke. Down inside the hole, not a glint off the surface of the black water.

Later, the major lights of the night sky shine crisp in the dry air. Long over their quarrel, Dolores and Frank sit cross-legged under the same blanket and eat a jar of stewed tomatoes and the last sleeve of crackers. For dessert, most of a jar of apple butter, dark with brown sugar, but no bread to spread it on. They sing some more songs, learned from Maddie and the crank record player and the big radio. "Knoxville Girl." "I'll Take You Home Again, Kathleen." "Try Me."

They count the Seven Sisters like Luce taught them, and they say words to each other. Some are common words, and some are of their own devising. But they are like wary people in a foreign country where a language they know imperfectly holds sway. They hide what they do know, except from each other. Whatever anybody says, stay blank. They don't talk about where they are. They're right here all over again. Circling back, when they thought they were gone.

They let time flow right now, and they don't worry about the black hole. It lacks interest. They can sit alone in the dark at the brink of a spooky pit in the woods and not give it more than a passing thought. The stuff they fear is unrelated to a hole in the ground and dirty water. They don't have to make up horror-movie visions to give themselves an entertaining shiver. The horror is other people. The things they think up to do to you.

HOOFPRINTS KEEP ON GOING. Gaps, sometimes, when the trail crosses rocky ground or open south-facing slopes. But you cast about, walk zigzag in the direction they've been heading, and before long there they are again, leading forward.

The afternoon stays clear and warmish. Get to an open shoulder of mountain and look back up to where you've been. High ridges grey as the bones of mountains in the sun, the highest peak still white with snow and frozen fog. You get justifiably proud of your survival. All those weak fuckers in their houses down in the valley. Watching their TVs with the heat blasting.

No telling how close the kids are now. Bud tries to get his mind right for rounding a bend and seeing a pony up ahead. No way to handle it but break it down into pieces, like any shit job. First you do this and then this. But if you start checking your watch and thinking all the way to the end of the day, you're lost. It's a sequence you're following, and the bad part is just one part. For that, quick is what everybody wants.

Bud gets sad again about his ineptitude with Lit. It's mainly doing it wrong that sticks in your mind afterward. If this wasn't going to be the last one, he'd want to buy a big-bore rifle, like the ones used by Civil War snipers he'd read about in his magazines. Sit up in a tree, scoping some enemy officer a half-mile away. A colonel or something. Tiny dude smoking a cigar, being a big shit in front of his lessers. With your magnificent art, you hold your breath and touch the trigger with the delicacy of touching your own eyeball. Before the sound of the shot reaches the colonel, his head's about like a big double handful of stew meat soaking into the ground, and the rest of him is barely starting to topple over like a sawed tree. And yet for the lucky colonel, the experience is no more than blowing out a candle. Happy, happy, dead. People lie in hospital beds worldwide praying for such a perfect end.

No use planning for the future, though. This is, for sure, the last one. Afterward, a new life.

Bud walks on until the sun drops and disappears in the trees. Suddenly, all the warmth of the day drains into the ground. It gets to a point of darkness where you don't know what to call it. Dusk or night. Twilight fits in there somewhere. People used to have a word, *gloaming*, but that's only a snatch of memory from a song. Wait a few minutes, though, and like so many things, it quits being an issue. Night falls, too dark to see your feet at the bottom of your legs.

Bud sits down in a level place by the trail. He's failed to learn the lesson of the coon hunters. Claim your space. Draw a circle of light around it. Push back against the dark. Don't just survive. Celebrate.

Impossible, though, with no chain saw, no bright-faced kindling fresh-split from a cylinder of pine with an axe. No childhood buddies sharing the heat and light.

Bud draws together wet rotting twigs and squats with his last matches. He achieves smoke for a few seconds. Says, Fuck it, and wraps himself in his blanket on his piece of Visqueen. He lies mostly awake through the night, listening to all the swirling languages the night-woods speak.

When he drifts to sleep, it's not really enough to interrupt his train of thought. And when he drifts back in, the voices are always murmuring against him, and he's always thinking about two quick sweeping movements.

No denying the ugliness. But swear you're done and move forward. Bud touches the necklace, then his arm.

Blood. It covers the earth. Animals and humans in their billions, their skin like the membrane of a balloon or a rubber. A thin scurf trying to keep the liquid from spilling out, but doing a poor job of it.

Touch a needle to your finger and see how bad it wants to get into the air. If God wanted things different, he'd have coated us in armor. Or made us pray to a face pulled apart by pain, screaming.

But he wanted us to bleed. The flow of blood, a red bleeding heart. That is beautiful.

AT THE FIRST SUSPICION OF DAWN, Luce takes off alone. The earth and the lake and the sky still grade only slight shades of color apart. Bare November trees pitching in the wind against a charcoal sky, and the lake charcoal too, with little waves breaking against the shore rocks. Maddie and Stubblefield dozing at the kitchen table.

Alongside the trail, the lush growth of summer droops over, dead brown. The tops of giant hemlocks disappear in fog, and their roots probe deep in the moisture below the creek banks. Galax leaves, transformed by frost, shine glossy maroon.

She has slept once in the past three days, and Stubblefield even less. He's taken an hour now and then, leaned against her on the front seat of the car somewhere way up a fire road. The afternoon and evening of horrible weather—rain falling hard, ashy sideways streaks of rain in the headlight beams—they drove into the mountains until the roads got so rough they dragged the muffler off the Hawk and figured the oil pan would be next. By the time they returned to the Lodge, she was too tired to argue when he put her to sleep. When she woke, early that morning, the rain had become big wet flakes of snow, melting as they hit the ground, but by the time the sun was up over the eastern ridges, the clouds were breaking apart. More empty searching that whole day, but with the sky blue and the high peaks white all morning with snow. Searching in the car and on foot, knocking on farmhouse doors and asking the same question over and over. Driving to check the phone at the store every few hours. All the time, trying to hold a

positive picture in her mind and entertain imaginary hope. By late afternoon, sundogs and bare trees.

Now, walking in the cold fog, Luce doesn't even try to track the
children. Short of a dropped sweater, all trace of them will have been
erased by rain and snow. So she walks with nothing at all in her mind
and tries to feel which way they might have gone. But she isn't the
least bit telepathic; no vibrations reach her other than the general
shimmer of sleeplessness.

Many turnings present themselves, plenty of opportunities for
choosing one faint passage over another. These mountains are no wilderness. They have been lived in for thousands of years. Many old
nobodies, long gone to earth, left their marks on the land, subtle or
not. Gameways stretching back beyond buffalo days to a distant ice
age became Indian trails, little foot-wide hunting paths and broad valley trails linking towns, each with its pyramid. Roads broad enough
for helmeted Spaniards and their horses and scores of pigs and cap-
tives to make twenty miles a day in their traverse through here. Two
hundred years farther on, many paths for horny colonial merchants
and botanists and preachers coming to the highlands to make money
and mixed-blood babies. And then American soldiers burning the villages so that the townhouses at the tops of the pyramids became nothing more than a layer of charcoal. Some of those same roads became
exile trails for the Cherokee, endless trails for the many who never
reached the end. On the same mule tracks and wagon roads, the deluded greyboys traveled to war. Then, sunken logging roads and skid
paths from the end of the previous century, and narrow-gauge rail
beds from the early clear-cut years of this century. Everywhere Luce
looks, the ground lies webbed with lines of passage, a maze for the
children to get lost inside and never come out.

Numb and hopeless, Luce walks in the direction of the black hole.
At the trail tree, she sees hoofprints and starts running. When she
gets to the dry ridge of hickory and locust, she smells smoke in the
woods and runs downhill into the wet cove and into the shadows

under the hemlocks. Running across the beds of needles so quiet the loudest thing is her breathing.

At the hole, near the lip, a fire smokes, burned down mostly to coals. Stubs of Franklins, half-burned at the edges of white ash. Like they had no more value than yesterday's sports section crumpled to light a fire. Bud stands between the fire and the hole, looking off into the woods, a long bright-edged blade drooping from his hand. Burnt edges of bills sticking out his jacket pocket.

Luce can't see the children until she follows Bud's line of sight. Dolores and Frank stand together on the far side of the hole, right at the edge. Sally shifts about, off in the trees behind them.

Bud turns around and looks at Luce. He says, Jesus Christ.

Luce tries to breathe. She says, What have you done?

—Not a damn thing yet. They keep running around this quarry.

He starts moving toward Luce, and she angles away. For a few moments they mirror each other, like a slow dance separated by twenty feet. Bud moving in and Luce moving away, skewing out of reach. Until they stop with the circle of fire between them, Bud standing near the hole, Luce with her back to the hemlock woods. Bud kicks at the burnt ends of bills, shoving them toward the live coals.

—Look at it, he says. I could have lived high forever. But now, nothing.

Luce glances quickly at the bits of paper igniting in the coals, confused. Then back to Bud. Waiting for him to move again.

—Y'all haven't left me a lot of choice here. I'm going to do what I have to, and then get gone.

—You don't have to do anything, Luce says. Just go now. Never see you again, that's all I want.

—How dumb do you think I am?

—What?

—You can say any kind of lie right now. But I'm not leaving a string of witnesses.

—I haven't witnessed anything, Luce says.

Bud looks across the hole to the kids. He says, Stuff piles up. Probably, they'll try to blame Lit on me too.

—I know you did it. But I can live with that. Leave us alone and go.

—No. From right here, there's one way it's got to be.

Out of frustration—the endless circling of the hole trying to catch the kids, figuring they would eventually act like prey animals and get nervous and flare off into the woods in fear and then he would run them down, but them never panicking, keeping always one-eighty degrees away, circle after circle—Bud makes some bullshit calculation in regard to the smaller circle of fire. He tries to leap it to get to Luce.

Midway in the crescent of his jump, as he realizes one foot is going to land in the fire, the machete slips his grip. It spins behind him to the edge of the hole, jangles on rock, and falls over the lip. End over end, down into the black water, which receives it without comment, neither splash nor ripple.

Bud steadies his footing, one boot muddy and the other ashy. Says, I'll kill you with my hands.

He comes at Luce, but not rushing. Moving wary and uncertain without his blade.

Luce pulls her birthday razor from the pocket of her coat and flips the hook at the end of the handle. Holds the razor angled, like a barber ready to shave a face. The steel of the rectangular blade ripples in the light. Along the edge, it's almost transparent.

The Adam's apple makes a good round target, a knot of gristle under the skin to mark exactly where the windpipe runs. Luce moves at him and swings hard, wanting to go deep.

Instinct. Bud steps back and throws up his hands. The blade passes across both palms with hardly more resistance than through air itself. For a second Luce thinks she hasn't gotten him at all. But Lit said the blade seeks bone. The faint ripples she felt through the handle means it cut to every one. She stares at Bud's hands, the marks thin as paper cuts.

Luce squares up in case she needs to make another go, but then the blood comes. Two dark sheets running from the heels of Bud's hands and down the wrists where all the suicide veins tangle. The fingers extend spectacularly white above the blood. Blood falls to the leaves and dirt.

BUD YELLS IN SHORT BURSTS, just vowels, declining in volume. He keeps his hands up, and blood runs warm and sticky past the cuffs of his leather jacket and down the insides of the sleeves and pools at the elbows. He can't think of anything to say. His breathing becomes a problem. And there stands Luce with the razor, ready to come at him again. He turns and looks at the kids. They stand pale-faced across the hole, in the shadows under vaulted boughs of hemlock. Watching him with no expression at all.

Bud runs. Takes off without benefit of track or trail in no preconceived direction whatsoever. All the wet dead shit of autumn grabbing limp and clammy at his feet. He runs until he can't do it anymore, and then he walks. He holds his hands pressed in his armpits and keeps going, sort of grunting and sort of sobbing. When Luce and the kids are far behind, he sits with his back against a fat hemlock trunk, the bark streaked black with rain, and reaches his hands into the air to slow the bleeding.

Under the hemlock, everything lies dark and quiet. Needles not rustling in the breeze like leaves, just a hissing in the air. Around the trunk, a circle of shadow denser than other shadows. Listen hard and you hear a sound like the ticking of many wristwatches, the fall of dead needles, building in tiny increments a deep thousand-year bed to kill weaker things that try to grow underneath.

Bud can't help it, he wants to watch. He cups his palms in his lap, and counts how many times he breathes until they fill with blood. Then, reach for the sky again.

It doesn't even hurt much, but his thumbs no longer work right. His fingers hardly move. They're like flippers. He swipes the bloody fingertips under each eye, marking his face like a high school football player on a Friday night. Works his necklace over his head and tries to throw it off into the woods, but his hands don't cooperate, and it goes only six feet and falls into the bed of hemlock needles. That's good enough. Ten thousand years from now, what a mystery for somebody to find a fossil shark tooth at the foot of a mountain.

Bud sits a long time studying his bleeding. When he decides it might be slowing down some, he walks until he comes to a creek. Plunges his hands into the cold clear water and watches tendrils of blood flow downstream, trailing away across smooth mica-flecked stones. Eventually, you can't tell blood from water, but what beautiful shapes it makes before it disappears.

Fresh from the creek, the edges of the cuts are clean and chalk white. Look deep down, though, and the details get as messy as an anatomy chart before they fill and overflow with blood again.

Moss grows dense on the creek bank. Bud peels two patches of it from the ground like scabs and puts them back to back and presses his palms hard against this green poultice.

He waits for something good to happen. And in an attempt at sympathetic magic, he tries to think back to a pure moment in his life. Cleanliness and innocence is what he's trolling the past for. Being at the beach when he was a kid, maybe. The end of the day. Tired and sunburned and salty from the water. Or, better yet, this sweet, round-faced girl at the end of a teenage date. September. Sitting in the driveway of her house, the engine off and key switched to Alt. The radio glowing on the dash. And yet, neither of them at all in the mood for groping. Just talking and laughing. Her face open and sweet. Bud remembers washing the car that afternoon, whisk-brooming the interior. Remembers fog in the air that night, a whole sequence of songs on the radio, but he can't remember the girl's name. Yet he thinks maybe he should have married her. Her big smile and small teeth. Deep happiness elusive as always.

His hands come away from the compress of moss still bloody. But maybe the optimistic word in regard to the state of his cuts would be weeping rather than flowing. Possibly, death has taken a step back.

How to get the fuck out of here, Bud wonders.

He unfolds the cornmeal map with some difficulty and spreads it across the bloody lap of his pants. It's like a child scribbled random lines with a crayon. He could be anywhere amid this useless landscape rising all around. No matter how hard he studies the old boys' markings, the map and the world remain irreconcilable.

DOLORES AND FRANK sidle wary around the hole. Sally side-passes off in the woods, a dark shape far back in the hemlock shade. Exactly matching their movement, but at a farther circumference.

Not wanting to spook them, Luce doesn't run to the kids. That old wisdom Stubblefield taught her. Don't chase it, and it will come back. She waits by the fire. Kneels down and puts her hands out to the warmth. Pushing back hurt mama feelings, like what they were running away from was her and she ought to feel upset about it. They got scared and took off into the woods. Nothing but natural. Pretty much what she would have done. Had done.

Dolores and Frank ease their way around the circle and stand near the fire. No hugs. Certainly no tears. Sally stops at the edge of trees, bobbing her head. Impatient.

Luce, trying to sound like everything is fine, says, Go get your pony and let's head on home.

Luce doesn't try to lead Sally. She follows close behind, the razor closed in her palm with her thumb on the hook to flick it open fast. Listening deep into the woods and looking for any movement. When the trail becomes wide enough, she walks alongside Sally. Tells the children, I was so worried. It must have been . . . She starts to say *terrifying* but settles on a different word. Cold, she says.

Dolores talks about the swapping of the hat, the lighting of the great dead balsam. And Frank tries to say something about dawn and the ice in the trees. His arms rise, and he flutters his hands. Luce can translate only a few fragments, but it's like some of her important music. You can't make out most of the words, but the message is clear.

She says, Next time, you have to take me with you.

———

BARE WOODS STRETCH ENDLESS, the night sky cold and deep with stars. The Dipper slides down toward the treetops and everything coming up after it is nothing but random. The stars have shapes that mean something if you know the code, but Big Dipper is it for Bud.

Out here, the deadly shit seeking your blood and meat is not confined to snakes and bears and weather. Other forces resent your presence too. Ghosts of long-gone wolves and buffalo and Indians and pioneers, dead in the service of implacable history. If you stop and camp early, while it's still daylight—claim your space, plant your flag, build your fire—you push them back into the past. But alone in the dark, the minute you sit your ass down they circle close around. Lie on the ground, and the cold seeps up as they try to equalize your temperature with theirs. Get quiet, and you hear the voices. A few words in English, but mostly other languages. The ones that came before the Indians. Words the long-gone animals thought to one another. Words flowing against you. Wishing you ill. Yet, somehow, all gentle as an outbreath. Mumbles and sighs.

And their vehicles of communication? Creek water over rocks, wind flowing through bare trees and across dead leaves. And that's exactly what the old speakers want you to be. Dead in the ground, exactly like them.

At some point, stars wheeling through the tree limbs and the voices humming around him, Bud makes up a short story. Maybe, some future day when he has a minute, he'll write it up. Send it to one of his magazines. Won't take up much space.

Fellow takes a walk in the beautiful mountains. Pick any season you want, with its many details. Colors, for example. The world is full of colors, even in winter.

Fellow trips on a small rock. Falls forward. Busts his head open on a larger rock. And then what happens? Think ripe cantaloupe. All that tangled mess spilling out into the daylight.

Boom. The whole world goes away, never to return. Black peace. Happy ending.

At least, if you think about it in the context of all the common ways to check out. All that screaming final shit in hospitals. Deluded people in white clothes watching the dying and feeling superior, like they're immune to death forever. But still awfully interested in the process. Like these hillbilly mountaineers watching some deer they just shot blink its last vision of the world while its blood soaks the leaves.

So if Bud ever writes his story, the moral is, Make it quick. No more than switching off the porch light before bed. Happy, happy, dead.

Then lie on the woods floor through winter, freezing and thawing. Rain and shine. In summer, a stand of Indian pipes growing pale and ominous like skin underwater from melted flesh. The sacred heart tattoo fading into the ground.

A wandering fisherman or hunter gets curious about a funnel of birds in the sky beyond the lakeshore. At the place where the spout touches down, he finds a dozen rumpled buzzards standing around hunch-shouldered, acting polite with one another. Nothing to get excited about, just another piece of work. Might as well take turns.

CHAPTER 5

STRINGS OF COLORED BULBS and greenery wind around
the drooping wires crossing Main Street to hold up the three stoplights. Red, green, blue, and yellow streaks on the wet black pavement.
When the Hawk passes underneath, the streaks slide up the hood and
illuminate the beads of water on the windshield. Luce gets lost in
childhood memories, that one magical year Lola and Lit roused themselves from their immersion in each other to go buy a couple of baby
dolls to unwrap.

In the backseat, the children busy themselves with a new game
where they shape three fingers of each hand into claws and interlock
with the other and grapple. As soon as somebody gets hurt, game
over. Luce's rules. On WLAC, "Papa Ain't No Santa Claus (Mama
Ain't No Christmas Tree)" drifts into "Merry Christmas Baby."

THE METHODISTS EXCHANGE presents by way of a Santa in faded
red flannel and dingy white fake fur. He sits in a metal folding chair in
front of the decorated tree near the pulpit and pulls wrapped packages
from his sack and draws folded strips of paper and calls out numbers.
Odds and evens, boys and girls. One by one, children run down the
sloped aisle between rows of pews to claim their prizes. It goes on and
on. Now and then, a choir in blue robes sings one of the old songs. A
pale brown-headed boy, small for his age, unable to wait any longer for
his toy, shouts out, Don't forget little Vincey.

Luce, sitting near the back, all of this new to her, likes to believe her children are nothing like a pair of copperheads amid a field of sweet brown mice. She reminds herself that it's not just one or the other. There's a range, and you can slide either way. The whole point of being here is to begin shaping a place in the world around them.

But Dolores and Frank don't care about Santa or what's in his sack. It's the many burning, dripping candles in tall holders that fascinate them.

Soon Stubblefield has to make an end run around the pews to keep the smolder of burgundy drapes from spreading to burgundy carpet and oak pews and burgundy cushions. He stomps out the tinder, wadded-up copies of *The Upper Room*, the cover a colorful, cartoonish depiction of Baby Jesus in the manger. Barely averting sirens from the fire station, three blocks up.

—We'll keep working on that, he whispers to Luce after he sits back down.

AS THEY LEAVE TOWN, Stubblefield drives around back of the sheriff's office. The green pickup still sits in the parking lot where it was towed more than a month earlier, about the same time the sheriff tried questioning the kids, who sat before him like the Tar-Baby, saying nothing. When Luce took her turn, she told of a knife fight and a mysterious hole in the woods that nobody had ever heard of.

Many days later, when the coon hunters finally came down from the mountain to resume dreary daily life, their recollections of seeing Bud were vague and inconclusive. It was only for a few hours, and they had been impaired to a high degree. The best most of them could do was confirm that somebody showed up in the middle of the night and left in the morning while many still slept and the rest were hungover and hadn't even finished their first cup of coffee. Only old Jones made a firm identification, but, of course, he might hold a grudge. The search of Bud's rented bungalow had yielded only a few money rolls, a bootlegger's notebook, and a long ribbon of dirty bandage.

For the sheriff, it was simple. Lost kids happily found. Some guy in town for a couple or three months decides to move on. The truck and the money remain a puzzler, but the truck is worn out and people get in a hurry and forget things. As for Lit, with his many enemies, maybe he'd had it coming for a long time.

BACK AT THE LODGE, Luce leads the children upstairs. Past 202, Maddie's room when she cares to use it. Sometimes she's there as high as three nights a week, and sometimes she checks out for eight or ten days at a time. No plans. You see her when you see her. Tonight, you don't. But probably midmorning tomorrow she'll show up with a bowl of festive holiday collards and gifts of fruit and hard candy.

The children have 203, and Luce tucks Dolores and Frank into bed under a deep pile of quilts. She reads the one about the heifer hide and the one about the goats. And for this particular night, she summarizes as best she can the poem with all the reindeer names, though she has to make up three of them on the fly. She concludes the storytelling with the one line she remembers exactly. *Away they all flew like the down of a thistle.*

As soon as she closes the door, Luce immediately begins planning ahead to next October. A docent walk in an abandoned field on a dry afternoon, weeds shoulder-high and some locusts and pines starting to come in. The subject will be all that hopeful business of forest reclaiming its place, the sequence of plants from bare ground to cove hardwood forest. She'll break off a stem of dried bull thistle for the children to admire the structure of its flower. Then hold it up to her mouth and say the magic words. Draw a deep chestful of breath and blow the down into the world to fly away with the air and fall to earth.

Downstairs, Stubblefield sits reading, the radio faint and the fire burning old and slow. The .32–20 on the end table. Luce sits next to him on the settle and leans against his shoulder and reads his book. Something about beatniks climbing mountains. Outside, a noise. Probably a limb falling from one of the old oaks. Stubblefield doesn't look up from the book but moves his right hand to the arm of the settle, a foot from the pistol.

Doors locked, weapons close. But every day that passes, Bud's presence fades. Nothing but a feeling. No telling for sure whether he is still going or long gone. Fled into the distance or absorbed into the landscape, which does not punish or reward but cleanses all bones equally.

CITY OF LIMERICK PUBLIC LIBRARY
C 99382

93335

ABOUT THE AUTHOR

CHARLES FRAZIER grew up in the mountains of North Carolina. *Cold Mountain*, his highly acclaimed first novel, was an international bestseller and won the National Book Award and the Sue Kaufman Prize for First Fiction from the American Academy of Arts and Letters. His second novel, *Thirteen Moons*, was a *New York Times* bestseller and named a best book of the year by the *Los Angeles Times*, *Chicago Tribune*, and *St. Louis Post-Dispatch*.